Tristan lowered his mouth, captured hers.

A feather-light touch that rapidly became firmer, deeper, called to her.

'Kiss me again,' she whispered, pulling his head down to hers, whispering against his firm mouth. 'One last time. No one is here. Tomorrow will be too late.'

He lowered his mouth again, and this time the kiss was harder, more insistent. Penetrating. Sensation coursed through her body in hot, pulsating waves.

Her breasts strained against the confines of her corset. Ached. She felt the material give and his cool fingers slide against her fevered skin. She sighed and parted her lips, drunk on the scent of him. His lips trailed down her neck, tasted her skin, and began to slowly travel lower.

'Unhand that woman, you…you cad!'

Dear Reader

This story came about because my daughter loved and adored a secondary character in A CHRISTMAS WEDDING WAGER. She begged and pleaded that Lottie Charlton needed to have her own story, and so, wishing to keep peace and harmony within my family, I agreed. It turned out to be a real pleasure to write, and I am delighted that it will be published during Mills & Boon's centenary year.

As ever, I love getting reader feedback, either via post to Mills & Boon, my website, www.michellestyles.co.uk, or my blog, www.michellestyles.blogspot.com

All the best

Michelle

AN IMPULSIVE DEBUTANTE

Michelle Styles

MILLS & BOON®
Pure reading pleasure™

First published in Great Britain 2008
Harlequin Mills & Boon Limited,
Eton House, 18-24 Paradise Road, Richmond, Surrey TW9 1SR

© Michelle Styles 2008

ISBN: 978 0 263 86278 2

Set in Times Roman 10½ on 12¾ pt.
04-0908-77901

Printed and bound in Spain
by Litografia Rosés S.A., Barcelona

Although born and raised near San Francisco, California, **Michelle Styles** currently lives a few miles south of Hadrian's Wall, with her husband, three children, two dogs, cats, assorted ducks, hens and beehives. An avid reader, she has always been interested in history, and a historical romance is her idea of the perfect way to relax. She is particularly interested in how ordinary people lived during ancient times, and in the course of her research she has learnt how to cook Roman food as well as how to use a drop spindle. When she is not writing, reading or doing research, Michelle tends her rather overgrown garden or does needlework, in particular counted cross-stitch. Michelle maintains a website, www.michellestyles.co.uk, and a blog, www.michellestyles.blogspot.com, and would be delighted to hear from you.

Recent novels by the same author:

THE GLADIATOR'S HONOUR
A NOBLE CAPTIVE
SOLD AND SEDUCED
THE ROMAN'S VIRGIN MISTRESS
TAKEN BY THE VIKING
A CHRISTMAS WEDDING WAGER
   (part of *Christmas by Candlelight*)
VIKING WARRIOR, UNWILLING WIFE

For the students and teachers of Crystal Springs Uplands School, class of 1982, in particular for the head of the English Department—Mrs Norma Fifer. Truly an inspirational teacher.

Chapter One

1847 Haydon Bridge, Northumberland

'I kept my promise, Father.' Tristan Dyvelston, the new Lord Thorngrafton, placed his hand on his father's grave and his fingers touched the smooth black marble, tracing his father's name. He glanced down at the weed-infested grave.

'Your brother has died,' he said solemnly, repeating the vow he had made on this very spot ten years ago. 'I have returned to take the title. I will be above reproach now. But while my uncle was alive I wanted him to think the worst about me and to fear for the future of his beloved title.'

He bowed his head and stepped back from the grave. One part of his oath was complete.

The late morning sunlight broke through the cloud and illuminated the ruins for a single glorious moment, making it seem like he had stepped into one of John Martin's more evocative paintings. Tristan tightened his grip on his cane. Here was no picture to be admired. The scene showed how much had to be done. How much would be done.

He was under no illusion about the enormity of his task. His parents' graves lay under a tangled mass of nettles and brambles. In the ten years since he had last been here, the entire churchyard had fallen into decay, echoing the state of Gortner Hall, some fifteen miles away. He would put that right, eventually. His uncle was no longer there to object.

He traced the lettering on his mother's grave. How would the county greet the return of the black sheep? He had heard the tales his uncle had spread—the gossip, the scandal and the plain twisting of the facts. His uncle had sought to deny him everything but the title and the entailed estate, a dry husk, long starved of any funds. Tristan took great pleasure in confounding his expectations.

The clicking of a gate caused him to turn. Irritated.

A blonde woman with a determined expression on her face tiptoed into the churchyard, glanced furtively about and raised a shining object into the air. The sunlight glinted on it, sending a beam of light to dance on the yew trees. Tristan relaxed slightly. She was not someone he had ever encountered before and therefore was unlikely to recognise him. But there was something about the way the petite woman held her head that intrigued him.

Why would anyone come here?

She wrinkled her nose, fiddled with the object again and finally gave a huge sigh of satisfaction. 'I told Cousin Frances that a moonlight aspect would work better than a Gilpin tint, and I was correct. She will have to retract her scornful words. The church could be romantic in the moonlight. One would have to imagine the hooting owl, but it could be done. It could be painted.'

Tristan jumped and considered how best to respond to the statement. Then he gave an irritated frown as he realised that the woman was not speaking to him. He regarded her for another instant as she peered intently at the object in her hand. He gave a wry smile as he realised the object's identity—a Claude glass, a mirror that prettified the landscape and allowed the viewer to see it at different times of the year, or hours of the day, simply through changing the tinted glass. It all made sense. She had come in search of landscapes.

If he was lucky, it would be just the Claude glass and a few ladies to coo and ahh at the ruins. If he was unlucky, they would have brought their watercolour paints, brushes and easels, the better to capture the romantic ruins. He lifted his eyes towards heaven. God preserve him from ladies wielding Claude glasses, their pursuit of culture and their self-righteous indignation that others should not share their same view of the world, interrupting his first chance to pay his respects to his parents. Tristan frowned. Not if he acted first.

'Precisely how many more of you are there?' he asked, making sure his voice carried across the disused churchyard. 'How many more are there in the horde?'

The woman spun around, her mouth forming an O. She had one of those fashionable china-doll faces—blue eyes and pink cheeked in a porcelain oval. The lightness of her complexion was highlighted against the darkness of the yew hedge, giving her almost an angelic appearance, but there was a sensuousness about her mouth, a hint of slumbering passion in her eyes. Her well-cut walking dress hinted at her rounded curves as well as revealing her tiny waist. A temptress rather than a blue stocking.

'You are not supposed to be here,' she said, putting her hands on her hips and gesturing with her Claude glass. 'Nobody ever comes here. Cousin Frances told me emphatically—Haydon Church is always deserted.'

'Your cousin was obviously mistaken. I am here.'

'My cousin dislikes admitting mistakes, but she will be forced to concede this time.' The woman hid her mouth behind her hand and gave a little laugh. 'She much prefers to think that since she has her nose in a book all the time, she knows rather more than me. But she can be blind to the world around her, the little details that make life so interesting and pleasant.'

'And you are not? Looking at the world through a mirror can give a distorted view.'

'I am using both my eyes now.' She tilted her head to one side. 'Are you up to no good? Cousin Frances says that often you meet the nefarious sort in churchyards. It says so in all the novels she reads. It is why she refused to visit.'

'But she thinks it deserted.'

'Except for the desperate. Are you desperate?'

'I am visiting my parents' graves.'

'You are an orphan!' The woman clasped her gloved hands together. 'How thrilling. I mean, it's perfectly tragic and all that, but rather romantic. What is it like not to have family considerations? Or expectations? Is it lonely being an orphan?' Her face sobered. 'How silly of me. If it wasn't lonely, you wouldn't be visiting your parents and attempting to derive some small amount of comfort from their graves.'

'There is that.' Tristan allowed the woman's words to flow over him, a pleasing sound much like a brook.

She came over and stood by him, peering at the ground. 'You should tend their graves better. They are swamped in nettles and brambles. It is the right and proper thing to do. An orphan should look after his parents' graves.'

'I intend to. I have only recently returned from the continent after a long absence.' Tristan stared at her with her ridiculous straw bonnet and cupid's-bow mouth. Right and proper? Who was *she* to lecture him?

'That explains the entire situation. You had expectations of another's help, but that person failed you.' She gave him a beatific smile. 'Orphans cannot depend on other people. They can only look to themselves.'

'How very perceptive of you.'

'I try. I am interested in people.' She modestly lowered her lashes.

He straightened his cuffs, drew his mind away from the dark smudges her lashes made against her skin. 'How many more shall be invading my peace? Ladies with Claude glasses have the annoying habit of travelling in packs, intent on devouring culture and the picturesque.'

Her pink cheeks flamed brighter and she scuffed a toe of her boot along the dirt path. 'I am the only one. And I have never hunted in a pack. You make society ladies sound like ravening beasts, longing to bring men down when, in fact, they are the ones who provide the niceties of civilisation. They make communities thrive. When I think about the good works—'

'Only you? Are you sure that is prudent?' Tristan cut off the discussion on good works with a wave of his hand.

Even though Haydon Bridge was rural Northumberland, the woman did not appear the sort who would be allowed to roam free and unaccompanied. Her pink-and-white-checked gown was too well cut and her straw bonnet too new and finely made. Her accent, although it held faint traces of the north-east, was clear enough to indicate she had been trained from an early age by a succession of governesses.

'I am able to look after myself. I know the value of a well-sharpened hat pin.'

'You never know what sort of people you might meet.'

'It is the country, after all, not London or Newcastle.' Her cheeks took on a rosy hue and she lowered her tone to a confidential whisper. 'I am aiding and abetting a proposal. At times like these, positive action is required, even if there is an element of risk.'

'A proposal?' Tristan glanced over his shoulder, fully expecting to see some puffed-up dandy or farmer advancing towards them. 'Tell me where the unfortunate man is and I shall beat a hasty retreat.'

'Not mine. My cousin's.'

'The one who is mistaken about graveyards,' Tristan said, and struggled to keep his face straight. It made a change to speak about things other than the state of Gortner Hall's leaking roof, the fallow fields and the other ravages that his uncle had wreaked on the estate.

'That's right.' There was a sort of confidence about the woman, the sort that is easily destroyed later in life. 'All Frances ever does is read Minerva Press novels and sigh about Mr Shepard's fine eyes and his gentle manner. What is the good with sighing and not acting positively? She needed some help and advice.'

'Which you have offered…unasked.'

She held up her hand and her body stilled; an intent expression crossed her face. 'There, can you hear it?'

The sound of a faint shriek wafted on the breeze. Tristan lifted an eyebrow. 'It sounds as if someone is strangling a cat. Is this something you are concerned about? Should I investigate?'

'My cousin Frances, actually. She is busy being rescued from the Cruel Sykes burn.' She tilted her head, listening and then gave a decided nod. The bow of her mouth tilted upwards. 'Definitely Cousin Frances. We practised the shriek a dozen times and she still managed to get it wrong. She needed to gently shriek, and to grab his arm, but not to claw it. I do hope she has not pulled him in. That would be insupportable. Truly insupportable.'

'All this is in aid of?'

'Her forthcoming marriage to Mr Kent Shepard.'

The woman drew a breath and Tristan noticed the agreeable manner in which she filled out her gingham bodice. But he knew she was also well aware of the picture she created. A minx who should be left alone. Trouble. He would make his excuses and depart before he became ensnared in any of her ill-considered schemes.

'Cousin Frances has to get engaged. She simply has to. Everything in my life depends on it.'

'Why should it matter to you?' His curiosity overcame him.

'I was unjustly banished.' The woman wrinkled her nose. 'It was hardly my fault that Miss Emma Harrison kissed Jack Stanton in a sleigh in full view of any passing stranger.'

'Jack Stanton is well able to look after himself.' Tristan gave a laugh. His impression had been correct. She was the sort of woman to stay away from. Trouble with a capital T. 'I hope your friend was not too inconvenienced, but she picked the wrong man to kiss. Jack is a good friend of mine and not given to observing the niceties of society.'

'Do *you*?'

'When the occasion demands. I was born a gentleman. But Jack…is immune to such stratagems. It is amazing the lengths some women will go to.'

'It all ended happily as they were married, just before Christmas.' Her eyes blazed as she drew herself up to her full height. 'You obviously do not know your friends as well as you think you do.'

'I have been travelling on the Continent. But if it ended happily, why were you banished?'

'My brother Henry was furious. He turned a sort of mottled purple and sent me out here to Aunt Alice until I could learn to keep my mouth quiet. "Lottie," he said, "you have no more sense than a gnat," which was a severely unkind thing to say.'

'And have you? Learnt to keep your mouth quiet?'

'Yes.' Lottie Charlton looked at the elegantly dressed man lounging against a yew tree with exasperation. Who was he with his dark eyes and frowning mouth to sit judgement on her? He was not her brother or any sort of relation. She snapped the Claude glass shut and took as deep a breath as her stays would allow her. 'I have, but Henry refuses to answer any of my impassioned pleas. He ignores me. And Mama is being no help at all. She keeps going on about her nerves and how unsettling family disagreements are, but she refuses to do anything.'

'And you dislike being ignored, forced to the margins.'

Lottie retained a check on her temper—barely. They were not even formally introduced and already this man had picked her character to shreds. 'This is my best chance, my only chance, to get back to Newcastle this season. I know it is. My dream of a London Season has vanished for the moment, but there are appearances to maintain. And some day I shall visit all the great cities—London, Paris and Rome. I plan to be the toast of them all.'

'How so? Haydon Bridge is very far from these places.' The man lifted one eyebrow, seemingly unimpressed with the brilliance of her scheme.

'I am well aware of geography.' Lottie pressed her hands together. She had to remain calm. 'Aunt Alice will have undying gratitude to me if I arrange this marriage between Cousin Frances and Mr Shepard. Mr Shepard has been making sheep's eyes at Cousin Frances for weeks now, and the only thing Cousin Frances can do is blush and readjust her pince-nez.'

'And you are an expert in these matters.' His eyes travelled slowly down her and Lottie fought against the impulse to blush. 'You look all of seventeen.'

'Twenty in a month's time. My sister-in-law sent me the Claude glass for an early birthday present. It is quite the rage, you know.'

'Nineteen is not a great age.' A smile tugged at his mouth, transforming his features. Darkly handsome, she believed it was called, like one of those heroes in Cousin Frances's Minerva Press novels. 'When you are my age, you will see that.'

'And your age is?'

'Thirty-one. Old enough to know interference in matters

of the heart brings unforeseen consequences.' The words were a great finality. Lottie frowned and decided to ignore his remark.

'I helped to arrange several proposals last season in New-castle. Proper ones as well, and not the dishonourable sort.' Lottie resisted the urge to pat her curls. 'I can number at least seven successful matches that I have helped promote.'

'Including the one that sent you here.'

'If you are going to be rude, I shall leave.' Lottie lifted her skirt slightly and prepared to flounce off. The man made her brilliant stratagem sound like a crime, like she was intent on ruining someone. Newcastle was not London, but at least there remained a chance of meeting someone eligible. It was the most prosperous city in the whole of the British Empire, everyone knew that. 'You must not say things like that. I *have* helped. Martha Dresser and her mother showered me with compliments when I brought Major Irons up to snuff.'

'Don't mind me. It is one of my more irritating habits.' A slight smile tugged at the corner of his mouth, making him seem much younger. 'Your scheme appears to be full of holes. And I doubt you would know the difference between a proposal and a proposition.'

'I know all about those. One learns these things, if one happens to possess golden curls, a reasonable figure and a small fortune in funds.'

'I will take your word for the funds. I can clearly see the other two.' His dark eyes danced. 'I agree that they can be a heady concoction for some men.'

'Yes, I know.' Lottie began ticking off the points. 'One has to be wary of the inveterates who stammer out marriage proposals at the sight of a well-trimmed ankle, the cads who try to get you into corners and steal a kiss, the let-in-pockets who only have an eye to one's fortune and clearing their vowels. I have encountered them all. But I am quite determined to be ruthless. Mama wants a title.'

'A title can be a difficult proposition. What makes you positive that you can snare one? What sort of mantraps do you intend on laying? It can take great skill and cunning to succeed when so many are in pursuit.'

Impossible man. He made it seem like she was some sort of predator. Lottie stuck her chin in the air and prepared to give the *coup de grâce*. 'I have rejected Lord Thorngrafton. He positively begged for my hand last November.'

'Lord Thorngrafton? The elderly Lord Thorngrafton?' The man went still and something blazed in his eyes. The air about him crackled.

'Not so very elderly.' Lottie kept her gaze steady. She refused to be intimidated. As if the only titled men who might be interested in her were on their last legs or blind in both eyes! 'Around about your age and you are hardly in your dotage.'

'When did he propose to you?' The man leant forward, every particle appeared coiled, ready to spring. 'I would like to know. It is most intriguing. I have been on the Continent until recently and am unaware of certain recent events.'

'Shortly before Christmas.' Lottie gave a small shrug and wished she had thought to bring her parasol. She would have liked to have spun it in a disdainful fashion. 'However, I do not think the proposal genuine as Mama never remarked upon it. I rather fancied it was the sort where the gentleman expects you to fall into his lap like a ripe peach, perfect for the plucking and tasting, but easily forgotten.'

'You'd be right there.' The man's eyes became hooded and his shoulders relaxed. 'I do not believe Lord Thorngrafton intends to wed any time soon. I should not try any of your tricks with him.'

'Are you acquainted with Lord Thorngrafton? Is he another of your friends that you have misplaced while you were on the Continent?' Lottie narrowed her eyes, peering at him more closely. Silently she cursed her wayward tongue. He did look like Lord Thorngrafton, if she half-closed her eyes. But this man had a wilder air about him. She would swear that he moved like a panther that she had once heard about at the Royal Zoological Society in London. 'You look somewhat similar—dark black hair, same eyes, but he was shorter, more squarely built. He had fat, doughy hands and he spoke with a slight lisp.'

A muscle twitched in the man's jaw and a cold prickling sensation trickled down the back of Lottie's neck. What had Lord Thorngrafton ever done to this man?

'We are acquainted. Relations.'

'And you are?' Lottie clutched her reticule tighter to her bosom. She knew the information should make her feel more secure, but somehow, it didn't. The man knew both Jack Stanton and Lord Thorngrafton, but that did not mean a thing.

'Tristan Dyvelston,' he said and his dark eyes flared with something.

Tristan Dyvelston. The name rang in Lottie's ears. She glanced about her and the giant yews began to press inwards, hemming her in. The notorious Tristan Dyvelston. Cousin Frances, in one of her more expansive moods, had whispered about him and the scandals he had left in his wake. She peered more closely at the weed-choked graves and picked out the Dyvelston name. The tale on balance was true. Why would anyone pretend to be Tristan Dyvelston? Even after ten years, the wisps of scandal clung to his name. A scandal so great that Frances only knew the barest of details.

She made a pretence of straightening her skirt. Life's little problems were never solved through panic. She had to find a way to retreat in a dignified manner. She doubted if society's rules and niceties would constrain Tristan Dyvelston. He would take, and pay no regard to the consequences. That was a woman's job—looking towards the consequences of her actions.

'But he went to the Continent, pursued by several angry husbands.' The words slipped out. She wet her lips, drew a deep breath. 'Are you funning me? Who are you really?'

'Tristan Dyvelston.' A faint hint of amusement coloured his dark features. 'I have returned…from the Continent. It is no longer necessary for me to be there.'

'But the scandal.' Lottie made a small gesture. 'The shame, the dreadful, terrible shame. Those poor women. Cousin Frances was most particular on the shame.'

'She knew what she was on about, the lady I left with. And I use the word lady lightly.' Tristan Dyvelston's mouth turned down and his face took on the appearance of marble. 'No husband pursued me. I believe he was thankful to get rid of the encumbrance of his wife. The affair cooled before we reached Calais. Last seen, the woman in question had found solace in the arms of an Italian count.'

Lottie measured the distance between herself and the

gate. She wanted to appear sophisticated and unconcerned, but if she was caught here alone in the company of a notorious womaniser, any hope of regaining a social life would be gone. She might as well learn to do tatting and resign herself to looking after Henry and Lucy's children. She had to leave. Immediately.

'An Italian count—imagine that. Really, it has been very pleasant speaking with you, but I must be going…'

'And here I thought we were having a pleasant conversation.' He took a step closer to her. A smile tugged at the corner of his mouth as if he understood precisely why she had decided to depart. 'I regret that I disturbed you.'

'You didn't. I have seen all that I came for. I will return one day with my paints. There is a certain melancholy air about this place.' She cautiously took a step backwards, then another; her foot slipped and a bramble snaked around her boot, holding her fast.

She attempted to free herself but only succeeded in catching the skirt of her dress. And it would have to be her new checked gingham. Fine lawn. Easily torn. She could hear Frances's clucking and Aunt Alice's sighing now. Then there would be explanations, ones she did not want to make. The dreaded Carlotta would be used in terrible tones. Carlotta—a name more suited to her aunt in Alnmouth than her.

Lottie shivered slightly and redoubled her efforts, wincing as a thorn pricked her through her glove. Her reticule with the Claude glass dropped to the ground with a slight crash. Lottie cursed under her breath. Everything was going wrong.

'Allow me, Miss Lottie.' Tristan Dyvelston bent down,

and his long fingers caught her ankle, held it firm, while his other hand freed her from the bramble. He handed her the reticule and Lottie clutched it to her bosom. 'No harm done and no need for unladylike utterances.'

'You know my name.' Lottie stilled, the reticule dangling precariously from her fingertips.

'You said it earlier.' He stood up, but did not move away from her. 'You should be more cautious.'

'Is this a warning?' Lottie's heart began to pound in her ears. He was very close. Earlier she had failed to notice the breadth of his shoulders or his height. She wondered how she had failed to do so. Wondered briefly what it would be like to be clasped in his arms, and she knew this was why he had his scandalous reputation.

'An observation from one who has lived a bit longer than you.' He looked at her. 'I have met women like you before. They need to learn life's lessons.'

'And do you propose to teach me them?' Lottie crossed her arms and forced her back straight. She gave her curls a little toss. They were back on familiar ground. She had endured such propositions before, although none given in such a warm voice. She supposed he practised it, but a small part of her wanted that voice to be just for her.

'Do you wish me to?' His eyes blazed with an inner fire. 'Forgive me, but it is dangerous thing to do—provoking a man when you are quite without a chaperon.'

'Forgive me, Mr Dyvelston—' Lottie inclined her head '—we travel in different circles, but that line has been tried on me at least four times. You are not the first to use it and no doubt will not be the last. I may give the impression of being a silly blonde, but I am not. I might be not as sophisticated as some, but I can take care of myself. I have no intention of learning life's lessons from one such as you. Or indeed any of your kind.'

He raised both eyebrows. 'You speak in a very forth-right manner for one who is barely out of the school room.'

'Men such as you are an occupational hazard.' Lottie smoothed the folds of her dress. A cold fury swept over her. Why was it that men expected women to swoon when confronted with something? Or to recoil in horror? Flirtations were fine, but men always went that little bit beyond. She cleared her throat and assumed an air of haughty superiority. 'The agreed answer is that I am quite satisfied with my life at present, so thank you for the honour, but no. I shall wait until I receive the perfect proposal.'

The corner of his mouth twitched upwards as if her words amused him. Amusement! How dare he!

'And having received this set-down, I am supposed to walk away, and not gather you up in my arms. Is that what they taught you?' He paused and his hand brushed her gloved one, sending tingles throughout her body. 'Or would you rather a demonstration?'

'A demonstration?' The word emerged as a high-pitched squeak. Lottie held up her reticule like a shield. But she was torn between the knowledge that propriety demanded that she should flee, and the desire to stay and see what he might do. What would it be like to be held in the arms of a man who knew what he was doing? 'I have no wish for you to demonstrate *anything.*'

'Don't you?' The words wrapped around her like a silken rope and held her.

Slowly Lottie shook her head, but she watched Tristan

Dyvelston's smile increase. Lottie took two steps backwards. Perhaps she had made a mistake. The sound of Frances's shriek was far too distant. She had been over-confident. 'I will be going now. Straight away.'

He threw back his head, and his laughter startled a wood pigeon out of a tree. Broke the spell. He had intended on frightening her. She wanted the earth to up and swallow her. She had been naive.

'I fail to see the amusement in this.'

'Your expression is that of an outraged kitten with spiky hair.'

'My hair is not spiky.' Lottie opted for an expression of haughty disdain. 'I have had odes written to my hair. Lord Thorngrafton sent me an ode about the gold in my curls.'

'Not from me. Never from me.' The colours of his eyes changed and she wondered that she had thought them deep black. They appeared full of hidden lights, shifting, dancing. Never the same, but spellbinding to watch. 'I never write odes to hair. Never write odes at all if I can help it.'

He crossed the distance between them in one stride. His hand brushed her curls. 'Definitely not spiky. I retract.'

'Oh.' Lottie put a hand against her throat. Her heart had begun to beat very fast. She parted her lips and closed her eyes. What would it be like to feel his lips against hers? She had only been kissed twice last Season, and neither time had been what she would qualify as a success. They had been somehow dissatisfactory, particularly after she had learnt that Lieutenant Ludlow had gone around trying to catch Caroline, Diana and Leda under the mistletoe as well. She waited, lips pursed and poised.

'Virtuous virgins hold little attraction, even those with

strawberry red lips. You may lower your mouth, Miss Lottie, and next time, wait.'

Lottie opened her eyes and hurriedly lowered her chin. She could feel the heat beginning to rise on her cheeks. A mocking smile twisted his mouth and his face became like carved marble.

'Do they indeed?' she asked in her frostiest tone as she drew her body up to her full height.

'Too many complications. Too many considerations.' He gave an elegant shrug of his shoulders.

Lottie released the air from her lungs. She should be relieved, but a small stab of regret ran through her. She had wanted to experience his arms holding her. 'You make me sound positively frumpish. Highly unattractive.'

'Not plain. Just a young lady who is far too aware of her charms and wants to play games, dangerous games that lead where neither party is prepared to go.' His eyes darkened. 'Women such as you provide complications, complications any sensible man would be well advised to give a wide berth, if he wished to retain his place in society. Even among my kind, we have a certain honour. I prefer someone who knows how to play the game.'

Lottie inclined her head. 'Goodbye, Mr Dyvelston. It has been enlightening.'

'Until we meet again, Miss Lottie.'

'I doubt that very much.'

'One never knows. When you are older, perhaps…'

He captured her hand, raised it. His lips brushed the exact point where her glove gapped, and touched her naked flesh for the briefest of instants. It seared through her.

Lottie jerked back her hand, and fled to the echoing

sound of laughter. She ran straight into Frances, who wore the look of a disgruntled hen as she squelched along the lane. Her straw bonnet dripped muddy water.

'Ah, Cousin Carlotta, at last we discover you.'

'I was regarding the old church through my Claude glass.' Lottie held up her reticule with a smile. How many times had she told Frances that she hated the name Carlotta? And how many times had her cousin ignored the request? Her hand went around the reticule. She winced as she realised that she had dropped the Claude glass and returning to the ruins was impossible. Not while Tristan Dyvelston was there. 'The moonlit aspect was quite unusual. I shall have to show you some time.'

'You mean now?' Cousin Frances held her hands as an alarmed expression crossed her face.

'Impossible, Fanny dear, as you appear a bit damp and I have no wish for you to catch a chill.'

'I hate the name Fanny.'

Lottie gave a small smile. 'I always have difficulty re-membering that.'

'We thought we heard voices, Miss Charlton, just now.' Mr Shepard's Adam's apple bobbed up and down. He appeared to have a very damp, dead sheep look about him and Lottie was positive that she detected a tinge of pink to Frances's cheeks. 'Yours and someone else's.'

'Yes, a male voice, Cousin, and yours answering him.' Frances gave her a piercing glance. 'Is there anyone of our acquaintance there?'

'How did you find the bridge at Cruel Sykes burn?' Lottie asked quickly. They had to get away from here before Mr Dyvelston appeared with a sardonic twist to his lips. When Frances was in one of her moods, everything would come out. Then she would never get back to Newcastle. 'Was it easy to cross?'

'Wet,' Frances replied. 'Very wet. Cold and slippery.'

'Miss Frances fell in.' Kent Shepard puffed himself up. 'I had to rescue her.'

Lottie did not miss the slight change of name. Some good had come of this afternoon after all. Her scheme showed definite positive signs.

The golden portals of society and triumph beckoned. Tristan was wrong. She glanced behind her at the seemingly empty churchyard, biting her lip. As long as her little encounter went undiscovered. It had to go undiscovered. No one would believe that a notorious rake like Mr Dyvelston had gone to the churchyard of his own volition. He supped with the devil, according to Cousin Frances.

Why was it that the attractive men were always among the most unsuitable?

Lottie gave automatic answers as the conversation turned towards pleasantries about the weather. Her hand went to the place his lips had touched her wrist. She shivered involuntarily. She had had a lucky escape. Mr Dyvelston represented danger and she had best remember it. She would lead the sort of life that her mother and Henry wanted her to, if only she could return to civilisation. It was her destiny. She knew it.

Tristan watched her go. He heard her bright laugh and artless explanation and then turned back to his parents' graves. A small case winked up at him. He reached down and pocketed it.

There was very little point in going after the woman now. Tristan closed his eyes. He had lied when he'd said that Lottie's hair was ordinary. It was the colour of spun gold. He could see how men could have their heads turned. But there was something else about her. Something that called to him.

'We will meet again, Lottie, you and I. And on my terms,' he said, fingering the Claude glass and staring down at the village. 'But first I need to determine who the false Thorngrafton is.'

Chapter Two

'I had expected my sister to be here.' The sound of Henry's pompous voice greeted Lottie as she entered Aunt Alice's house. 'You know, Aunt, what sort of mischief Lottie can get into when left to her own devices. It is precisely this sort of thing that I warned you about.'

Her aunt's soothing reply was muffled behind the door to the parlour.

Typical, Lottie thought, the one time her brother decided to make the journey here, she was out, gallivanting across the country with an ungrateful Cousin Frances. It could have been worse. Frances could have spotted her with Mr Dyvelston. But Frances showed a singular lack of interest in her whereabouts or in the church. And nothing had happened, nothing at all.

Lottie's fingers explored the underside of her wrist. The imprint of his touch still burnt her flesh. What was it about that one particular man? Was it the danger he represented?

'Do you have any idea of when she might return?' Henry's pompous voice brought her back to reality with a bump. 'I have business to attend to and cannot wait around for ever. The train leaves for Gilsland in two hours. And there is not another one until morning.'

'Henry, is that you? Are Lucy or Mama with you?' Lottie called out as she removed her gloves and bonnet with trembling fingers. Why was her brother here? Had something happened? She would be brave.

'Ah, Lottie, you make an appearance.' Henry turned from her aunt and Lottie was surprised to see how fat he had grown. 'Come and greet me. What do you have to say to your brother?'

He had a well-fed look like a trained seal. If anything, the last five months had made him sleeker and fatter. She noticed he wore normal clothes and not mourning ones. Lottie gave a sigh of relief, thanking God for small mercies.

'You should have sent word, and I would have been here.'

'I had expected you would be here, doing your needlework or making another one of those pincushion mottos that you and my wife are enamoured with.'

'Why?' Lottie blinked rapidly and refused to let his cutting words hurt. She would have been here, sitting, doing needlework if only he had let her know. 'We keep different hours in the country. I went for a stroll with my cousin. The fresh air is reputed to be good for most constitutions. You should try it some time.'

Henry harrumphed. 'I suppose there is no harm in a quiet walk.'

'Now, tell me, Henry what is the news?' Lottie came forwards and caught her brother's hands. 'How are Mama,

Lucy and the children? They send letters, but it is not the same as hearing it. I do miss them so. Do say they are all well and that you are not here because of them.'

'Lucy sends her regards. The children are well, or so Lucy tells me.' Henry's face softened. 'Mama has gone to Gilsland Spa for the waters.'

Lottie concentrated on her aunt's patterned Turkey carpet. It could be that this was her best chance, far better than the marriage plans for Frances and Mr Shepard. She had to show that she had learnt from her exile. 'Is my dear sister-in-law planning to come out to Haydon Bridge? There are some fine walks around here. I can tell her the legend of Cruel Sykes burn and she can look for the blood in the water.'

'Yes, Carlotta and I went to the Cruel Sykes burn today.' Frances nodded and her cheeks flamed to a bright pink. 'It is quite a pleasant walk. I nearly fell in the burn, but Mr Shepard rescued me. Fished me out.'

'I had no idea that Mr Shepard had accompanied you.' Aunt Alice's voice was chilling. 'Who arranged this?'

'He did not accompany us, exactly, Mama. We met him on the pathway and Carlotta suggested that he walk with us for a while.'

'One can hardly be rude to one's acquaintances, someone one has been formally introduced to.' Lottie shifted uneasily. Perhaps she should have discovered Aunt Alice's feelings towards Kent Shepard first, beyond noticing the warmth with which he was greeted at church.

'Niece, are you going to explain further?' Her aunt tapped her fan against the small table. 'Is this some new scheme of yours? Why precisely did Mr Shepard join you and my daughter? Had he experienced difficulty with one of his cows? Goodness knows I have tried many topics with Mr Shepard but he always returns to his irksome cattle and their breeding.'

'Our paths crossed,' Lottie said, trying to forestall more of Frances's confidences. From the thunderous look on Aunt Alice's face, she was beginning to think that perhaps she had been mistaken. Perhaps Aunt Alice had not wanted the match for Frances. 'And I…that is…we suggested that he might like to join us. He appeared quite willing to do so and in a jovial mood.'

'Yes, yes, Carlotta made the suggestion. Mr Shepard is very good at rescuing, Mama.'

'Ah, and did he rescue you from the burn as well, Carlotta?' Her aunt gave her an icy stare, one that caused her to shift uneasily in her boots.

Suddenly Lottie was very aware of the glaring and obvious flaws in her matchmaking scheme, fundamental flaws that she should have anticipated. She could not lie, but to tell the full truth would invite disaster. She had no wish to explain about Tristan Dyvelston, and the kiss on her wrist.

'You might well ask that, but the truth is…'

'Niece, none of your smoked gammon and pickles for me. You appeared to have outgrown the tendency once you were away from your mother and under an altogether steadier influence. Did or did not Mr Shepard fish you out of the burn?' Aunt Alice raised her spectacles. And her piercing gaze appeared to look into the depths of Lottie's soul. 'You are rather less damp than my daughter. Your clothing shows no sign of being rumpled.'

'No.' Lottie kept her chin high, but she swallowed hard. How was she going to explain this away, particularly as Henry had put Aunt Alice into one of her moods? 'He did not.'

'He couldn't.' Frances gave a high-pitched giggle that echoed around the room. 'She wasn't there.'

Lottie heard her aunt's little screech of horror and wished the floor would open up. Why had she ever considered that today could be called a good day?

'Was not there?' Her aunt's voice sounded like a church bell tolling out a funeral march. 'Why not there? You depart together. You come back together. But Lottie was not with you at the burn when Mr Shepard oh so gallantly fished you out.'

'Lottie, what were you doing?' Henry thundered. 'Are you up to your old tricks? I warned you.'

'I had gone to look at the old church's ruins with the Claude glass that Lucy sent me as an early birthday present and I could have sworn they were right behind me.' Lottie opened her eyes, and used the slightly singsong voice she adopted whenever her mother accused her of anything untoward. 'It was only when I arrived that I discovered my mistake. They had taken the turning to Cruel Sykes burn. Seeing that I was there, I had a look about the church… Cousin Frances had extolled its virtues as a…subject for a watercolour…'

She glanced between Aunt Alice and Henry to see if they were going to accept the story. Cousin Frances made encouraging noises about the Claude glass.

'Mr Shepard and Cousin Frances soon caught up with me.' Lottie wiped her hand across her mouth and hoped. 'And that is all to the story. A simple misunderstanding.'

'Carlotta Charlton,' her brother thundered, 'how could you do such a thing!'

'We were right behind Lottie. Only but a moment, once we realised there had been a mistake,' Frances agreed, nodding vigorously, impressing Lottie with the way she entered into the spirit of the thing. Perhaps she had mistaken Frances's intentions. Perhaps they could become friends. 'Mr Shepard thought he heard voices. Lottie's and a man's.'

Lottie put her hands over her ears and turned her head away as everyone began to speak at once. No, definitely not friends.

'That settles it, then.' Her brother's tone boomed out over the rest.

'Settles what?' Lottie asked into the sudden silence.

'Haydon Bridge has singularly failed to curb your wayward tendencies.'

Lottie curled her fingers as she tried to suppress the wave of hurt that washed over her. 'I think you are being harsh, Brother. I have led an exemplary life. Ask Aunt Alice, or Cousin Frances.'

'Carlotta Charlton, you have been attempting to do mischief, serious mischief.' Henry stabbed his forefinger into the air. 'I told you at Christmas, I have had enough of your minx tricks! You treat your reputation with a casual contempt and a woman without a reputation might as well not live. Polite society certainly will not recognise her.'

'I…I am entirely innocent,' Lottie said through gritted teeth as Cousin Frances gaped, opening and closing her mouth like some demented cod fish. Right at that instant, she was not entirely certain whom she hated more—Cousin Frances, Mr Shepard or Tristan Dyvelston.

'It is no matter.' Henry brushed an imaginary speck of dust from his frock coat. 'Mama is determined that her daughter will marry a title. There is no reasoning with her. You know what she is like with her enthusiasms.'

'I am hardly likely to catch an aristocrat in Haydon Bridge.'

'True, true.' Henry gave an exaggerate sigh. 'Mama has been bending my ear about the very subject. I had hopes when she left to take at the waters at Gilsland Spa that she would be distracted, but her experience has only served to renew her determination. She has sent me letter after letter on the subject. Hardly a post goes by without yet another epistle arriving.'

'Do you mean to send me to London?' Lottie felt the room tilt slightly. Perhaps today was not terrible after all. Perhaps everything was a blessing. She attempted to keep the eagerness from her voice. 'I know I have missed the Queen Charlotte Ball, but a number of events remain in the Season. Mrs Fullen did say that she might be prepared to sponsor me and she is the sister of Lady Rowland. She knows the patronesses of Almack's.'

'Lucy considers otherwise. She thinks Mrs Fullen exaggerates about her connection with the patronesses.'

'Lucy forgets what Mrs Fullen did for Ann Mason only two years ago. Lady Rowland is a respected member of the *ton*, Henry. I read her antecedents in *Burke's Peerage, Baronetage and Knightage,* and if she is in Burke's…'

Henry held up his hand. 'I am unprepared to countenance you set loose in London. Lottie, you would be ruined within moments of stepping on a dance floor. Were very nearly, by all accounts, ruined by an unknown man in a deserted churchyard. You have no sense with men, Sister.'

'Then Newcastle? You are taking me back home.' Lottie refused to let the disappointment of London bow her spirits. Once she returned to Newcastle's society, she could work on her mother. Mama would realise the true importance of having a London Season to securing a title.

'Gilsland Spa where Mama is taking the waters.'

'Gilsland?' Lottie's heart sunk. 'What is at Gilsland? *Who* is at Gilsland at this time of year? It is fine for Mama, but does she intend to marry me off to some gouty lord or a creaking count from some unknown European principality?'

'Lord Thorngrafton currently resides there. He has taken a suite at Shaw's Hotel, as have several other members of the aristocracy. Mama has sent a list of the titled currently residing there. The prospects quite excite her and I must say that they make for quite intriguing reading. I had never considered Gilsland Spa as a possibility before.' Henry puffed his chest out. 'I am given to understand that Lord Thorngrafton was very interested in you at an Assembly ball last autumn, Lottie.'

Aunt Alice gave an audible gasp and Cousin Frances's eyes gleamed as Lottie gave a sigh of relief. Here at last was an opening.

'I believed Lord Thorngrafton's attention was of a dishonourable nature than honourable.' Lottie settled on the horsehair sofa, crossing her ankles and arranging the folds of her gown. If she could turn Henry's attention away from Lord Thorngrafton, she might be able to return to Newcastle after all. It was a matter of persuasion, applying the right sort of pressure. He would yield.

'Our mother believes otherwise. She has had a conversation with the man in question and he remarked on your fine eyes and how much he admired them.'

'Lord Thorngrafton spent most of last November speaking to my bosom. I do not believe that he once noticed my eyes.'

'Carlotta!' her aunt shrieked. 'Unmentionables in front of Frances! Cover your ears, Daughter!'

'I have done so, Mama.'

Lottie crossed her arms and glared at them. 'It is true.'

'Mama stated in her letter that he asked after you particularly.' Henry's eyes narrowed. 'Do not play the sly puss with me, Carlotta. I have it on good authority that Lord Thorngrafton is possessed of a more than agreeable fortune. He saw the possibilities of railways, long before I. He is a business associate of Jack Stanton, a partner in some of his ventures. And you know how rich Stanton is. I have done some investigating.'

'So rich that Mama would have happily forgone a title.' Lottie made sure that her smile was sweet. 'Letter or no, Lord Thorngrafton is up to no good. Why should a titled gentleman possessed of an agreeable fortune wish to ally himself with our family?'

Aunt Alice began to fan herself rapidly at the outburst as Henry's face turned a sort of mottled purple.

'Explain yourself!'

'I simply feel there are other better places where I could go.'

'You do, do you?' Henry jabbed his finger at her. 'Let me tell you this, Miss Butter Would Not Melt in Her Mouth! Should you fail to bring Lord Thorngrafton up to the mark, I will marry you off to the next person who asks.

In fact, I am tempted to marry you off to the next person—Lord Thorngrafton or whomever—after this latest outburst. I have it on good authority that Mr Lynch is currently on the lookout for a wife, or should I say nursemaid, for his brood of seven children.'

Lottie stared at her brother in horror. He could not do that. Could he? She fought against the panic that swept over her, struggling to breathe against the confines of her corset.

'Where is Mama? Let me speak to her. You cannot do that, Henry. I forbid it. Mama will be distraught when she learns of your unkind and uncharitable attitude.'

'Mama is at Shaw's Hotel, waiting for your arrival. And despite Lucy's misgivings, I must conclude that it is the best place for you. You will catch a titled husband there, so help me God.'

'Why are you doing this, Henry?' Lottie asked in a small voice. 'Why are you doing this to me?'

'My sister's marriage is a matter of business. You have two weeks, Lottie. I am not an unkind man, but it is all the time I wish to be away from my family. You and our mother together…'

'But…but…'

'Perhaps we send for Mr Lynch now?'

Lottie stared at her brother. Once she had thought him a god, but now she knew he was a hard, unfeeling monster. He did not care for her future happiness, merely for what prestige or power her marriage could bring to him. What business opportunities might arise. Her value on the marriage market. Lottie refused to cry or give way to temper. That, she knew from bitter experience, would not help the situation. She had to be calm. Somehow, she would find a way.

'I will go,' she whispered.

'Good.' Henry turned his back on her. 'Now, Aunt, may I have another of your esteemed muffins?'

'Lottie, dry your eyes.' Cousin Frances patted her shoulder. 'Things like this are always happening in my Minerva Press novels and they turn out all right in the end.'

Lottie gave a small hiccup. Somehow, Cousin Frances's sudden solicitude made everything worse.

'Time to wake up, Lord Thorngrafton.' Tristan strode across the darkened room, pulled apart the curtains and let the fresh air enter the wine-soaked room. 'Or should I say, Cousin Peter? I had wondered who I might find at Shaw's and had suspected that it might be you.'

The prone figure on the bed groaned, mumbled a few incoherent words before pulling the pillow over his head. 'Go away. It is the middle of the night.'

'Time to be up, Peter. Three o'clock in the afternoon. Play time has finished.' Tristan controlled his fury at his first cousin. 'Quit your shamming or you will have cause to regret it. Can you give me any reason why I should not summon the parish constable?'

At the mention of the parish constable, the man sat straight up. His florid complexion paled as Tristan regarded his first cousin with a dispassionate eye. There was a vague family resemblance, but nothing remarkable.

'You…you…you are supposed to be on the Continent. Or, better yet, dead in some alleyway.' Peter's hand trembled as he passed it over his eyes. 'I was sure you would never return to England. And Uncle swore it when I changed my name from Burford to Dyvelston.'

'Changing a name and being acknowledged as his heir does not change the order of succession, Peter.'

'I know that, but…'

'I returned, Cousin, as I promised I would.' Tristan stared at him. 'I always keep my promises…unlike some.'

'Allow me some moments to dress. This is quite a shock to me. You here. Alive.'

'Not as big of a shock as it was to me to discover that Lord Thorngrafton had been responsible for a variety of actions. What amazes me is how brazen you have been about it.'

His cousin stood up and started to dress.

'Don't begrudge me, Tris,' he said. 'I thought you dead. I was sure you were dead. Uncle Jeremiah swore it as well. He told me that you were seriously ill in Florence… or was it Venice? Don't matter, but I didn't expect you to appear.'

'Reports of my demise were premature.' Tristan paused and brushed a speck off his frock coat. 'And never call me Tris. It implies a familiarity that does not exist between us.'

'But I am your heir. There ain't no other and if you were dead…' Peter ran his hand through his hair. 'Be fair, Tristan. Uncle's obituary, of course, made the papers and everyone naturally assumed that I would be the one… Who am I to dissuade them?'

'And who are you charging all this to?' Tristan made a sweep of his hand. 'The best suite at Shaw's is ruinously expensive.'

'You need not worry. I only borrowed the title.' Peter

shook his head. 'I am not that let in the pocket. And one has to speculate to accumulate.'

'Good use?'

'Exploring business opportunities…' Peter gave a practised smile. 'I have a plan about lead mining, and I just need a little capital. There is a piece of property.'

'And it has nothing to do with the card game I heard about being arranged at Mumps ha' not a mile from here. Or the two aged widows Lord Thorngrafton pursued without success last month.'

Peter winced and ran his hand through his hair, making it stand up on end. 'You heard about that.'

'Certain parties were keen to inform me of this development once I enquired. I am not without friends, Peter.' Tristan regarded his cousin. 'I warn you, Peter, the current Lord Thorngrafton will be above reproach, his name unblemished. I intend to restore the estate to its former glory, to undo the damage our uncle did.'

'But…but scandal dogs your footsteps.' Peter blinked. 'It is why you went to the Continent. You killed a man.'

'He failed to die.'

'But you shot him.'

'For cheating at cards. I had had too much to drink and my aim was less than true.' Tristan gave a cold smile. 'It has improved. Now your exploits are at an end.'

'You remind me more and more of Uncle Jeremiah! He had the same aptitude for a chilling phrase. The same ice-cold eye.'

'Shall I forget we are related?' Tristan asked, raising an eyebrow.

'Please, Tristan, for old time's sake, let me do this one

thing. I have prospects. There are three youngish widows whose heads are turned at the thought of a title. Then there is this businessman, whose mother is impressed with titles, but if I can persuade him to invest in the old lead mine, it will return a thousandfold...' Peter laid his hand on Tristan's shoulder. 'When we were young, we used to help each other out. I helped you escape to the Continent. You can't deny it. You owe me, Tristan. I was the one who aided you and Suzanne. Made things possible.'

Tristan regarded his cousin. Peter's body was already starting to run to fat and his face showed a certain thickening. Perhaps the widows and the businessmen deserved what they got. But neither was he ready to forgive Peter's observation. He and his uncle did not share a temperament.

'You did indeed. Perhaps I do owe you for that. I recall precisely why I was there as well.'

'A simple misunderstanding.' Peter held up his hands and began to speak very quickly as he dressed. 'It is my best chance of getting the readies I need. I have spent time conversing with the businessman's mother. She is here taking the waters. He is coming to visit and bringing his sister.'

'His sister?'

'She has a small fortune in funds... A week—that is all I want and then I shall never trouble you again.' Peter's eyes grew crafty.

'Who exactly is this businessman?'

'Henry Charlton. His sister is mad for titles.' Peter gave a laugh. 'I had thought to seduce her last November, but she slipped through my fingers. Then her mother appears here, an odious woman with aspirations, and informs me of her daughter's fortune in funds.'

'You tried to seduce a number of women last November.'

'Yes, but they knew what they were on about.'

'As long as you are sure. Virgins and the like can lead to unforeseen complications.' Tristan paused. 'We leave now.'

'This very instant? But it will take me a time to pack and it is past checking out. I will have to pay for tonight's room.'

'That is your problem.'

Peter's eyes grew crafty. 'You will need a place to lay your head. Stay here tonight. One night and see if I can't persuade you to invest. For days gone by. Please.'

Tristan regarded his cousin, with his face pleading. 'I want no more of this deception. You will put matters right.'

'If I must…' Peter's face showed signs of clear relief.

'I positively insist. You will follow my lead. Do not attempt to cross me, Peter. The next time, I will forget that you are kin.'

'Have you memorised the list I gave you, Lottie, so you will know which gentlemen to dance with?' Her mother grabbed Lottie's elbow as they descended the stairs at Shaw's Hotel the next evening. 'You must make sure that you speak very loudly to Lord Crawley. He is as deaf as a post. And Sir Geoffrey Lea…'

'Mama, I have read the list and committed it to memory. You have asked me this twice already.' Lottie fought the temptation to roll her eyes heavenwards.

'I know how inattentive you can be, Carlotta. This is a serious campaign. I had expected you two days ago.'

'Aunt Alice sends her apologies, but the packing took time.'

'Not when I do it.' Her mother gave a loud sniff and muttered something about the incompetence of sisters-in-law.

Several hours at Shaw's Hotel and Lottie come to the conclusion that her options were limited. Nearly every person she had encountered was well past the age of fifty or appeared to be suffering from a weak chin and watery eyes. Or both. The only possible glimmer of an idea she had was to steer the men towards other women. If they all found wives, she would be free.

'But Mama, the men here are more likely to want a nurse than a wife. I will make a very bad nurse.'

'A young titled widow is always in demand, Lottie. You can marry for other things later.' Her mother caught Lottie's chin between her thumb and forefinger, twisting Lottie's head to the left and right before releasing it. 'Your looks should hold another five years at least. Plenty of time. You need to think towards the future. I would see you married well.' Her mother went down the stairs with a determination that Wellington would have admired.

'Are you sure this neckline is not a touch too low?' Lottie asked Henry as they followed in her wake. 'Mama appears to have forgotten the lace. Perhaps I ought to go back.'

'You never bothered about such things before,' Henry said. 'I feel certain that Lord Thorngrafton will appreciate the...dress. Or one of the other gentlemen. I dare say Mama was correct. There are any number of titled widowers here.'

'They are all about one hundred years old except for Lord Thorngrafton, and I warned you, Henry, about him.'

'You appear to know a great deal about Lord Thorngrafton all of a sudden.' Henry frowned. 'And he has yet to make an appearance.'

'We encountered each other last November. Martha Irons saved me from disaster with her timely swoon.' Lottie demurely lowered her eyelashes. 'But my lace, Henry. Is the neckline not a bit daring? The dress is two seasons old.'

'It looks lovely from where I stand.' The low rumble of a voice washed over her. Lottie froze as she felt a hot tide of red flush her face. He was not supposed to be here. He was supposed to be safely in Haydon Bridge or wherever rakes went. Certainly not here.

'Are we acquainted, sir?' Henry's voice had become frigid.

'Tristan Dyvelston.' Tristan's voice was cool. 'Perhaps, Peter, you would be so good to introduce us.'

'My cousin, Henry, my cousin.' Peter Dyvelston, Lord Thorngrafton, came forward and caught Henry by the arm. 'It was my mistake. Tristan, I told you about Henry Charlton and his charming sister, Miss Charlton. Where is your delightful mother? I was looking forward to speaking with her again. We had such an amusing conversation the other night.'

Lottie stared at the impeccably dressed gentleman standing next to Lord Thorngrafton. Her pulse began to race and she struggled to remember how to breathe. She had told herself that she had been mistaken, that Tristan could not be that handsome. But her memory had lied.

He was far more.

The darkness of his frock coat contrasted with his face, and his cream trousers skimmed his figure. But what was he doing here and in the company of Lord Thorngrafton? He had given the impression the other day that he had very little to do with the man. Lottie tightened her grip on her fan and hoped that he would not make any untoward remarks about their last meeting.

'I am delighted to make your acquaintance, Mr Dyvelston.' Lottie held out a gloved hand, prayed that his lips wouldn't brush it, then prayed that they would.

Chapter Three

Tristan regarded the trio in front of him. The mother and the brother were types he was used to, but Lottie Charlton in an evening gown was a piece of shimmering blue confection. The form-fitting bodice bowed out at her waist and her petticoats swirled about her ankles in a sea of white foam. Tristan wondered if his hands could span her waist or would there be a gap? Would her flesh feel as warm between his fingers as her wrist had felt against his mouth the other day?

Her ear bobs swayed gently and her blonde ringlets were artfully placed on the top of her head. No expense had been spared. She was obviously angling for a husband, but which one of the geriatrics did she want? And what would happen if she knew his title? Would she use their earlier meeting against him? A pulse of anger ran through him. He would not be so easily ensnared into marriage.

'I am delighted to make your acquaintance at long last, Miss Charlton. I was confused as to your identity.' Tristan bowed low over her hand. His breath touched the thin kid of her glove, though Lottie drew back before his lips encountered her palm. But he had seen the slight flaring of her nostrils. 'I have heard a great deal about you from my cousin.'

'What are you doing here?'

'Lord Thorngrafton has taken a suite of rooms here and my cousin is permitting me to share them.' Tristan watched the comprehension grow on Peter's face. The masquerade would continue for tonight, until the precise nature of the situation was clear. It paid to be cautious.

'How did you get here?' Lottie asked in a furious undertone, pointedly ignoring his arm. 'You were in Haydon Bridge looking after your parents' graves and hopefully feeling remorse at the state you allowed them to get into.'

'I could ask the same of you.' His eyes stopped at her neckline and flicked up to her generous mouth. 'What did you come in search of? A husband? Your gown is admirably suited for the hunt.'

The corners of her mouth turned down and her blue eyes took on a mulish expression. 'You do take the strangest notions into your head, Mr Dyvelston. Do you always give lectures in this manner?'

'My cousin is here but for a short while.' Tristan gestured towards where Peter stood, rapidly expounding on the virtues of lead mining in the district to Lottie's brother. An unforeseen complication, but one he intended to his advantage. If Lottie discovered his true status, would she tell her mother about the incident in the cemetery? Would the mother use it as an excuse to ensnare him? He refused to take the risk. Peter would keep silent, he was certain of that. 'I do not feel that he would be good husband material.'

'And is there anyone you recommend in his place?' Her tone was light, but her eyes narrowed as she fluttered her fan.

'I have not been here long enough to advise properly,' Tristan said, allowing his eyes to dance.

'You should not assume, then.' Lottie snapped her fan shut. 'I declined your cousin's offer before Christmas.'

'So you did. I had forgotten.'

'I am here because my brother brought me.' Lottie risked a glance at Tristan's unyielding profile. It irritated her that he thought her so blindingly obvious in her husband-hunting. And if he had made that assumption, how many of the other guests had also come to the same conclusion? Her mother could be terribly indiscreet. 'My mother is taking the waters. She swears that they do her nerves a power of good. She enjoys the company.'

'The sulphur water at Gilsland is renowned as is its matchmaking Popping Stone. I believe the numbers are about even.'

Lottie gritted her teeth. 'My mother desired a bit of company. I shall not be following the footsteps of Sir Walter Scott.'

'Did everything work out as you had planned for your cousin?' he asked in an arch tone, seemingly amused rather than quelled by her remark. 'Is your aunt pleased with your interference in matters matrimonial?'

Lottie examined the pattern of the carpet. He would have to bring that up. 'I maintain hopes, but I misjudged the situation slightly. It was felt that perhaps I was better off departing as Mama was desirous of me arriving here. I am to be the belle of tonight's ball, so I understand.'

'Ah, you are here for the matchmaking.'

'No, I am here to prove to my mother and brother that I can be trusted. I wish to make my mark in London.'

'Do you think you will be able to? Many young ladies vie to become to the Incomparable, the Diamond of the Season. The vast majority are condemned to be wallflowers.'

She glanced up and noticed that his dark eyes were fringed with impossibly long lashes, the sort of lashes that were wasted on a man. But his gaze held no malice, only concern. A queer trembling overtook her. He, a near stranger, cared. 'I think there are other places where I stand a better chance of achieving my goal.'

'And the goal is...'

'To make a brilliant match.' She threw back her shoulders and made sure her eyes danced. 'And you do not need to worry. I have no designs on your virtuous name. Mama is insistent on a title.'

'That fact relieves me no end.' He gave a short laugh.

'I thought it would.'

'Who are you hunting?'

'Mama has made a list, but I fear she has not consulted Burke's recently and is doomed to disappointment.' Lottie rubbed her eye, relieved to be explaining the problems. Tristan Dyvelston, at least, was a sympathetic ear and he might have a solution to her problem. 'I distinctly heard Lord Foster mention a wife and she has him down as a widower. I am not sure if she has been careless or if she simply made a mistake. These things can happen even in the best ordered of campaigns. But it doesn't really matter as I have no intention of marrying, simply demonstrating to Mama that I can behave properly. There will be no scandals clinging to my skirts.'

'Sometimes scandals happen whether one is trying to avoid them or not.'

'What does it feel like to be on the outside of society, Mr Dyvelston?' Lottie tilted her head to one side, making her smile sweet.

His eyes became a deep black as the barb hit home and he inclined his head. 'It is a cold and bleak place, Miss Charlton. You would not care for it. And yet women are easily banished there. Too easily.'

Lottie grasped her fan tighter and struggled to breathe against the tightness of her corset.

'No, I probably would not, but then it is unlikely I shall have to encounter it.' She gave her ringlets a little toss. 'I plan to be at the very heart of society. It is my natural place.'

'Are you determined to marry a title, then? Against the odds?'

'It is as easy to love a titled man as an untitled one.' Lottie glanced over her shoulder and dropped her voice. 'One of Mama's little sayings, and it does seem to mean so much to her. She has aspirations.'

'So your sights are set on Thorngrafton, as much as you try to deny it. I will warn you for the last time, Miss Charlton, my cousin is not to be trusted. Please consider long and hard if he does make an offer.'

'His title includes a baronetcy, one of the original ones purchased from Charles I, or so Henry says.' Lottie tapped her fan against her mouth, suddenly aware that she had perhaps revealed too much. 'It is an honourable title, but I hope to do better. I want to convince Mama that a London Season is what I need.'

'Then why are you here?'

'Because I have yet to convince my brother.' Lottie held up her hand. 'I know what you must think of me. Cold-hearted, unemotional and obsessed with titles, Mr Dyvelston, but may I remind you that you are hardly a person to be sitting in judgement.'

'I never judge my fellow human beings, Miss Charlton.' A dimple flashed in the corner of his mouth. 'Particularly when the person in question is as refreshing about her intentions as you.'

Lottie's breath caught in her throat. Why couldn't Tristan Dyvelston have a title? It would make life much simpler. She would not have minded setting her cap for him, despite saying otherwise. He was exciting, different. He did not melt at a flutter of her eyelashes, and, more importantly, he did not treat her as an inanimate object or speak exclusively to her breasts. 'I hardly see any point in pretence, Mr Dyvelston.'

'Will you save a waltz for me?'

Lottie turned her face towards the corniced ceiling as she tried to resist the sudden quickening of her pulse. A waltz in his arms. 'If you like...'

'Lottie, do hurry up. Lottie!' her mother called. 'There are a number of people who are desirous of meeting you.'

'One should always be careful about whom one meets in a hotel, Miss Charlton.' His eyes held something hidden. 'There can be no telling if they are the genuine article or not.'

'One should be careful about whom one meets in a ruined churchyard, Mr Dyvelston.' She tilted her chin upwards and prepared to sweep away.

'One meets all the best sorts of people there.' His voice held a note of amusement that rose around her and held her spellbound.

'Lottie, why do you dally?' Her mother's voice re-sounded across the foyer, recalling her to her duty. 'There is someone here who insists on making your acquaintance. I am certain you will find him most agreeable.'

'My mother calls. She will wonder why I have been detained.'

'Do not let me keep you, Miss Charlton. I have no wish to cause a scandal.'

'I thought that was what you did best.'

'You mistook me. My scandalous days have long past. I lead a sober and uneventful life.'

'Mr Dyvelston.'

Lottie picked up her skirts and hurried over to her mother. She stopped short as she saw the wizened man that her mother was sitting next to. Her heart sank. Sir Geoffrey Lea. The name that was proudly written below Lord Thorngrafton's. He was over seventy. How could her mother do this to her?

She forced her shoulders to stay straight, refusing to glance back at where Mr Dyvelston stood.

Why were men such as he always dishonourable and forbidden?

Tristan bided his time during the early part of the evening, observing the current guests of Shaw's Hotel, waiting and watching. They were a mixed group and, as far as he could tell from the accents, not from the general vicinity. It was becoming clear why Peter had been able to carry off his impersonation.

Many of the men were elderly and comfortable in their own self-importance. He felt sorry that Lottie Charlton was going to be sacrificed to one of them. But he had to trust that her family would not marry her off if she objected.

He watched as Lottie's blue gown with its swirling lace flashed by and heard her laughter float out over the crowd. A number of matrons and their other less well-endowed daughters clicked their tongues, but Tristan sensed a sort of desperation in her moves as if she was determined to show that she was having fun. He had been tempted to confess the truth about his title and watch her face. But there was also the mother to consider. One false step and he could find himself shackled.

'Congratulate me, Thorngrafton.' Sir Geoffrey Lea, one of the more decrepit denizens of Shaw's came up to Tristan.

'My cousin—' Tristan gestured towards where Peter stood, speaking about his lead mine to any who would listen.

'Is plain Mr Dyvelston. Being adopted does not mean inheriting the title.' Sir Geoffrey tapped his nose. 'I am not past it yet, whatever anyone might say. Took me until I saw you to put my finger on why I did not trust him. I dare say that most people have forgotten which cousin would inherit, particularly as your uncle was so marked in his preferences. Won't enquire into the game you two are playing either, it is not my place. But your cousin will not get the Charlton heiress. You may inform him of that.'

'I never intended that he should.' Tristan tightened his jaw. The elderly gentleman made Lottie sound as if she was some sort of bone to be fought over. He had forgotten quite how depressing the English marriage market could be. 'I have my reasons, Sir Geoffrey, please respect them. I ask this as a gentleman.'

He held out his hand and, after a moment, Sir Geoffrey took it.

'I shall keep your identity secret while you are at Shaw's, Thorngrafton. I give you my word. We are both men of honour.'

'Thank you.'

'There was bad blood between you and your uncle. Shouldn't happen in families, but it does.' Sir Geoffrey gave a wheezing laugh. His watery eyes narrowed as he peered at Tristan. 'You are like your father in many ways, but I see your uncle as well. You had best be careful. You know how life treated him. A pity—he showed such promise at Eton.'

'What should I be congratulating you for?' Tristan said firmly, drawing the man from his reminisces. He refused to be compared with his uncle. He knew what a bitter and twisted man his uncle had become.

'Pipped your cousin at the post. Pipped everyone. That's what. I have spoken to that vision's mother.' Sir Geoffrey used his walking stick to indicate where Lottie danced with an elderly man. 'She is as charming in person as she is to look at. A true picture, an ornament worthy of appreciation. Her mother assures me that she is an excellent nurse.'

'Does she, indeed?'

'She also assures me that her daughter is every bit as virtuous as she is good-looking. She will make an admirable wife. I shall have to make a visit to the Popping Stone with that gel.' Sir Geoffrey gave a wheezing laugh.

'And virtue is important to you, Sir Geoffrey? I would have thought conversation, wit and a general attraction.'

'Virtue is everything. Without virtue, the woman has nothing.' Sir Geoffrey thumped his cane on the floor.

'Except a fortune in funds.'

'The fortune allows me to overlook other certain less favourable aspects about the match.' Sir Geoffrey cleared his throat. 'Did you know her paternal great-grandfather was in trade? A grocer!'

'I had no idea, but the family, I believe, has high aspirations.'

'It is true.' Sir Geoffrey nodded and a twinkle came into his eye. 'She will make an admirable companion for my waning years, don't you think? Quite a well-turned ankle. It will show them at the club that I am not past it, that I can still attract the fillies.'

'Some might entertain that notion.'

A huge bubble of pleasure coursed through Lottie. She had forgotten how much fun it was to waltz, polka and generally be the centre of attention. True, Shaw's Hotel was not London or even the Assembly Rooms in Newcastle, but there was dancing. Ever since the five-piece orchestra had begun to play, she had had no time to sit down. One after another the gentlemen had begged for the favour of a dance. Lord Thorngrafton had staked his claim to the Sir Roger de Coverley before disappearing to converse with Henry about lead mines.

Her only disappointment was that Tristan Dyvelston had not come near, not once. She had seen him following her with his eyes, and twice he led other ladies out onto the dance floor. Stately widows with well-upholstered bosoms and braying laughs, the sort one might dance with if one was looking for a wealthy wife who would not be picky about his lack of a title.

Was that in truth why he was there? That he was seeking a wealthy wife? It made a certain amount of sense, but it annoyed her that he had made remarks about her husband-hunting.

She redoubled her efforts to be charming and to forget him, but it appeared her body had developed an acute awareness when he was around. Each time she circled the floor, she wondered what it would be like to have his hand on her waist, clasping his fingers instead of her partner's.

'Shall you dance with me next?' a bewhiskered elderly gentleman asked. 'Your mother has proclaimed how divinely you waltz.'

'This waltz is already spoken for.' A shadow loomed over her.

Lottie glanced up into Tristan's darkly intent face. Her body tingled as her breath caught in her throat. 'Is it?'

'You agreed to waltz with me earlier,' he said. 'Have you forgotten?'

'So I did. I cannot think what might have come over me.' Lottie tried to ignore the frisson of pleasure that rippled through her. She wanted to waltz with him. She wanted to forget everything else, to forget her future. She simply wanted to dance and take pleasure in the moment. 'Shall we waltz then, Mr Dyvelston? They are playing one of the Strauss waltzes.'

'It is not one of the most fashionable, but it has a pleasant enough melody.'

He put his hand on her waist and they started off. Somehow, dancing with him was different from every time she had danced before. His steps were perfect—not overly showy like a dancing master's or clumsy. She concentrated on his shoulder rather than on his mouth.

'Where did you learn to waltz like this?'

'In Vienna.'

'One day, I should like to travel. I have only been as far as Yorkshire. Mama does not believe in foreign travel, but I think it must be tremendously exciting.' Lottie was aware she was babbling, but it kept her mind off the gentle pressure on her waist and how their bodies fitted exactly, moving in time with each other.

She looked down at the smooth floor. Less than a week ago she had had no idea of his existence, but by ten o'clock this evening, she could think of nothing but him. She wanted to say that it was Cousin Frances's scandalous tales but there was something else that drew her to him. She had seen the way he'd looked at his parents' graves.

'You are not attending me, Miss Charlton,' he said. 'I just gave you a witty sally about Vienna and you remain silent. Not even a smile passed your lips.'

'I shall try harder.' Lottie glanced up into his face and saw the crinkles around his eyes. She swallowed hard and struggled to think beyond his hand upon her waist. 'Was there something in particular that you wished me to be amused at? Repeat it and I will attend. You will find me the perfect conversationalist from now.'

He gave a husky laugh and she felt his hand tighten, pull her closer so that their bodies collided. His breath fanned her ear. 'Sir Geoffrey Lea. He was in a very self-congratulatory mood.'

A stab of fear went through her and she missed a step.

Her fingers clutched at his shoulder as if it were a life raft as the ballroom tilted sideways. Her slippers skidded into each other. 'Sir Geoffrey? Congratulations?'

'He is very pleased with what he has done. Matrimony.'

Lottie looked wildly about her and tried not to panic. She had to remember to breathe, and not to give way to wild imaginings. Such things were for Cousin Frances, not for her. Her mother would not have done such a thing without speaking to her.

'Is there some problem?'

'He figured highly on my mother's list. My mother's list of eligible men.' She struggled to draw a breath and found she could not. Her fingers curled around his arm. 'Please say his congratulatory mood had nothing to do with me, that he has found some well-endowed widow of about fifty. I saw him with my mother earlier. He is more than three times my age.'

'I would say that is an accurate assessment.'

'You are not providing much comfort, Mr Dyvelston.' Lottie tried to draw a deep breath and mentally cursed her corset and the need for a fashionably tiny waist. She should not have insisted that they be done up so tightly. She had to do something or she would faint. She swallowed hard.

'You become pale. The air in here is close.' His arm came around her, an iron band of support. Lottie leant back against it, grateful. 'I must insist we go outside.'

'A breath of fresh air would be helpful, Mr Dyvelston.' Lottie concentrated on putting one foot in front of the other as she leant on his arm. Around her the sound of the waltz swelled, mocking her.

How could she have taken such pleasure in such a transitory thing?

Her life teetered about her, threatened to collapse. Mama would insist and Henry would agree. He had already begun to make noises about the expense of staying here and how he longed to be back within the bosom of his family. And she would be sentenced to a life of misery.

Tristan threw open the French doors and led the way out onto the terrace. The blackness of his hair and coat mingled with the darkness that surrounded him.

The cool air rushed out to meet her, caressing her fevered skin. In the distance she could hear the River Irthing. Above her were the first faint glimmerings of stars. The whole world was at peace. She was aware of Tristan coming to stand by her. Not touching her, just standing close enough that he could act if she fainted. Lottie pressed her lips together. She would not faint and give way to her feelings. Such things were for women like Frances. When one fainted, one lost all control. She drew in another breath and concentrated on the shadows in the lawn.

'Have you recovered, Miss Charlton?' His hand hovered at her elbow. 'We may go in if you like. I am certain no one noticed us coming out here. Your virtue is quite safe.'

'Who has Sir Geoffrey found to marry?' she asked in a strained voice as she dug her nails into her palms. 'Exactly which widow will look after him in his declining years?'

She glanced up and saw the sombreness of Tristan's face. Slowly he shook his head and his eyes showed pity. 'The woman in question is no widow.'

She clutched the balustrade, forced her lungs to strain against her stays. 'Does it have anything to do with me?'

'Would it matter if it did?'

'Several days ago, I played a game, Mr Dyvelston, an innocent game.' Lottie looked out into the blackness. She could make out the vague shape of the trees. 'I sought to help my cousin to become engaged to a man whom I felt she had affection for. This afternoon, my mother gave me a list of eligible men, men I have no affection for, but one of whom I am supposed to marry. It is my task.'

'Does affection have anything to do with marriage? I would have thought security and status were high on your list.'

Tears pricked Lottie's eyelids. She blinked rapidly. He was being kind. It had been a long time since anyone had been kind. She wanted him to be cruel or to laugh at her. Anything but be kind. He knew what her mother and Henry had planned for her. It felt as if great prison doors were swinging shut.

'I used to think, like my sister-in-law, that security was important, but then I saw how happy Emma Harrison was…is and knew I was mistaken. Emma waited years for the love of her life. She is adored.'

'Is being adored something you wish?'

Lottie nodded mutely. She half-turned and her cheek encountered the starched front of his shirt. She rested her head, listening to the reassuring heartbeat, the steady thumping. His hand went under her chin and raised it so she could look into his eyes. They were larger than she remembered, warm. She could drown in eyes like that.

'Lottie, you must be strong.'

'I will try.' She gave a slight sniff.

'That's my girl.'

She knew that propriety demanded that she move away. She was anything but his girl. She was nothing to him. She was about to be promised to Sir Geoffrey Lea. Sacrificed on her mother's altar of social ambition. Ever since she had made her début, she had paid attention to the consequences. But for what? To be married to a fossil, a man older than her late father. To submit to his horny-handed embrace. Fate was cruel and she wanted to cheat it.

Her feet stayed still as he placed a strong hand on her shoulder, drawing her closer. She struggled to breathe, to remember her name, to remember anything beyond the shape of his lips. She raised a hand in mute appeal. Touched his shirt front.

He lowered his mouth, captured hers. A featherlight touch that rapidly became firmer, deeper, called to her. She felt her body arch towards his, wanted it to continue. But he lifted his mouth and regarded her.

His face was all shadows and angles. Moonlight shone down, giving it another glow. In the distance she could hear the faint strains of a polka, but much closer she heard the pounding of her heart. Her tongue explored her aching lips and a sigh escaped her throat.

His arms tightened about her again, held her there against the length of his body. A fiery glow built inside her. She was alive in a way she would never be again, if she were married to Sir Geoffrey Lea or whichever other titled fossil her mother might discover.

'Kiss me again,' she whispered, pulling his head down to hers. Whispered against his firm mouth, 'One last time. No one is here. Tomorrow will be too late.'

Her hands came up and clung to his shirt front. He

lowered his mouth again and pressed kisses along her neck and then returned to recapture her mouth. This time the kiss was harder, more insistent. Penetrating. Sensation coursed through her body in hot pulsating waves.

Her body collided with his as the meeting of lips stretched. His hand tangled in her hair, holding her face. A warmth grew deep inside Lottie, melting her limbs, forcing her to seek the support of his body. Her breasts strained against the confines of her corset. Ached. She felt the material give and his cool fingers slide against her fevered skin. Her entire world had come down to this one moment, this one point in time. She sighed and parted her lips, drank in the scent of him. His lips trailed down her neck, tasted her skin, and began to slowly travel lower.

'Unhand that woman, you…you cad!'

The words pierced her inner core. Lottie froze, hoping they were directed at someone else. Tristan raised his head, looked over her shoulder towards where the voice resounded. He put her away from him. Lottie looked up at him, unable to turn around. His face changed, became hard, but his arm remained about her, holding her. She resisted the temptation to bury her face in his shoulder. Both enormity of what she had done, what she had been discovered doing, and the knowledge that if it had continued for much longer, she would have been powerless to stop it, weighed in on her.

'Is there a problem, Sir Geoffrey?' Tristan said, drawling the words.

Lottie flinched and moved out of the circle of his arms. He made no attempt to keep her in them. She turned and looked back towards the French doors. Sir Geoffrey stood there, leaning on his cane, surrounded by other figures. How long had they been standing there? How much had they seen? She glanced down to where her bodice gaped open, brought her hands up and tried to rearrange it. Her curls tumbled in disarray about her shoulders, the artful hairstyle her mother's maid had arranged earlier this evening gone in a moment's passion. She winced, knowing the wanton picture she must make.

'What is going on here?' Her brother's voice floated over the rapidly increasing crowd. 'Oh my God, Lottie, what have you done?'

'He has seduced her.' Sir Geoffrey's voice boomed out over the rest. 'He coldheartedly took her innocence and virtue. Look at her state of undress.'

'It all depends on your definition of seduction.' Tristan's voice dripped with ice.

'Mr Dyvelston was helping me because I felt faint.' Lottie forced the words from her mouth. She looked up at Tristan for confirmation. His eyes blazed black. 'I needed a breath of fresh air. Nothing happened.'

'It looked rather different to me,' Sir Geoffrey thundered.

'I kissed her, yes. I overpowered her.' The words exploded from Tristan Dyvelston.

'Did you kiss this man, Carlotta?' her brother asked. 'Did you allow him to kiss you?'

Lottie's tongue explored her lips—full, swollen and aching for the pressure of his mouth once again. She dreaded to think what the front of her gown looked like. They had been caught. Denial was impossible. Everything appeared to be happening from a long way away. She nodded as she crossed her hands over her chest. Waited.

'Charlton, our bargain has ended.' Sir Geoffrey's voice resounded across the veranda. Strident. Furious. 'She is damaged goods, sir. Given towards lewd and licentious behaviour. I wish you luck in finding a husband for that baggage. No gentleman will have her. Thank God I discovered what she was like before I married her. She'd have run away with her dancing master, soon as look at you.'

Lottie heard the swell of voices rise around her, echoing Sir Geoffrey's harsh sentiments. Everyone speaking at once. Ruined. She was ruined. The dreaded consequences that Lucy had so confidently predicted for her all those months ago had happened. There would be no London Season. No triumphant return to Newcastle. Nothing, all because she had not been able resist the temptation of Tristan Dyvelston's mouth.

'I...I...' Lottie put a hand to her head and groped for words, something that would explain it all and that would restore everything to its natural order. Her mother and Henry had to see that it was not the end of the world, that she was still an asset to the family. In time, she might once again have marriage prospects.

She scanned the rapidly expanding crowd for a friendly face and found none.

'What do you intend to do about it, Dyvelston?' Sir Geoffrey shook his stick at Tristan. 'You have ruined this young person. Taken advantage of her youth. The tales they whispered about you were true, even though I have always vigorously denied them. No son of your father would behave in such a libertine manner.'

'Do? Why should he do anything?' Lord Thorngrafton

came forward. 'All he did was kiss the girl. She asked for it. There was that incident in Newcastle—'

'Stay out of this, Peter!' Tristan Dyvelston thundered. 'You have done enough damage already.'

'Lord Thorngrafton is right. He simply kissed me. Nothing more.' Lottie hated the way her voice shook. She tried for a smile. She might be ruined, but Tristan should not be held entirely to blame. 'Might this whole thing be…?'

The faces turned towards her were less than encouraging. Several of the old ladies lifted their fans to gossip behind. The tale was already being embroidered. By morning she'd be a harlot and there would be no hiding from the scandal.

Lottie took a step backwards, encountered the railing. The enormity of what she had done washed over her. She had kissed a man, passionately kissed him, without expectation or forethought. A huge gaping hole opened in her middle. She wished she could turn back the hands of time.

'Oh dear, oh dear, whatever shall we do? All the love and attention I gave her and she repays me like this.' Her mother stood next to Sir Geoffrey, white-faced and wringing her hands. Her ample bosom trembled as she raised an accusatory finger. 'Carlotta, look what you have done to the family. To me. It is not just your reputation you have tarnished. You have shamed the family.'

'I didn't mean to.' Lottie held out her hands and willed her mother to smile at her, to make some small sign that she would stand by her. Her mother buried her face in her hands and the sound of sobbing increased.

'You only have yourself to blame, Mother.' Henry put

a hand on their mother's shoulder and turned his furious gaze on Lottie. 'You encouraged her far too much. I knew one day she would go too far and she has. You have disgraced us, Carlotta.'

Lottie kept her back straight. She had to get through this somehow, and then she'd decide what she could do. Perhaps there was a way to hush the whole thing up. If only everyone would stop yelling at once.

'He has ruined her, I say. I demand to know what he intends to do about it!' Sir Geoffrey drew himself up to his full height. 'I may be old, sir, but I am not without influence. I will have it known that you are debaucher of virgins, a man not to be trusted. What are you going to do? Are you totally devoid of honour?'

Tristan stared at the elderly man as the diatribe washed over him. He knew Sir Geoffrey was correct. Doors would be closed to him. He'd spent ten years in the wilderness. He did not intend to go there again. He glanced at Lottie Charlton. At first she had winced every time someone said something, but now she stood, straight, not moving a muscle. It would not just be he who was ruined, but also this woman.

He gave an ironic smile. He should have remembered his own advice—virgins were complicated. He should never have tasted her lips. He wanted to taste her skin again. He wanted her lips to softly yield under his again.

'Marry her. I will marry Miss Charlton.'

The veranda went silent.

'You are going to do what?' Mrs Charlton squeaked and began to furiously wave her fan.

'As I have ruined her, there is only one course open to

me, I will take the responsibility and marry her. My honour demands it.'

'I knew you had it in you, Dyvelston,' Lottie's brother said, clapping him on the shoulder. 'There, Mama, problem solved. Dyvelston will marry Lottie. We will have a quiet wedding and no one in the business community will turn their faces from us. While Dyvelston might not be what we would have wished, he will at least do the decent thing.'

'I am so grateful you solved the problem, Sir Geoffrey.' Mrs Charlton grabbed on to the elderly man's arm. Her plump face was very close to his. 'Eternally grateful.'

Sir Geoffrey patted her arm absentmindedly. 'My pleasure.'

'Where will the marriage take place?' Henry Charlton's eyes became crafty. 'It is all well and good to agree a marriage, but does he have any intention of actually marrying her? I know how these rakes operate. When do you intend to marry my sister?'

Tristan rubbed his chin. He could see Mrs Charlton's eyes gleaming. How much did she know? How much of this had been planned? 'I don't want banns. It might cause talk.'

'Let it be a special.' Mrs Charlton's eyes lit up. 'I always wanted my daughter to be married by special licence. So much more status than an ordinary license.'

'Oh, yes, Mama, a special licence would be splendid.' Lottie clapped her hands, like a child in a sweet shop. 'What a wonderful idea. Can you arrange that, Mr Dyvelston?'

'No special,' Tristan said through gritted teeth.

'What are you saying?' Her bottom lip trembled like a

child who had sweets taken away from her. Her blue eyes shimmered with tears. 'We are going to marry, aren't we? An ordinary licence, then.'

Tristan looked at where Lottie stood. It would be easy to indulge her when she looked at him like that. He wanted her to go on looking at him like that for the rest of his life, but he was a realist. Lottie Charlton, through no fault of her own, had all the hallmarks of a spoilt child who would grow into a spoilt woman. He knew what sort of trouble a woman like that could cause, if left unchecked. He would marry her, but she needed to be taught a lesson. If he confessed now who he really was, he would always wonder.

Had tonight's events been fabricated for her benefit? Did she really know who he was and was that the reason she had kissed him so passionately? And asked him to kiss her?

He needed to know; until he discovered the truth, he would keep his identity a secret.

'Gretna Green is but a few miles from here.'

The entire crowd fell silent.

'You mean to elope?' Mrs Charlton's shawls quivered. 'You are proposing to elope with my daughter.'

'It is the most sensible solution in the circumstances,' Sir Geoffrey said, giving a decisive nod. 'I will vouch for this man's honour, madam.'

'My sister is to elope? Married under Scottish law?' Henry Charlton's face expanded and he bore a distinct resemblance to a walrus. 'Do you know what you are on about, man?'

'I have agreed to do the decent thing and marry the woman, but it will be at Gretna Green, and not in some church wedding.' Tristan straightened his cuffs. 'It will save gossip.'

He took great pleasure in watching Henry Charlton's mouth open, but have no sound come out. Three times he started to say something, but somehow the words would not appear. He tried jabbing with a finger. 'You…you bounder. You will create a scandal if you marry her in that fashion.'

'I have agreed to marry your sister. I am hardly a bounder. And there is already a scandal of sorts.' Tristan gave a shrug. 'I am sorry if the terms of my offer are not to your liking, but there they are. You must decide which is the greater scandal—your sister unwed but kissed, or your sister married at Gretna Green.'

'But…'

'You must decide. Or, better yet, let your sister decide. It is her life and reputation we are discussing.'

'I suppose you do have a point.' Henry Charlton gave a harrumph. 'Carlotta?'

Tristan watched Lottie. What would she do? Would she risk it? A wild exultation grew within him. The risk. The gamble. What would she choose?

'Thank you for allowing me to make the choice, Henry.' Lottie came forward and tucked her hand into Tristan's. He glanced down at her, impressed with her dignity in the face of her brother's blustering and her mother's shrieking. She appeared to have accepted her fate. 'Mr Dyvelston is correct. Banns and the like will simply point to a harum-scarum marriage. I will make a runaway match. Far more romantic.'

Chapter Four

'Not the watercolours, Lottie. And only one satchel, you heard Mr Dyvelston.' Lottie's mother hurried into the room where Lottie sat packing. 'You will need a complete new wardrobe now that you are married. I dare say that he plans to buy it. It is the best way.'

Lottie tucked the watercolours and brushes into her bag. The first words her mother had said to her were a complaint. 'I heard Mr Dyvelston the first time, Mama, and I intend to paint on my wedding trip. I am being practical.'

'You have dashed all my hopes and plans for your future.' Her mother gave a loud sniff. 'And now all you can talk of is painting. Have you no consideration for my nerves? For what you have done to your brother? To me? You were supposed to wed a titled man. It was to be the culmination of everything.'

'I am getting married, Mama. He is connected to a title.'

'Yes, but will anyone know? I should never have let Sir Geoffrey sway me. I should have insisted on a proper marriage.' Her mother buried her face in a handkerchief.

'Lucy warned me that you would come to a bad end with your tricks and you have. You are a lucky woman that Mr Dyvelston turned out to be a gentleman. Goodness knows what you were thinking…Sir Geoffrey had made an offer for you. How could you do this to me?'

Lottie slammed another pair of stockings into the satchel. She refused to dignify her mother's remark with a reply.

'Well, Carlotta, what do you have to say for yourself? How can you explain away what you did? The man has no title, nothing to recommend him. Why did you kiss him?'

'You were quite prepared to marry me off to Jack Stanton.'

'Lottie, you ungrateful child!' Her mother gave a sharp intake of breath, went white and she waved her hand in front of her face, choking. 'My medicine, Lottie.'

Lottie rushed to the washstand, picked up the small vial, pulled off the stopper and held the smelling salts under her mother's nose. Her mother inhaled deeply; gradually, her colour returned to normal. Lottie breathed again. 'Are you better, Mama? I did not intend to give you another attack. You should take more care.'

'Me? You are the one who should have been cautious. I had everything arranged.' Her eyes narrowed. 'You threw it all away, you ungrateful spoilt child. Well, young lady—'

'I am marrying Mr Dyvelston, Mama.' Lottie fastened the satchel. She adjusted her pelisse and bonnet. It made a charming picture over her paisley silk afternoon dress. The cut was fashionable and Lottie had made sure the corset was laced extra tight in order to show off her waist. She wanted Tristan to look again at her with those smouldering eyes. 'Neither of us planned it, but it will save me and the family from ruin. I cannot undo the past. And Tristan does have connections, Mama. He is Lord Thorngrafton's cousin.'

'Lottie, Lottie. I cannot help but worry. Though Sir Geoffrey says that this is the best way and I must trust him.'

'And it saves the expense of a London Season. You might remind Henry of that, if he intends on huffing and puffing.'

Her mother gave a loud sniff. 'Yes, I suppose Dyvelston is doing the decent thing. But I care about my daughter's future. You were given every advantage.'

'I believe in my case, if I fail to marry, the advantages will mean nothing. I will be ruined, Mama. And won't I spend my life repenting that as well?'

'Oh, you young creatures are all the same. You think you know everything.' Her mother threw up her hands and Lottie wondered if she was going to have to retrieve the smelling salts again. She shifted uneasily, hating the disloyal thought, but she had seen how her mother had used the attacks before. 'A man should respect his wife. If you keep giving in to your passion, it will be the road to ruin. Your poor papa and I had a good marriage based on mutual respect and duty.'

And what about love? Or desire? Lottie stopped the words and allowed the remainder of her mother's diatribe to flow over her. She did not love Tristan, but she knew that there had to be more to a marriage than respectability. And she certainly did not want a title if Sir Geoffrey Lea was offering it. She was not a pawn to be sacrificed for her mother and brother's social ambition. She would lead her own life.

'You are not attending, Carlotta.'

'Mama, it is time to go.' Lottie leant forward and kissed her mother's cold cheek. 'I am getting married today to a good man. I can sense it in him.'

'Lottie, Lottie. There is more to being a good man than a pair of broad shoulders and a smooth dancing step.' Her mother's hands grasped Lottie's upper arms and she made a clucking noise at the back of her throat. 'You are such a child, Lottie. I blame myself. There is so much I should tell you, warn you about. Men do not like wanton creatures. They use them and discard them. When I think of your poor dear departed papa...'

'Papa would have wanted me to be happy.' Lottie stared at her mother, seeing for the first time the attempts to hold age back, the slightly over-garish jewellery, the petulant expression. Then she shook herself, hating the disloyal thoughts. Here was her mother, the woman she should revere above all others, but who had wanted to sell her for a title and reflected status. 'It was all he ever wanted. It is why he worked so hard. He wanted to give us everything we wanted.'

'Happiness is a fleeting thing. Security and connections are all.' Her mother shook her head and buried her face once again in a handkerchief.

'It just happened, Mama.' Lottie touched her lips, remembering the sensation of Tristan's lips against hers and knew that she would yield again.

'That is no excuse. I trust you will remember where your duty lies. A woman must take responsibility for a family's status. Remember that and behave accordingly, if nothing else. Try to grow up, Lottie...before it is too late.'

'Mama, I will be a good wife.' Lottie curled her fingers

around her satchel. 'I will make sure the marriage prospers.'

She marched out of the room, head high and shoulders back. She would show her mother that her dire predictions were wrong. She would make this marriage a success.

Lottie sat opposite Tristan in his borrowed carriage and watched the sunrise begin to appear on the horizon. Her bonnet had slipped over her nose and the wild exhilaration she had felt as she'd waved goodbye to the assembled throng of people had vanished. Her back ached and her feet were numb.

What had she done? Had she done the appropriate thing? She had done the only thing.

Each turn of the carriage wheel took her farther away from her mother, her family, her former life and closer to Gretna Green and marriage, marriage to Tristan. She would snatch a sip from the cup of happiness. Somehow. She refused to believe her mother's dire predictions about marrying for passion.

The carriage hit a rut, and her shoulder met the side of the carriage with a thump. Lottie winced at the pain, stifled the gasp behind her gloved hand.

'Careful.' Tristan, from where he sat, put out a hand to steady her. The touch of his hand burnt through the thin material of her dress. 'You don't want to injure yourself.'

'I will be fine.' She sat up straighter. Her hands curled around the edge of her seat, holding her there. 'I was unprepared. The road to Gretna Green is heavily rutted.'

'It is a well-travelled route.'

'Yes.' Lottie agreed. Well travelled. As if she needed reminding how many people went there to get married because they had to or because their families objected. Some might call it wildly romantic, but the doubts had started to circle around the edges of her brain. The Tristan Dyvelston who sat opposite with his top hat, black frock coat, cream-coloured trousers and hands lightly resting on a cane was very different from the excitingly attractive man who had kissed her earlier. No less handsome, but somehow more reserved, as if he were waiting and watching for something. Self-contained.

Lottie searched her mind. What did one say politely to the man who was about to become one's husband, but appeared now more than ever to be a stranger? And in such a fashion? How could she explain that she was terrified of what the future might hold?

She had no wish to appear a ninny or a brainless fool. She thought of topics like the weather or music, only to reject them. Some were too impersonal. Others far too personal. It was difficult, particularly as she simply wanted to curl up next to him and feel his arms about her. The silence seemed to hang between them, growing with each turn of the wheel until it was a palpable living thing that threatened to crush her.

'Wasn't it kind of your cousin to lend us his carriage?' she said, finally, in desperation.

'My cousin?' He raised an eyebrow and his face did not invite further enquiries. 'What does my cousin have to do with this carriage?'

'His arms are on the carriage door,' Lottie said, sitting up. Her hands adjusted the ribbons of her bonnet and tension appeared to ease from her shoulder. Finally a subject they could discuss—social niceties. 'I noticed it when we got in. Little details make the world go round. It eases social tensions, if one does not have to explain everything. It is something one learns rapidly when you are required to do as much visiting as Mama and I.'

'I had not considered that.'

'It was obvious to any who had eyes. Why else would someone paint their arms on a carriage unless they wanted to be noticed? Unless they were proud of the title?'

'Why indeed?'

Tristan's hand tightened around his cane and his mouth became a thin white line. Was he ashamed of borrowing his cousin's carriage? Was he worried that others would mistake him for his cousin and cause embarrassment? How awful would that be—to be mistaken for a peer when one wasn't.

Lottie folded her hands on her lap and crossed her ankles. Considered the possibility and decided against it.

Anyone who had met the two would know they were different. Tristan could never be Lord Thorngrafton. They had similar looks, but their temperaments were not at alike.

She never would have allowed Lord Thorngrafton to take her in his arms or even escort her outside into the darkness for a breath of fresh air. The air of a snake hung about him. He had presumed much last November and acted as if she was a naive miss who had no idea of what going to see etchings entailed, as if his title and status was all the reassurance a woman needed.

Lottie concentrated on taking a deep breath, and not letting her fury at the memory overwhelm her. But he was to be family now and she needed to be charitable. She might have mistaken him, but in any case, when they next encountered each other, she would be married and related to him. Family was different.

But she could not expect Lord Thorngrafton to apologise. It was up to women to mend bridges. And at the same time she would make Tristan see that there was nothing to be ashamed about when it came to using family connections. It was positively *de rigueur*, according to Mama.

'When did your cousin inherit the title?' she asked, assuming the voice she used for the more important At Homes when she wanted to make a suitably genteel appearance. She would find a way to build the bridges without revealing her distaste for the man.

'I doubt we will be seeing my cousin often.' Tristan's tone was less than encouraging. 'The present Lord Thorngrafton inherited the title within the last year. I was travelling on the Continent at the time.'

'But he is family.'

'Yes, of a sort. The old lord was my uncle.' The merest hint of a smile touched Tristan's lips. 'One cannot pick and choose one's family as easily as one's friends.'

'That is why family is all the more important.' Lottie batted her eyes and made her voice sugar sweet. It was obvious to her that there had been a quarrel between Tristan and his cousin. Perhaps she could do something to get them to make up. It was never good to quarrel with those who might be in a position to help you. 'Friends may come and go, but families are always there.'

'You are not encumbered with my relations.' Tristan's reply was crushing. He tilted his hat over his eyes and stretched out his legs as if to indicate the conversation had ended and the topic was no longer up for discussion.

Lottie looked out of the carriage window at the darkened countryside sweeping past and felt the prick of tears. This ride was not going as planned. He was not behaving how he ought. She swallowed her annoyance at Tristan's obstinacy and tried again. She had to explain why this overture from his cousin had to be treated with respect and gratitude. Why it was the only way. Anything to keep her mind off the closeness of Tristan and how she wished he'd take her in his arms and tell her not to worry.

'But he is your cousin, and titled,' she said, trying again. This time she ran a hand down the horsehair seats. 'It was very kind of him to lend us his carriage and driver. Most unexpected and done with such grace. Does he do this sort of thing often?'

'Kindness had nothing to do with it.' Tristan lifted his hat and peered at her. His dark eyes flashed with some barely suppressed emotion, but then he leant forward and touched her hand briefly. The tiniest of touches, but one that made her heart pound slightly faster. 'Lottie, my cousin Peter has never done anything for the benefit of others. It is part of his creed.'

'I suppose you are right. You have known him longer than I have.' Lottie resisted the urge to put her glove to her cheek and savour the lingering imprint of his fingers. 'He must have been pleased that you were finally going to settle down.'

'I expect he was.' There was a note of surprise in Tristan's voice. 'I had not considered it. He is probably pleased to see me gone from Shaw's. I was not adding to his general state of well being. Destroying his ambiance, as he put it to me before we came down to dinner. I believe he rather wished I had stayed on the Continent.'

'I am certain you are wrong.'

'I know I am right.'

Lottie shifted, sliding slightly on the horsehair seats. He was not making this easy for her. All she wanted was some reassurance that he would make his peace with his cousin. And maybe, one day, when Tristan and she had children, his cousin would ease their way in society. Lottie drew in a breath. Children. Babies. Lying in Tristan's arms. Suddenly the carriage appeared to shrink, to push her closer to his chest, his lips. This topic was supposed to keep her mind off such things, not bring it back to his kisses.

'The carriage is very new,' she said, searching for another topic, one which did not lead her thoughts on such dangerous paths. 'He obviously thought enough of you to lend it. He trusts you.'

Tristan's hands tightened on his cane. 'You are very observant, but your conclusions are wrong. Neither of us trusts the other further than he can toss him. There is much that lies between my cousin and me. He wished me gone with all speed.'

'I try to be observant.' Lottie cleared her throat, pleased that she had found a subject they could converse on, a chance to show off her social skills without suddenly blurting out that she wanted to be kissed or held. Already, she could imagine introducing him to her friends: my husband—not only is he handsome but also a cousin to a lord. Martha, Caroline and the rest would forgive the elopement once they had met him. 'It makes it easier when

I go calling. Fifteen minutes is barely any time and the hostess is often tired of repeating the same story over and over again. It saves idle chit-chat or speaking about the weather. Some days it seems I never speak about anything but the weather. There is only so much one can say about the rain.'

'Is there? I never participate in At Homes if at all possible.' A shudder went through him. 'On point of principle.'

A sudden pain coursed through Lottie as her future plans crumbled to dust. Not participate. But the After the Marriage calls were some of the most significant calls a woman could ever make. She might not be having the wedding of her dreams, but she thought she'd at least have the calls and the attention. She had dreamt of making such calls ever since she had first been allowed to participate in At Homes.

'But you will have to.' Lottie leant forward, placing her hands on her knees to keep them from trembling. 'We will need to make calls when we get back to Newcastle. The After the Marriage calls are a necessity, or how else will anyone know that we will continue to see them socially? And all of my friends will be anxious to meet you. I dare say they will be quite green with envy. Pea green.'

'We won't be living in Newcastle.' Tristan regarded the woman sitting opposite him. Her head was full of society and outward appearances. At Homes. Dances. Positions. Furthering her status at the expense of others. She had to be made to realise that there was more to life than such things. He wanted to glimpse again the woman who had berated him for not looking after his parents' graves.

'Where? London? Or on the Continent? Paris, maybe? I do think I would quite like Paris and its salons.'

'Not there,' Tristan said firmly, gritting his teeth. He would test her, and she would learn the lesson. He would reach the woman from the cemetery.

'Where will we be living?'

'My uncle left me an estate—Gortner Hall. I have a fancy to settle down. It is up in the North Tyne Valley, about fifteen miles from Haydon Bridge.'

'Then I will be expected to make calls on the various ladies who live near there.' Lottie folded her hands in her lap with maddening complacency. 'It will be expected. You will have to go calling with me. There must be someone I know from Newcastle who could smooth our way…'

'No one of any consequence lives near.' Tristan paused. 'It will not be expected. It is the country, not the town.'

'Aunt Alice and Cousin Frances are bound to know several.' Lottie waved a dismissive hand. 'Aunt Alice knows positively everyone in the Tyne Valley. She can offer introductions. It may be the country, but there is always somebody. Calling and socialising is what makes the world go around.' Lottie sat up straighter. She shook out the folds of her dress. 'It is the lifeblood of the community. I plan to play my part as your wife. I will show them the right and proper way to behave.'

'I have been on the Continent for years. And as your cousin quite rightly pointed out to you, I led a somewhat scandalous life in my youth.' Tristan struggled to maintain his temper. He would give her one more chance. 'I am uncertain how many might wish to acknowledge me.'

'Oh. How truly thoughtless and terrible of me.' Lottie sat back against the hard seat and her face crumpled. She reached out and touched his hand. 'No doubt we shall meet them in due course and convince them of our worthiness to be befriended.'

'It may take some time.'

'But working together, we will convince them in the end. For our children's sake.' Her cheek flushed scarlet. 'You have proved your worth to me. You have saved me from ruin.'

'It was something any gentleman would have done.' Tristan shifted slightly. His plan would be harsh, but it should work. She had a good heart.

Lottie drew a shaking breath. Why was he making it so difficult? Tears pricked at her eyelids. He had to understand what she was attempting to do and why. He had to accept her apology. She would try much harder in the future, truly she would, but right now she needed reassurance—reassurance he appeared reluctant to give.

'Not anyone. I can name a half-dozen officers who would not have done what you did. They would have left me to my fate.'

'I kissed you. It very nearly went much further, Lottie.'

'You saved me from a life of cats and skirts being subtly drawn away. I do not think I would care for being my mother's companion either—fetching and carrying all the time. We would have driven each other mad within a fortnight.'

She stuffed her hand against her mouth and looked out of the window at the grey landscape. Yesterday on the train coming to Gilsland Spa everything had seemed so fresh and new. She had never imagined that she would be sitting here, facing an almost complete stranger on her way to be married.

'Yes, in due course, we will encounter the neighbours.' Tristan reached forward and caught her hand with his, interlaced his fingers with hers. The slight pressure sent tremors along her arm. 'Try to sleep now, Lottie. It has been a long day and we won't be in Gretna Green for a few more hours.'

'As long as that?'

'Would it be easier if I came over and sat next to you? You may put your head on my shoulder.'

He moved over and sat by her. The pressure of his leg against hers somehow made everything appear better. He wasn't angry with her. He did not blame her for what happened. It was not what either of them had anticipated, but she would do her best. Surely being married to him would be pleasant. A great wave of tiredness washed over her. It seemed liked for ever since she had kissed Aunt Alice and Cousin Frances goodbye. What would Frances say when she learnt her cousin had married the notorious Tristan Dyvelston? She gave a small sleepy smile and settled her back more firmly against the seat. There was at least that.

'I will close my eyes for a moment. It is really quite pleasant to be able to lean against someone. Comforting.'

His arm came around her and held her. 'It will work, Lottie. You must see that.'

The sun had risen and the road teemed with carts, carriages and various livestock by the time the carriage reached the outskirts of Gretna Green. Tristan's muscles ached from the journey and his arm had gone to sleep. However, Lottie had snuggled close. Her warm body touched his. He looked to where her red lips had parted, soft and inviting. Her lavender scent rose around like a perfumed cloud.

It had taken a vast reserve of Tristan's self-restraint not to pull her more firmly into his arms and make love to her in the carriage.

He forced his body to wait, to remember that she was a virgin and unused to such things. He would have the rest of his life to get to know her.

But first he had to be certain of why she had married him so quickly, why she had agreed to his suggestion. Did she know his true identity? Had she seen this as her only remaining chance to fulfil her mother's expectations and marry a title? He was under no illusions how powerful an incentive such expectations could be, but he wanted to know that she had married for the man, not the status. He had to know.

The carriage slowed down to a crawl and the noise of the town resounded in the enclosed space. They had arrived in Gretna Green and Tristan knew he had to act, he could no longer afford to sit and cradle his wife-to-be. He gently eased the sleeping Lottie from his shoulder and banged on the roof with his cane. Instantly the carriage halted. Tristan stepped out and closed the door behind him.

'Market day, my lord,' the coachman said, coming down to stand beside him. 'There are drovers and farmers all along the road. I am thankful today is not a hiring fair as the town must heave then.'

'I can see the carts and the cattle. The drover's bellowing echoes off the carriage walls.' Tristan stretched, trying to clear his mind. Today he needed all his wits about him.

'Where are we headed for, my lord? The headless cross? A quick marriage and then back to London?'

The coachman's voice jerked Tristan fully awake. 'Robinson, we had words earlier.'

The burly coach driver's cheek tinged pink. 'That we did, sir. I had forgotten. I don't understand the ways of the aristos, that I don't.'

'You are not paid to.'

'But what do you want me to do now?' Robinson rubbed the back of his neck. 'Are you going to marry her, like? You can always send her home.'

'Of course I am. I am going to marry the girl, and I am going to tame her.' Tristan glanced over to where Lottie softly slumbered, her red mouth now pouting slightly and her golden curls tumbled about her face. He had to admire her irrepressible spirit. 'I have to know, Robinson. I have seen too many women forced into marriages against their will. I have seen what it does to them, what it does to their husbands. She must want to marry me for me.'

Robinson gave a long whistle. 'It never did your uncle any good.'

Tristan's jaw tightened. 'That marriage brought misery to everyone.'

'What am I to do, sir? I mean, it is not right leaving you alone like this here. The London dockyards are refined compared to this place.'

'You are to put us down, that inn will do.' Tristan pointed towards the disreputable-looking coaching inn. 'Then take the carriage back to London. Wait for my word. We will take the train to Hexham. I have sent word to Mrs Elton at the hall. There will be a cart for us at the station.'

'As you say…sir.' Robinson's voice betrayed his uneasiness.

'You need not worry. I am well used to looking after myself.' Tristan reached into his jacket pocket, pulled out several notes and handed them to Robinson. 'These will see you to London.'

'And beyond.' The man gave a soft whistle.

'I want you to leave directly, Robinson. No hanging about.' Tristan looked pointedly at Lottie. Lottie stirred slightly in her sleep and murmured something indistinct.

Robinson ran his finger around his collar.

'It is the part of the plan I am uneasy about, sir. The lady is Quality. You can see it from the cut of her clothes and the way she speaks. She could be in danger.'

'Nothing is going to happen, Robinson. I promise that.'

'It is not you that I am worried about. It is that lass. How will she react? Someone ought to watch over her, like.' Robinson assumed a pious expression that was at odds with his former occupation as a boxer.

'Hopefully, she will reject temptation and obey my instructions, but if not, her lessons in life and treating people properly begin now. The ride in the carriage convinced me of it.'

'If that is what you want.' Robinson resumed his place, grumbling about the swells and their peculiar ideas.

Tristan stepped back into the carriage and smoothed a damp curl from her forehead as the wheels began turning again. 'Time to wake up, Lottie. We are nearly there. See. It's the headless cross.'

She wrinkled her nose and pushed at his hand.

'It is far too early for such things, Cousin Frances.' Her

eyes flew open and widened at the sight of her hand clutching his. Her cheeks took on an even rosier hue. And she rapidly dropped his hand. 'Oh. It's you.'

She sat up and began to rearrange her dress and bonnet.

'Did you have a pleasant slumber?' Tristan asked.

'I fear I fell asleep on you. Our limbs became entangled and I may have mussed up your shirtfront. You should have woken me. It was presumptuous of me.' She clasped her hands together. 'Do say that you forgive me. Please do.'

'We will be married today, Lottie. Man and wife. No one will say a word if you fall asleep on my shoulder.'

'I suppose not.' She bent her head so that all he could see was the crown of her straw bonnet and its elaborate blue ribbon. 'I keep forgetting. It is all very sudden. It is the best thing. I know it is the best thing.'

'Good.' Tristan lifted her chin so he looked her in the face. For an instant he drank in her luminous beauty. Then he hardened his heart. He wanted her beauty to be more than skin deep. He wanted her to want him for more than a title and his worldly goods. He had to carry out his experiment. He had to show her that there was more to life than social calls and pincushions. Life was to be lived, and not reflected in a Claude glass. 'I want you to stay here while I procure us a room.'

'Here? In this carriage? On my own?' The words came out as a squeak. Her eyes widened and she clutched her reticule to her chest. 'I have never been left in a coaching yard on my own before.'

'You will be quite safe in the coaching yard…as long as you remain there. No one will harm you. Your dress is of a certain quality.' Tristan forced himself to walk away from her, not to take her by the arm and lead her to another inn. He had to do it, for the sake of their future.

Chapter Five

Lottie watched Tristan walk away from her. She half-raised a hand to beg him to stay or at least to take her with him, but he never glanced back. She gazed about the coaching yard where several drovers discussed cattle in heavy Scots accents. The smell of manure and sweat seeped into the carriage. Lottie put her handkerchief over her nose and hoped the inn would be better than its yard. 'This is a fine mess you have landed yourself in, Lottie Charlton. What happens to you now? Why did you let him go like that?'

'You will have to get out, miss.' The large coachman with the broken nose opened the carriage door. 'Orders is orders. It ain't my business to contradict Lord Thorngrafton. He says to me, leave when you get to Gretna Green.'

Lottie blinked. 'Excuse me? Why? Mr Dyvelston is getting a room. Surely you may wait a few moments. I wish to stay in the carriage, away from the gaze of ordinary bystanders. It wouldn't be proper for me to wait in the yard on my own.'

'I am only a coachman. I know nothing about the ways of gentlefolk.'

'Your master will understand if you wait. You must wait.' Lottie tried to give her words all the imperiousness of her mother, but she heard the undercurrent of desperation.

'I need to leave.' The coachman's countenance took on a mulish expression. 'My…master said that I needed to be in London with all speed once I had brought you to Gretna Green. He didn't say nothing about waiting until that there gentleman procured a room. He told me, go once you get to Gretna Green.'

'Can't you wait until Mr Dyvelston returns? Please? For my sake?' Lottie pressed her handkerchief more firmly to her mouth and willed Tristan to return. Her whole body tensed as she peered out of the carriage door into the crowded yard: drovers, farmhands and the odd woman, but no broad shoulders encased in a fine frock coat. Her insides shook at being cast amongst those people. 'I beg you to re-consider.'

The big man shook his head. 'It wouldn't be proper, like. I have me orders. I like my job, miss. I won't jeopardise it for no one.'

'Why not? Mr Dyvelston charged you to look after me. I am sure he did. You cannot intend to leave me here with those ruffians.' Lottie bit her lip, aware that the words had come out more harshly than she had intended. But he had to understand that she had been cosseted and looked after. She was of gentle birth.

'No, he didn't, like.' The coachman lifted a bag from the back and set it down on the muddy cobblestones. 'This is all there is, miss. I am sure he will return in a few moments. If you please, miss. I am on my way to London to wait for Lord Thorngrafton's instructions. It is a week's journey in good weather and I'd like to get on my way.'

'But you have been driving through the night. Surely you will need time to rest. Mr Dyvelston will return in a few moments.' Lottie clasped her hands together. 'I beg you. Have mercy.'

'That is true and you should be safe in that time. I want to be well into England afore I do that. If you please, miss….'

Lottie looked at the single bag. Her mother had said that she would send her things on. It appeared that Tristan had not bothered to pack a trunk or even a bag. She reached down and picked the satchel up. The yard blurred for a moment, but she stiffened her back. Regained her composure. She would be fine. Tristan would return before she knew it. She held out her hand and the coachman helped her from the carriage. 'Thank you. It is very kind of you.'

She reached into her reticule and drew out a halfpenny. 'This is for you.'

'It's all right, miss, Lord Thorngrafton pays me well, so he does. Best of luck.' The coachman twisted his hat. 'Begging your pardon, but this here is from Lord Thorngrafton…in case you change your mind. In case…'

Lottie regarded the bank note with a sinking heart. Lord Thorngrafton must believe that Tristan was planning to abandon her. 'Don't you trust Mr Dyvelston?'

'I trust him all right, but…just the same. Best to be prepared, miss.'

'I couldn't, really.' Lottie turned her face into her handkerchief.

'Take it, miss, for my sake. Lord Thorngrafton has a right temper if his will is crossed.'

Her throat closed. She had wronged Lord Thorngrafton last November. He had thought about her comfort and had not been sure of his cousin. He had sought to protect her. She fingered the note and placed it in her reticule. 'You must thank Lord Thorngrafton for me. I will thank him myself when I can.'

'As you wish, miss. God speed.' The coachman touched his hat and went back to his place.

He snapped the reins and the carriage started to move. It made its way through the jumble of carts and horses, rolling away from her. A single tear ran down her cheek, but she pushed it away with impatient fingers.

Lottie stood there, her head held high and her fingers clutching her satchel and reticule in the centre of the yard, aware that people were looking at her and her much creased clothes. Aware that she had rapidly become an object of interest and curiosity. Lottie tightened her grip. She refused to stand there, being gaped at like some spectacle in a diorama or other cheap entertainment. She had to act.

She walked towards the inn and peeked into the public room, hoping to discover the familiar shape of Tristan's shoulders or his top hat floating above the crowd. The entire room appeared full of farmers, day labourers and drovers. High-pitched female laughter came from a dimly lit corner where Lottie could just make out a flurry of petticoats and entangled limbs. She stared for a heartbeat at the brazenness of it. The stench was worse than the yard. Lottie gave a soft cry and buried her face more firmly in the handkerchief.

'Is there something you want, dearie?' an old crone

asked, leering at her with a one-toothed smile. 'Sell your ear bobs, or your pretty hair? I pay top price for golden curls like yours.'

'Not my hair. Not my ear bobs.' Lottie blanched and rapidly made her way back into the coaching yard. She heard the crone's laughter chasing her as she went.

Lottie paused by the stable entrance and tried to get her breath as she scanned the yard for any sign of Tristan. But it remained stubbornly free of her future husband. She closed her eyes and wished. Opened them. Nothing. The sun beat down on her bonnet and her shift stuck to her back. Maybe Lord Thorngrafton's surmise was correct and Tristan did not intend to come back for her. He had only taken her here to abandon her to her fate. He would then claim she had run away and he'd be free to live his dissolute life.

Abandoned at the altar to a life of sin.

Cousin Frances had taken great pleasure in describing several Minerva Press novels where this was a main feature. The villain lures the heroine with blandishments, only to abandon her after he has had his wicked way with her, forcing her into a Life of Degradation…if it were not for the hero.

Lottie gave a tremulous smile. She had to think logically. Tristan had not had his wicked way with her, beyond the kiss they had shared on the terrace. If he had been planning to abandon her, he would have done so then, instead of taking her here. She had to be logical, and not give way to panic.

A sob built in her throat and she muffled it with the handkerchief. She refused to give way to wailing here despite the longing in her breast. She scrubbed her eyes with the now-crumpled handkerchief, replaced it in her reticule and took a fresh one as she made a slow circuit of the yard. When she returned to the stables, there was still no sign of Tristan. It was as if he had vanished.

Had something happened? Had some evil befallen him? An ice-cold hand went around her heart.

She counted to thirty and then thirty once more. Looked again hard at the door Tristan had disappeared through. Tristan failed to appear.

She bit her lips and attempted to think clearly as a pain pounded against her eyeballs. Something had happened to Tristan. She had to find where he had gone and determine if he did intend to marry her. She would search for him, all day and night if she had to, and, if he remained lost, she would return to Newcastle, much chastened, hoping for charity. She would use Lord Thorngrafton's money to purchase her train fare back to Newcastle. The first thing she would do when she did arrive home would be to raid her savings and send the money back to Lord Thorngrafton. It would be the polite thing to do, and she would not mention the scoundrel-like behaviour of his cousin.

Henry and her mother might not be pleased to see her, but they would not turn her from their door. She was certain of that. She was part of their family, in spite of everything.

She cringed, thinking of the words Henry would use, and how Mama would cry and how Lucy would look and sigh. Behind her skirts, everyone would whisper that she had deserved it, that pride came before a fall.

Emma Stanton had had it lucky, looking after her mother. Lottie caught her lip between her teeth. She wished she had never made fun of her last Christmas. Social success was such a transitory thing. Maybe Emma would be kind and send a list of books for her to read in her exile.

But somewhere deep inside her, a little voice told her that Tristan would look after her. She had to trust him. He had no reason to abandon her like this.

'Where is the market?' she asked an elderly lady with a well-lived-in face. 'I wish to find a constable. I have lost someone. He needs to be returned to me.'

The lady appeared surprised to be addressed. 'Lost someone? A man? Mother Hetts is good at finding men for pretty doves.'

'Yes, my fiancé appears to have gone missing.' Lottie was unable to prevent the slight catch in her throat. She swallowed hard before she continued in a steadier voice, 'It is imperative I find him. I am worried that something might have happened to him. It is unlike him to leave me for so long and in a place like this.'

'Men are like that, pet. They come. They go. You will find another soon.' The woman's eyes roamed over Lottie's dress. 'Particularly in them there togs.'

'I don't want another. I want to find my fiancé, Tristan Dyvelston. I thought the parish constable might be able to help.'

'His box is that way. But you won't be catching him in his box today, mind. Market day, me pet.' The old woman's eyes grew crafty. 'Of course, I could be wrong. It might be best to check. Make sure you take the third turn on your right. It will take you straight there. Otherwise it is a long ways around and there are bad folks about.'

'Thank you, thank you.' Lottie pressed the woman's hand. 'I really appreciate your kindness. I am sure I will find him now.'

'I hope you do, pet. There are them that don't.' The woman smiled, a cruel smile. 'You can always come back and finds me. I will offer you a good home. You come back here and tell that there landlord Mother Hetts will give you a place to rest your pretty golden head.'

Lottie stepped over a pile of muck and turned her back on the woman and crowded yard, hurrying away from that evil place as quickly as she could. She would not think about 'them that don't' and 'a good home'. She could do this. She was capable. It would be no worse than going for a walk in Haydon Bridge. She would find the constable and explain. He could discover Tristan's whereabouts while she waited. She would be safe.

The market-day crowd jostled her, but she kept on walking, relieved to be taking action instead of standing there panicking. She released her breath and tried to ignore the stares, acutely aware that her paisley dress was more fit for carriages than walking. Several women wrapped in woollen shawls and carrying baskets stared at her and put their heads together, whispering and pointing.

A carriage with a young girl and her mother in it swept past, splashing mud on the hem of her gown. Lottie gave a small cry and jumped back. Then she stooped and tried to wipe it off as men stopped and stared. A man said something unintelligble, but Lottie shook her head. She glanced back over her shoulder towards the inn, but it had been swallowed up by the crowd. She couldn't go back and she had no guarantee that Tristan would even be looking for her. Once she found a constable, things could be put right. All this unpleasantness would be a bad dream.

Several of the market goers jostled her. Lottie continued on, holding her reticule close, trying not to think about the beggars and thieves. She saw the opening, more of an alleyway than a street. She hesitated, then chided herself for being a ninny. The elderly woman had been quite specific with her directions. She plunged into the narrow street. It was imperative that she find the constable as quickly as possible.

'Going my way, my pretty dove?' a gin-soaked voice asked. 'See here, Fred, a fresh dolly bird has flown into our nest.'

'Ain't never been paid to do this before.' The innkeeper looked skeptical, but he pocketed the coins that Tristan pushed forwards on the bar.

'As long as it is done tomorrow morning, I don't mind.' Tristan pressed his hands against the bar and leant forward so that he was close to the unshaven jowls of the innkeeper. 'I always pay my debts, keep my promises and never forget a favour or an injury.'

'You had that look about you.' Sweat broke out on the innkeeper's face. 'I will do what you ask. And your lady friend, she is your wife, isn't she? I run a decent establishment.'

Tristan glanced around at the bar where a motley group of farm labourers, card sharps and ladies of the night were arranged. Blue smoke hung in the air. In one corner, a woman warbled a forlorn song. 'Your opinion and mine may differ as to decent.'

'Are you saying that I cheat my customers?' The man wiped his hand across his forehead. 'I ought to have you thrown out of here.'

'But you won't. I paid in advance and far more than that room is worth.'

The innkeeper licked his lips. 'That you did, that you did, and I don't say nothing to a paying customer.'

'It is how I want it.'

A moment of unease about the deception he was playing on Lottie passed over Tristan, but he pushed it away. He was doing what was right. One short sharp shock for Lottie Charlton and their married life would be far happier. It was easier if she learnt lessons now, before it was too late.

Tristan went back to the yard, filled his lungs with clean air and swore. Loud and long. No blonde in a paisley silk afternoon dress, straw bonnet with a satchel by her side. No woman of quality waited there.

Tristan pressed his lips together. He had expected her to be there—spitting fury with her eyes perhaps to be left in the yard on her own, but to be there. He tried to think clearly. Robinson would have obeyed him. He would not have taken her with him. Tristan swore again, wishing he had told Robinson to stop and explain once he had left the yard. A mistake, but one he could not undo.

He had been gone longer than he anticipated, but not that long. She had gone. He had been mistaken.

A hard tight knot came into his throat. He had counted on her being different. He did not think she would have abandoned him so easily, not after the stand she had made at the hotel. He gave one more sweeping glance of the yard. Next time he would remember about the perfidy of women.

'Lost something, pet?' an elderly woman crooned to him. 'A trinket? A pretty little dove? I know where you can find another. Mother Hetts knows everything about little doves, she does.'

'There was a woman here. A blonde woman, well dressed. Do you have any idea where she might have gone?'

'Can't remembering having seen anyone of that description.' The woman gave a shrug of her thin shoulder and her watery eyes turned crafty. 'Then my memory ain't what it used to be. Lots of folks searching for things today. Always asking Mother Hetts if she's seen this or that. Can't be expected to remember. It's market day.'

The old woman gave a cackle, reminding him of a demented hen. The crackle went straight through him. He swung back and advanced towards the woman, whose crackling abruptly ceased.

'You know something. Where did she go?' Tristan advanced towards, his hands flexing at his sides, longing for something to hit. 'Would a coin help to recover that memory of yours?'

'May do? May not?' The old woman rocked back and forth. 'It is amazing what silver coin can do for my memory.'

Tristan reached into his pocket and fished out a shilling, holding it beyond the reach of the woman. 'The truth. Quickly.'

'I sent her to the parish constable…if she can find him. Mother Hetts looks after the little doves, she does,' the woman said, holding her basket in front of her face. 'She was looking for someone who was missing. Right concerned she was. Nearly in tears. Poor little dove. Are you lost?'

Tristan tossed her the coin. She caught it with expert claws, tested it as Tristan's insides twisted. He had not considered the possibility that Lottie might wonder about his whereabouts and worry. He had to find her and quickly. There was no telling what trouble she might encounter.

'Bless and keep you, sir. You are a real gentleman. If you don't find her, I can always get you another pretty dove.'

Tristan pushed past a cart and horse blocking the entrance to the yard, and went out into the street. His blood pounded in his head.

She had to be there. She could not have gone far. That old crone would not spend for ever in the yard. He must have missed Lottie by a matter of moments.

Only farm labourers, cattle drovers and a few women wrapped in shawls and carrying baskets lined the streets. There was no sign of Lottie's brightly coloured straw bonnet anywhere.

He fought against the sudden stab of concern.

Lottie had gone looking for him. He would find her more than likely with the parish constable. He would keep her safe. Then they would marry. All would be well.

A woman's scream rent the air. Tristan raced towards it.

'Let me go.' Lottie twisted away from the evil-smelling man and screamed again. Her sleeve tore slightly as she elbowed the man hard in the stomach. His hands loosened as he doubled over in pain.

'Why did you have to do that? I didn't mean no harm, did I, Den?' the rough unshaven man said to his companion.

'No, Fred, you didn't,' the companion said, sticking his hands in his pockets and giving a low whistle.

'I doubt the truth of that statement.' Lottie kept her nose in the air; her stomach was in knots as she struggled to breathe. She wished her corset was not so tight, then she would have been able to run, but as it was, she could not draw sufficient air.

If she walked quickly, perhaps she would come to the constable's box…if it even existed, if the woman had been correct in her directions, something Lottie was beginning to have her doubts about. She should have never gone down this alleyway. She should have never trusted that old woman. She should have stayed in the coaching yard until nightfall and then demanded the constable be brought to her. That would have been the sensible thing to do.

Her slippers resounded on the cobble stones. Only a few more steps and she'd be back in the open. She'd be safe. One more step. Lottie resisted the temptation to turn around and see where the men were. The back of her neck pricked, but she forced her feet to move. They had to let her go.

'Playing hard to get, me little golden-haired beauty? Thinking yourself all prettified in those togs? Above the likes of me and me pals? Way aye, I have the measure of you.'

Rough hands grabbed her waist again, dragged her back into the alleyway, away from the light, and back into the dark. The scent of alcohol wafted over her. Lottie gagged and kicked backwards. But the man had lifted her off the ground and her slippers only encountered thin air.

'Not this time.' He wiped a dirty paw down her face. 'You won't get away so lightly, but I likes it when they plays rough, I do.'

'Let me go, you—you monster!'

'We will go somewheres quiet. You, me and Den. I knows a good game we can play.'

'Unhand me this instant or I will call the constable.' Lottie fought against the hands, saw her handkerchief, reticule and satchel fall to the ground and with them all her money. She gave a little cry of despair. But the arms continued to hold her tight. She kicked backwards and screamed.

'And what is the constable going to do about it, my pretty?' His companion laughed. 'See here, Fred, see if you can wake him from his box. Or is he snoring his head off?'

Lottie's throat went dry as she prayed for a miracle. She should never have gone off out of the yard. She should have stayed and waited. She whispered a prayer.

'The lady is with me and not with you.' Tristan's voice cut through the man's banter. 'Release her. Or I won't be held be responsible for what happens.'

Lottie froze as hope bubbled up inside her. Tristan. He was here. He had not abandoned her. He had found her. She turned her head towards the sound, hoping against hope that it had not been her imagination. He stood at the entrance to the alley, large and solid, formidable, his lips turned down in a furious expression.

'Tristan! I am here! Thank God you are all right. I thought something must have happened to you.' Lottie struggled against the imprisoning hands. 'Help me.'

'I said let the lady go.' Tristan advanced forwards. 'I am in no mood to repeat myself. No mood at all.'

'Why should I?' The man stood there, hands imprisoning her. 'I caught her first. Prove she's yours.'

'In the interests of your long-term health…release her.' Tristan's voice was calm and cold as if he were passing the time of the day. 'A friendly warning, if you like.'

'How so?' the man's companion asked. He advanced

towards Tristan, brandishing his fists. 'Fred found her, plying her trade. You best be about your business, you jumped-up Englishman. I'm a professional boxer, like. My punch is harder than a sledgehammer. Den Casey, Sledgehammer of the North, they calls me. Won five straight.'

A loud thwack resounded in the street as Tristan's fist connected with the man's jaw. The man tumbled backwards, lay on the ground. 'Remind me not to bet on any of your fights, then.'

'Den down?' Lottie's captor looked at his prone companion and back at Tristan. 'The Hammer is on the ground. Dead to the world. Felled with one punch. I ain't never seen the like.'

'Who is next?' Tristan straightened his stock. 'I want the lady released. Unharmed. Immediately.'

'It were only a bit of sport, your worship. We did not mean no harm.'

The hands were withdrawn so suddenly that Lottie stumbled forwards and encountered Tristan's hard body.

She gasped slightly at the sudden contact, but her feet refused to move as her entire body trembled. Safe. She longed to lay her head against his broad chest. Her knees refused to support her. She clung onto his arm and pushed all thoughts about what might have happened to her had Tristan not come by when he did out of her head.

'I…I…' Her throat closed and she found it difficult to speak. She swallowed and tried again, her voice barely audible. 'I should have stayed at the inn. I went looking for you. I was worried that something might have happened and that was why you didn't come back. I wanted to get help.'

'Are you unhurt?' His arm went about her waist, supporting her. Lottie gave into temptation and rested her head against his shoulder, felt his strength. She closed her eyes and breathed in his crisp, masculine scent. She was safe. He put her away from him and looked her up and down. 'Have they harmed you?'

'My…my reticule has vanished.' Lottie straightened her bonnet and shook out the folds of her gown. She glanced at the rip in her sleeve, winced, but it could be mended. 'My bag.'

'Give the lady back her reticule. And her bag,' Tristan said in the same deadly quiet voice to the man who was standing over his fallen companion, staring at them with fearful eyes.

'Look what you done to our Den. There ought to be a law.'

'There is and you are on the wrong side of it.'

'What you mean? The wrong side?'

'I have no little doubt the constable will be interested to learn of your whereabouts.' Tristan held out his hand. 'The bags. Now. And I might allow you to go.'

There was a shuffling of feet and her satchel was held out. Lottie curled her fingers around it, hugging it to her body. She opened it and saw everything her mother's maid had packed remained there.

'And the reticule.'

Much shuffling of feet and the reticule appeared. Lottie gave a small cry of joy.

'Is everything there, Lottie? Check it.'

Lottie opened it with trembling fingers and gave a little cry of delight. Lord Thorngrafton's money was there. 'It is all there. They took nothing.'

'You see, like I said, your worship, it's all a big misunderstanding. We was just taking her…'

'You were not just taking her anywhere. Next time, when a lady protests, you leave her alone. Do you understand me?'

'We didn't mean no harm like, your worship.' The thickset man held up his hands and backed slowly away from Tristan. 'We didn't know the lady was with you, like. It was just a bit o'sport. She seemed up for it, like.'

'I was not! I never!' Lottie balled her fists. She glanced up into Tristan's face, but all she saw was cold fury. At her? At the men? She tried to breathe. 'I would never. I was trying to get to the parish constable's box.'

'There ain't no constable's box around here.'

'I asked…the woman said…' Lottie paused. Tristan had to believe her. 'I thought something had happened to you. I wanted to make sure you were safe.'

His dark eyes stared at her for a long moment, searching her face, looking for something. The stern planes of his face did not change as he raised a single eyebrow. 'The lady says you were mistaken.'

'Maybe.' The man flushed and ran a finger around the neck of his shirt. 'Could have been. It were Den that—'

'Definitely mistaken.' Tristan's voice could cut through granite. 'You owe the lady an apology. The lady is my fiancée and deserves your respect. It is only the fact that it's my wedding day that puts me in a good mood.'

'I am…am sorry, your worship.' The man stumbled backwards, fell over his prone friend and scrambled to stand up again, touching his cap as he did so. 'I don't mean no harm like. I, that is we, had no idea. Many happy returns on your marriage.'

'Off you go.' Tristan gestured towards the prone figure of Den. 'Take your friend, he is cluttering up the pavement.'

'Right you are, your worship.' The man hoisted his friend on to his shoulder, and began to walk away, complaining loudly as he went that he did not mean any harm and how he was always hard done by.

Lottie's body began to shake. She wanted to sink down to the ground and weep. Tristan's arms came around her and held her against his body until the shaking passed.

'You are safe now, Lottie,' he said, his breath ruffling her bonnet. 'I am here.'

'Yes, you are.'

'And we are going to be married in a few moments.'

This was not supposed to be what her wedding day was like. She had had it all planned right down to the white silk dress, fashionable bonnet and veil and orange blossoms. Instead she had ended up brawling in an alleyway like a fishwife. She had been taken for a lady of the night.

Lottie moved backwards and Tristan's hold loosened. She wrapped her arms about her waist and attempted to control the shivers that now racked her body. She did not want to think about what had nearly happened to her. She took a deep breath and regained a small measure of control.

'Thank you for saving me,' she said when she trusted her voice would not quaver. 'Those men had evil intentions. I am sure of it. If you had not—' Her voice broke and she could only look up at the hard planes of his face, hoping he'd understand what she meant.

'You are safe with me now. Think no more about them.'

'I made a mistake. I should never have listened to that

old woman's directions.' Her voice held a pathetic quiver. She fumbled for her handkerchief, discovered she had lost it. With angry fingers, Lottie brushed away the tears. 'None of this was supposed to happen.'

He inclined his head, but his dark gaze searched her face. 'Did those men do anything to you?'

'They pawed at my dress and my face, but I will live.' She brushed a speck of dust from her sleeve, a small act, but one that did much to restore her confidence. She would not think about what might have been, but about the future. From now on, it would be the future she faced. And she would refuse to let Tristan leave her again like that. 'It is most aggravating to be touched in that familiar manner. Most unexpected.'

'The streets are unsafe for a woman dressed as you are. Gretna Green teems with drunks and ne'er-do-wells today. Far more than I thought possible for such a town.' His face turned grave. 'If you had stayed where I told you to, none of this would have happened. Why did you leave the yard? You were safe in the yard. You had no cause to go.'

'The coach driver went off. I was left alone. I became frightened and tried to find you. I went into the inn, but there was no sign of you. A woman offered to buy my hair.' A shudder went through Lottie at the memory. 'I couldn't stay there. I became worried, certain something had happened to you. I went to find the parish constable.'

'It took longer than I anticipated to arrange the marriage and our accommodation. I had not thought to be gone so long.' His fingers curled around hers. He brought them to his lips. Then let go. 'I regret that.'

Lottie resisted the temptation to put her hand to her face

and savour the touch. Was it an apology? She did not want to ask. All she knew was that he had not abandoned her. She hated her earlier thoughts.

'If you had not come when you did…' Another shiver convulsed through her.

'Forget the unpleasantness ever happened. It is over, truly. I swear it and I keep my promises.' He put his hand on her shoulder and looked at her with an intense expression. 'Remember that. If I say I will return, I will return. I will protect you.'

'Do you mean that?' Lottie asked in shaking voice.

'As best as I am able.'

'That is good to know.'

'And now if you remain willing, the blacksmith awaits.'

'The blacksmith?' Lottie tilted her head and tried to quell the sudden butterflies in her stomach. 'We have no horses that need shoeing.'

'We have a marriage that needs forging. It is where all the best marriages take place in Gretna Green, or so I am reliably informed.'

'We are not marrying in a church?' Lottie regarded her hands. 'I had always imagined that I would be married in church.'

He shook his head. 'We are marrying in Gretna Green, under Scottish law. Two witnesses are all the law requires. The blacksmith is waiting for us. All you have to say is that you don't want to, Lottie, and I will personally put you on a coach back to your mother and Newcastle.'

'No, I will marry you…even if it is a blacksmith's shop.' She drew a deep breath. Her wedding would bear no resemblance to the wedding of her dreams. A blacksmith's anvil and a torn dress. But it was a better prospect than the future those men had planned for her. 'Like you, Tristan Dyvelston, I keep my promises.'

He curled his fingers around her gloved hand, raised it to his lips. 'Thank you for that.'

Lottie allowed her footsteps to match his. She was getting married. It might not be the wedding she dreamt of, but she was determined to be the right sort of wife. She would make him see that she could be helpful. It was the details that counted. She gave one last backward glance to the alleyway and turned her face to the sun. Her footsteps faltered. 'Tristan, what sort of ring?'

'The blacksmith will take care of it. He is used to weddings. He informs me that he has already performed two this morning.'

'You mean it isn't going to be a gold ring?'

'Is a gold ring a requirement for a marriage in Scotland?' His gaze narrowed. 'Is it ever a requirement?'

Lottie wet her lips and said goodbye to the last of her dreams. 'I had only wanted to know.'

Chapter Six

Lottie twisted the iron band about her left ring finger, rather than look at her new husband where he stood speaking to the blacksmith. The ceremony had gone quickly, squeezed in between a horseshoeing and mending a plough. Nothing fancy. Simple and ordinary.

Her face burnt from the heat of the fire and her ears rang from the clanging of the hammer against the anvil. A quick brush of his lips against hers. Very correct. Very polite, but nothing more. But she wanted more. She wanted him to kiss her like he meant it, like he wasn't marrying her simply because he had to, because society forced them. Lottie concentrated on the iron band. Slowly she drew on her glove, hiding the ring, but her hand remained heavy with the unaccustomed weight.

'Shall we depart, Lottie?' Tristan said, coming over to her; the blacksmith started striking the anvil with his hammer again. 'Unless you want to stay and see the horses being shod, there is nothing here for us.'

Lottie shook her head and allowed Tristan to lead her from the shop.

'So we are married. Forged as it were.' She gave a small laugh once they had returned to the street. It looked as it had when they had entered the shop—people were still hurrying by, intent on their shopping, the mud still lay in pools. Nothing had changed. No one noticed what had happened to her. 'I had never thought about it. My friends will be all agog when I write. One only ever hears about going to Gretna Green to get married, and the precise details are never spelt out.'

'Yes, we are married. The ceremony was perfectly legal.'

'I never questioned it.' Lottie glanced quickly up at her new husband. His face was remote and held little of the warmth she had glimpsed last evening. She wondered how she could get it back. If he had looked like that, then she would not have been tempted to make this marriage. She wanted him to smile down at her, to do something to show that this marriage was more than an inconvenience caused by her own indiscretion. 'We have both been saved from ruin. The marriage will be a nine-day wonder, if that. Undoubtedly someone somewhere will do something worse and it will be forgotten.'

'I am no stranger to scandal but I had no wish to be outside society for ever. It is not good business.' His eyes showed no signs of softening. 'Neither of us had any choice in the matter, Lottie, but we do have a choice about the life we lead. Shall we look to the future, rather than live in what might have been?'

'The ice-cold wind of disapproval.' Lottie adjusted her bonnet and ignored the rip in her sleeve that appeared to grow each time she moved her arm. She hated the thought of being dressed like this in public, but there was nothing she could do. She had to hope no one would notice. She moved so her arm was next to Tristan's, hiding the worst. 'I need to know, Tristan. Why did you marry me, since you had already experienced society's disapproval?'

'Once you ruin a virgin…there is very little way back.' Tristan ignored her invitation to take her arm and stood staring down at her. His voice did little to restore her confidence.

'And did you want a way back?' Lottie asked. She wanted to believe that there was more to this, that he had wanted to marry her.

'I am no cad. And perhaps I no longer wanted to be an orphan.' A cold smile touched his lips. 'Does it matter about the reasons? We are married now, and we will go forwards without scandal. I will lead the sort of life my father had envisioned for me. Upright. Solid. The sort of life I intend to lead now that I have returned to Britain.'

'You appear to have made a number of promises to your father.'

'They were all part of the same promise. My father and my uncle were not friends.' He gave a bitter laugh. 'I wanted to torment my uncle.'

'And what did your uncle predict?'

'That I would come to no good, that I would blacken the family's name and die in an unmarked grave.'

'It is hard when families fight, particularly if one of them is titled.' Lottie placed her hand on his arm. 'Didn't your mother try to help? Or your aunt? It is the duty of the women in the family to mend quarrels.'

'My uncle's wife was concerned with…other matters and my mother died when I was three.' A flash of pain crossed Tristan's face and Lottie's heart constricted. In that instant she caught a glimpse of the young boy Tristan must have been. How truly awful to have this long-ago quarrel blight his life. 'I doubt she could have mended this quarrel, but I like to think she would have understood.'

'I am sorry. I lost my father when I was twelve. I cried for days on end. Buckets and buckets.'

'My father died when I was seventeen. I had stopped crying then.'

Lottie bit her lip, aware that she knew very little about the man standing next to her, very little about the man whose bed she would now share and whose table she would grace. She had always thought that she would have a long and proper courtship, but it had happened a different way. They would get to know each other in time. And some day, she would make him see that making social calls and being part of a community was important. It gave meaning to people's lives. It enabled people to help each other and to help their families lead better lives.

'We shouldn't be talking about sad things on our wedding day.'

'You are quite right—we should only speak of happy things.'

'It is the polite thing to do.'

'And you always do the polite thing.'

Lottie tilted her head. 'Whenever possible. It saves making a spectacle.'

'Then we had best move as we are beginning to make a spectacle.'

Tristan put his hand under her elbow and guided her away from the blacksmith's shop. Lottie saw the curious stares from several women. With his other hand he carried her satchel as they walked slowly through the streets of Gretna Green. The market crowd had dispersed somewhat, but the streets still heaved with people. Twice, Lottie had to walk around a drunk lying the gutter.

'Where are we going now?' she asked as he strode along, not looking left or right. 'What happens next?'

'You are my wife and I shall take you back to the inn where hopefully the innkeeper will have prepared rooms for us.'

'Do we have a private room?' Lottie asked. She attempted a smile. She did not want to think about what men and women did in bed at night. She heard whispered rumours from the servants, and once at Martha Dresser's house had come across *Aristotle's Complete Master Piece* in a box of books that belonged to Martha's grandmother. They had spent a half-hour giggling over the pictures before they'd been discovered and had their ears boxed.

'Is that important to you?'

'Yes.' The word came out a squeak. The thought of being with her husband for the first time in a room crowded with strangers had no appeal. And yet, she could not bring herself to explain, to confess to her complete ignorance about lovemaking beyond the few kisses she had shared. 'I know they must be at a premium, but somehow I don't fancy sharing a bed with a stranger.'

'And what would you call me?' He gave a short laugh, but his eyes were sombre. 'We are very much strangers to each other, Lottie.'

Lottie tucked her hand more firmly into the crook of his arm.

'My husband.' The words sounded new and exciting, but more than a little dangerous. 'I see no point in being old-fashioned and calling you Mr Dyvelston like Mama did with my father. It sounds so cold and formal. I...I want something more from our marriage.'

'Somehow I can't imagine you calling me Mr Dyvelston...ever.' A tiny smile on his lips. 'Tristan will suffice.'

Lottie tightened her grip on her reticule. Exactly who was her new husband? She had seen his controlled fury at the men earlier. She knew very little about him, about his prospects. And he appeared content to ignore Lord Thorngrafton's generosity to them. No, not content, but determined. But that was a problem to be solved later.

'And at least you call me Lottie. I loathe and detest Carlotta.'

'I will try to remember that, Carlotta.'

Lottie started and then she saw the devilment in his eyes. She aimed a kick at him, which he neatly side-stepped.

'But the rooms—will I be expected to go into a public room? It wouldn't be seemly.'

'My finances can stretch to a private room at that inn. I thought it would be better as we did marry this afternoon.'

'You never said about money.' Lottie stopped in the street, her slippers skidding into each other. Marriage meant sharing a bed. She forced her mind from that. 'You never agreed to a settlement with my brother. Will we need to ask for Lord Thorngrafton's assistance? You did borrow his carriage.'

'I have enough. I have no need for Thorngrafton's charity,' he said and his eyes slid away from her.

A pain gathered behind Lottie's eyebrows. He was trying to hide something from her. Had she fallen into a trap? She had not even thought about money; she had only thought about the shape of his lips and how they fit against hers. Mama had always told her to be sensible about men and she had failed, failed utterly and miserably. And now she was going to a mean inn for her wedding night. Her only comfort was that she remained respectable—barely.

'What is the estate you inherited like? Is it in good repair?' She placed a hand on his arm. 'Please, I want to know. Is it a place to raise a family?'

He looked down at her and his black eyes flared with some unknown fire, a spark of something that ignited a glow within her. And she knew she had asked the right words. Then the mask came down.

'It was a prosperous estate once, highly productive, but it has been neglected for many years. It has fine views of the river, a series of follies in the garden. It was quite well thought of in my grandfather's day.' Tristan looked ahead, rather than down at Lottie with her brave face and slightly torn dress. She had been battered more than he had intended before they were married, but here she remained firmly fixed on their social status. There were flashes in her of genuine concern, but he had to be sure. Too soon and he'd never know. Patience brought rewards. 'My uncle took a perverse pride in letting me know about its neglect. How the fields were fallow, and how the garden had become choked with weeds.'

'Neglect of good land is a crime.' Lottie turned her gaze

upwards and a furious expression came into her eyes. 'Why would anyone do that? Was it because of a will? Was the estate stuck in chancery? Why didn't anyone stop him?'

'It belonged to him. What do you know about estates and chancery?' A faint smile touched his lips as he realised a way to turn the conversation on to less rocky shoals. 'I thought you were a city woman.'

'I may look like just a pretty face, Tristan, but Mama was determined that I learn…as she was determined that I fulfil my destiny and marry a title or, failing that, someone very wealthy.' Lottie paused and gave tiny shrug. 'Not that it happened, but I needed to know something so I wouldn't be a ninny. My skills can be put to good use.'

'I think you are anything but a ninny.' Tristan resisted the temptation to draw her into his arms and confess. How much did she truly know?

'I thank you for the compliment.' Lottie gave a little wave of her hand. 'I know my limitations. I am not a blue stocking like Emma Stanton, nor am I the excellent house-wife that my sister-in-law is. But I plan to be a social asset and help further your standing in the community.'

'Whatever that is. I don't recall ever worrying about it before.'

'What did you do before you returned to England?'

'I gambled and led a disreputable life.' Tristan stopped and considered what to say. How much to reveal. How much to keep hidden until he was certain of her motives. 'Most of your cousin's stories contain an element of truth in them.'

'Are you ashamed of the life you led?' she asked. The

rim of her bonnet shadowed her face, making it impossible for him to determine her expression.

'Should I be?' He raised an eyebrow and turned their footsteps once again towards the inn. He would tell her the truth and then see her reaction. 'You probably think me wicked but, no, I am not ashamed. I did what I did for a purpose and I kept my promises.'

He waited for the gasp of horror, but instead she tightened her grip on his arm. A tiny furrow appeared between her brows. He resisted the temptation to smooth it away.

'Some people like my cousin would say yes, you should, but I am not sure. Keeping your promises is important.' She looked up into his face and he received the full blue gaze of her eyes. 'Does that make me wicked as well? Everyone says that I am, but I don't see it that way. My intentions are good.'

'I cannot change the past, Lottie. I did what I did to survive.' Tristan stopped by the inn's stables. He grasped her shoulders. 'Trust me?'

'But…but…' She pressed her hand to her lips, squared her shoulders. 'I will trust you. You are my husband. I am sure you have done your best and will look after me.'

A twinge of guilt passed over Tristan. What would she say when she actually knew what he had done? He dismissed it. His experiment would work. 'I will do well by you, Lottie.'

The smoke-hung public room fell silent as Lottie entered it. The crowd of drovers, workmen and ne'er-do-wells stared at them. Lottie shrank back against Tristan's arm. She turned her face towards his frock coat, breathed in, tried to rid her nostrils of the awful stench. He put a hand on her shoulder and lifted her chin as his dark eyes searched her face.

'Do I have to go through there? A woman tried to buy my hair! She appeared quite put out when I refused to sell it. Apparently golden curls are all the rage. I could get a good price for them, but they are mine.'

'If you want to get to the room, you will have to go through the throng, but I will be with you.' He touched her golden curls, a light touch, but one that sent a quiver arching through her. 'There should never be a need for you to sell your hair. Or your ear bobs. Trust me to provide for you.'

'How did you know she asked about those?'

'It stands to reason.' He gestured around the public room with its curling smoke and clanking tankards. 'In a place like this, people are looking to buy and sell whatever they can.'

'Do we have to stay here?'

'I have paid for the room.'

'I had rather thought it would be like the coaching inn that Mama and I stayed at when we went to Yorkshire once.' Lottie attempted a brave smile as she groped for a clean handkerchief, but could only find the crumpled one from earlier. 'Large clean rooms and an apple-cheeked proprietor. This inn has probably not been cleaned since the Jacobite rebellion. The ceiling is positively black with smoke.'

'I regret that it is not up to your standards but it is where we are staying.'

'It is not what was I was expecting.' Lottie tried to keep her skirts out of the unidentified puddle on the floor, but failed. A small cry of distress escaped her lips. 'It was my best afternoon dress.'

'The room is better than this.' His fingers tightened on her elbow.

'Have you seen it?'

'Dyvelston!' A voice hailed Tristan from a corner table. 'Here you are. Just the man for a game of cards.'

'A friend of yours?' Lottie asked, and her forehead puckered. Her husband was a gambler. He had to be if he was being hailed with such familiarity in an inn such as this one. She should have expected it, but she knew how much her father had hated cards. How he blamed them for his brother's downfall. For some men, cards was more than a pleasant pastime, they were a way of life, a religion.

'He is someone I knew once.'

'From your dissolute days.' Lottie strove to keep her voice light. 'Are you going to have a game of cards?'

Tristan paused, frowning.

'I will see you to the room. You need not worry about that.'

'And afterwards?'

'We are newly married, Lottie.'

'That is no answer.'

'It is all you will get.' He started towards the stairs. 'Are you coming with me or do you wish to be accosted by another buyer of hair? Or an owner of a nanny house?'

'I will come.' Lottie skirted around a second unidentified puddle on the sawdust-strewn floor and hurried after Tristan, reaching him just as he opened a door to the upstairs.

She followed Tristan up the stairs, along a narrow passageway, and then up another narrow flight of stairs. She tried to push away her fears. Tristan was taking her to their room. He had not abandoned her for a game of cards. Henry would have done that. Lucy was often left on her own. Ignored. Lottie wanted more from her marriage than Lucy had. She was determined to show Henry and Lucy that she could make a success of things.

Tristan opened the door and turned to her with a grim smile. 'How do you like the accommodation?'

Lottie started. She had expected a large poster bed with a roaring fire and a wash basin. This room was mean with bare floors and furniture that looked as if it had come from the early part of the last century. The sagging bed with its stained, greying coverlet took up a large part of the room and appeared to grow bigger with each beat of her heart. She would be expected to share it with Tristan.

For the first time in her life, she was alone in a bedroom with a man, a stranger. Lottie struggled to breathe. No, not a stranger, her husband, the man who had held her in his arms last evening. What would he expect of her?

Suddenly the public room was not as frightening as here.

Lottie wished she had had Lucy to ask about it, and Mama had been no help. All she had said was that all men were beasts and want to have their own way; women had to preserve their dignity. Beasts. Rolling around on that bed? Lottie winced, not liking to think of fleas or other insects lurking. She had enough to worry about without wondering if she would be bitten alive. She swallowed hard and risked a glance up at Tristan. His eyes were hooded, but watching her, his entire body stilled, waiting.

'You say nothing, wife. Does it measure up to your exacting standards?'

Lottie held back the arched remark she was about to make. This room was not his fault. It was quite probably the best he could afford. If he had known about Lord Thorngrafton's money, then perhaps he would have procured a better room, but he hadn't. And she had no wish to mock him. 'The room will be lovely for the night, I am sure.'

'It is a place to stay.'

'Yes,' Lottie said around the increasing lump in her throat. With every breath she took, it became harder and harder to pretend that this room was fine. Harder and harder to ignore the bed looming in the centre. 'No doubt your house will be better than this.'

'It may be. It may not be.' Tristan gave a little shrug. 'It has been vacant for years.'

Lottie did not dare reply. She wanted Tristan to take her in his arms again. She wanted it to be how it was last evening. She knew if his lips were against hers, she would not have to think or to worry.

'Is there some problem, Lottie?' Tristan put a hand on her shoulder, drew her to him. He pressed his lips to her temple. His breath against her cheek sent a pulse of warmth throughout. 'Confide in me. What troubles you? Why don't you like being here with me? Alone. You appeared to like being on the terrace with me last evening.'

'Nothing troubles me.'

She turned her face upwards and met his mouth. Their lips touched, parted and she tasted him. A jolt ran through her, igniting her insides. She moaned slightly in the back of her throat, felt her body begin to arch, and stiffened, stunned by her reaction. His hands dropped away. The kiss ended as air rushed between them. He regarded her with a question in his eyes, but made no move to touch her.

'Lottie, sweet Lottie.'

Lottie pressed her hand against her stomach, willed that the melting sensation would go away and tried not to think about what was to come. She knew her face flamed. What could happen if Tristan did not respect her?

The thoughts circled and circled in her head, making her dizzy. She had to find a way to breathe, to regain control of her thoughts and desires.

A distinct smell of wood smoke and cooking pervaded the room, gave her an excuse. 'Is there a possibility of food? I barely had anything for supper last night. I feel a bit faint.'

It was better than the truth. She knew she had done something wrong, but she had no idea what she had done. Why he had put her away from him.

'I will go and check.' Tristan's hand grasped the door. 'It will give you time to change, and to get comfortable.'

'Can you send someone to help me?'

'To help you?'

'I need a maid. I cannot undress myself.' She gave a small shrug.

He looked puzzled, then his face cleared. His voice became velvet soft. 'Unable to undress? Shall I play a lady's maid?' He came back over to her and trailed a hand along her shoulder. 'I have had a bit of experience in how ribbons and laces become undone.'

Him? He thought her a strumpet. Her mouth went dry

at the thought of his undoing her clothes. She remembered her mother's other words. A lady did not show passion. A lady submitted. Surrendered.

She had no wish to repel him. She knew she was not ready to give away her soul. Last night at Shaw's, his kisses had awakened something deep within her, a sort of hunger. But she wanted him to respect her. She was his wife, not his courtesan. She doubted if it would be possible to be both as much as she might like to be.

'My corset ties at the back. It can be very tricky. A serving maid would be best. More dignified.'

'If you wish, I only made the offer.' His voice lost its warmth and became correct. 'I have dealt with ladies' laces before…in my misspent youth.'

'Your misspent youth? It is different for a man. No one expects…no one makes comments…' Lottie watched him. Would he help her? What would it be like to have his long fingers stroke her skin? To feel his mouth move on hers like it had last night? She daren't ask in case he refused. She knew she was babbling, but anything to stop this growing dread inside her. What would he think of her without any clothes on? She hated her toes. Would he like her toes? Blind panic filled her. She knew nothing about lovemaking and he was an accomplished rake. He was used to women who knew how to please a man.

'Lottie, sweetheart, tell me what you want. It is our wedding night.' His voice played like silken velvet over her skin.

'It would be useful to have someone.' Lottie began to pace the room, unable to stand still, unable to think. 'Is there anyone at Gortner Hall? I shared a maid with Mama and then Cousin Frances and we helped each other. It was not ideal, of course, but I made do. It does not have to be a French maid. Any girl would do. I could teach her to do my hair. I am sure I could.'

She knew she was babbling and watched his eyes grow cold and his hands fall to his sides.

'I will send one of the serving maids with some bread and cheese. She should be able to help.' He bowed and closed the door. 'I will return shortly. That should give you enough time to make yourself decent.'

'Decent. Yes, I will be decent.'

'And, Lottie, there is no need to panic. I will send the maid. Remember to breathe while you wait.' He touched his fingers to his temple. 'It always helps.'

'I am not panicking.' She paused and smiled. 'I have no desire to faint.'

'That is a start.' He closed the door softly behind him.

Lottie breathed again. She would have time to get her nerves together. She would make sure that she did not give in to her passion. She would be dignified. Tristan would respect her for that. Men wanted wives that they could respect, who could help them. She had to remember that. She listened to the sound of his boots going down the stairs. The despair inside her increased with each step.

Had her passion doomed the marriage before it had started?

Tristan sat nursing his second pint of bitter. The inn-keeper had doctored the beer to a black sludge that gave no pleasure. He would give Lottie a bit of time before he returned to the room.

All around him, the dice rattled and the smoke swirled. Several ladies plied their trade. It was hard to imagine a more disreputable place, but it served its purpose. However, he wondered if he had made a slight error.

He had seen her face drain of colour when he suggested his playing the lady's maid. Silently he cursed her mother or whoever had told her about the facts of life. He had never lain with a virgin before, and most in particular had never lain with one who was his wife.

He had a responsibility to awaken her properly, to teach her about passion, and that meant going slow, and not forcing her here where the memory might be distasteful. Tristan regarded the bottom of his pint glass. He had to decide where it would be. He had to balance his desire against the need to make sure her first experience went smoothly. A great deal of responsibility rested on his shoulders. He was determined that his marriage would be a passionate one. He'd felt the passion in her earlier when they'd kissed.

Tristan gave the remaining dark liquid a final swirl. He was not ready for this. He tried to think about his other piece of unfinished business—his cousin, and how he could ensure Peter remained true to his word.

'Thorngrafton, it is you.' A large hand pinned him to his stool. 'I told Saidy that you weren't answering to Dyvelston any more, not since your uncle kicked up his heels. That was why you ignored him. It is amazing what some forget.'

'McGowan.' Tristan nodded as he finished his drink. The only thing he could be grateful for was that McGowan had failed to accost him while Lottie was there. He needed her to remain in ignorance for a few days longer. His experiment had to succeed. 'Is there some particular reason you are in Gretna Green?'

'Passing through, but I am most surprised to find you in a hellhole like this one. I would have thought you were more accustomed to staying at the finer coaching inns.'

'I have my reasons.'

'And it doesn't have anything to do with the beautiful blonde you were with—a real looker, that one. Golden curls, blue eyes and curves. You can pass her along to me when you've finished with her.' McGowan gave a coarse laugh.

'She's my wife.'

'Please give *Lady* Thorngrafton my compliments.' McGowan's leer told Tristan that he did not believe a word. 'Do she have a sister or three?'

'I will see that she gets your compliments.' Tristan gritted his teeth. He had no intention of explaining his actions to McGowan, an acquaintance from those long-ago days when he had taken great pleasure in making sure his name was as scandalous as possible. The difference between them was now marked. Once McGowan had been considered handsome, but now he showed the signs of overindulgence and too much high living.

'How came you to be let in the pockets?' McGowan fingered his chin. 'The last I heard you had done very nicely out of railways. One of the railway kings.'

'People talk too much, but I have no money worries.'

'Then why are you here? In this inn?'

'I have my reasons.' Tristan turned back to the barman, motioning for another pint. 'Allow me to pay for the next round.'

'Do you have time for a game of cards?' McGowan persisted. 'For old times' sake. I can remember how you and I would play until the dawn broke. You always knew when to stop, though. You had the coolest head I have ever seen.'

'You still play cards?'

'Avidly—you should have seen the money Saidy won off some high-flaunting lord lately returned from India. The nabob thought he were a king at cards, but we got his vowels in the end.'

'I will watch you play.' Tristan smiled as an idea on how to teach Peter a lesson came to him. Simple. Neat. It simply took a cool head and a steady nerve. The same approach he had to use with Lottie. 'There is a proposition I wish to put to you and Saidy. A little job that will put your…skills to good use, but you will be amply rewarded.'

'You interest me greatly.'

Dearest Henry and Lucy,

I cannot tell you what a splendid wedding Tristan and I had. You have never seen the like! You would have been so proud. My step never faltered and I said my vows so all could hear.

Lottie turned her face away from the letter and wiped a tear. She would allow no blotches on the paper. They would never know her wedding was anything less than marvellous. The shame would be unbearable. With a shaking hand, she added a few more lines enquiring about Mama's nerves, and her nieces and nephews. Then she sealed the letter and handed it to the serving girl.

'Will that be all, ma'am?'

'Your assistance is no longer required.' Lottie took the last few coins from her reticule. 'You have been most helpful. This should pay for the stamp as well as a little extra for your trouble. I do appreciate your help with the dress.'

The girl made another curtsy and left. Somewhere in the distance a door banged and loud footsteps sounded on the stairs. She hurried to the bed, dove in and pulled the sheets up to her chin.

'Where are you, Tristan? Why did you leave me alone?' she whispered and willed the door to open and her husband to appear.

Nothing.

A second set of footsteps came up the stairs, and several drunken voices argued about how much money was left in their purse and whether or not one or two of the lovely ladies downstairs would care to warm their beds.

Lottie clutched the sheet to her, and looked wildly about the room for a poker, for anything to defend her honour with. Her whole being longed for Tristan to appear and to cradle her. But when no one entered the room, she forced her hands to relax.

Her last waking thought before sleep overtook was that Tristan had not bothered to return. He was not interested in her. She wiped away a few tears and refused to cry. Crying only turned her nose red.

How everyone would laugh if they knew—the incomparable Lottie Charlton spending her wedding night alone in a filthy flea-infested coaching inn, fearful of drunken drovers and abandoned in favour of a card game by a husband who had married her out of duty. Married in a torn dress, a crushed bonnet and with an iron ring for a wedding band.

This was not how her life was supposed to go—at all.

Lottie slammed her fist into the pillow and resolved that, somehow, she would triumph. She would make this into a glorious match, if she could only figure out a way. She wanted a different way. She deserved better. She would find that way.

Chapter Seven

'Oy, you in there, get up. We need the room. You only paid until morning. It's first light now!'

A steady pounding on the door opposite them woke Lottie from her slumber. She pushed at the unaccustomed weight of an arm around her middle and suddenly realised that yesterday had been no dream. She was married. And Tristan was in bed with her. Not only in bed, but her bottom was snuggled up against him in a suggestive manner and her whole being infused with the warmth of him as his breath tickled the nape of her neck.

He must have come in some time in the night. And so great was her exhaustion that she hadn't woken. She should have done. Lottie bit her lip, regretting her late-night thoughts, regretting her damp pillow.

Had he noticed?

She resolved to be a better wife. She would give him no cause to run away and play cards. Her mother must have been right and her passionate response to his kiss disgusted him. She longed to have been wrong.

Half-turning her head, she caught his deep dark gaze watching her. The sight took her breath away and took all thoughts from her head. She could only drown in his eyes as deep hunger grew within her.

'Good morning,' he said, running a finger down her arm and sending a warm sensation pulsating through her. 'You were sleeping like an angel when I came to bed.'

'There is someone banging on all the doors,' Lottie said, hanging on to the last remnant of common sense. 'He wants money. Do we owe him money?'

'He won't come in here.'

'I rather think he means business. He will kick the door down.' Lottie fought against the tide of rising panic that threatened to engulf.

'He wouldn't want to damage his own property.' His breath tickled her neck.

'Tristan!' Lottie covered her ears with her hands.

'If you insist, I will see what can be done to preserve your sensibilities.'

Tristan removed his arm and stood up, totally unconcerned about his nakedness. His skin gleamed golden in the morning light. Lottie looked at his chest with its sprinkling of dark hair and then forced her eyes higher. She had been sleeping with a naked man and had brazenly pushed herself up against him. Was she a wanton creature?

He pulled his trousers on, and did up the buttons.

'How can you be so casual about this?' Lottie clutched the sheet and raised it to her chin. 'We will be disgraced! He is only next door. I am sure of it!'

'The room! Or more money!' The pounding increased. 'I will have the law on you.'

'We will leave in less time than it takes to get the constable!' a man shouted back. And a woman's voice hurled abuse at the innkeeper.

'Quit your blathering! You will wake the dead!' another yelled.

'Are you telling me to get the constable? I will and I will have every man Jack of you out of this inn. This here inn is a respectable place.'

Lottie regarded the door with horror. What was happening out there? Was the innkeeper demanding money from everyone? Was she going to be treated like some wastrel?

'Please, Tristan, I beg you—do something.' She made a little gesture as insults were exchanged between the innkeeper and the unknown guest. 'I am not decent. Goodness knows what sort of mood the innkeeper will be in when he knocks on our door. Please, Tristan.'

'Relax, Lottie. I have taken care of matters. We are safe, but if you are worried…' He opened the door, and stepped outside, closing the door behind him. 'Is there some problem?'

The reply was muffled, but the knocking ceased abruptly and the innkeeper went off, grumbling. Lottie rested her head against her chest. She was safe. She was not going to face the humiliation of being thrown out of the inn without any clothes on. But would the innkeeper come back? She tucked a strand behind her ear and tried to collect her thoughts.

Tristan came back to bed and put his hands on either side of her face. 'He has gone now, Lottie. You can stop trembling with fear. You won't have the innkeeper barging in.'

'The shame of it. I couldn't stand the shame.' She concentrated on taking steady breaths. 'That poor couple. Do you think they had just married?'

'I have no idea. They have nothing to do with me. I did not want you to be fearful of the innkeeper.'

'Thank you.' Lottie watched the muscles ripple on his shoulder and her lips ached.

'Perhaps I should have come back to bed earlier. Then you could have expressed your gratitude more properly.' He trailed a hand down her arm. 'But it is too late for regrets. We have to move. The day is wasting.'

'Where are we going?' Lottie asked quickly. If his hand continued to stroke her arm, she would lose all power of movement. All her resolutions would be forgotten before she had even risen from the bed. 'What are your plans?'

'To Gortner Hall, the house I inherited in the North Tyne Valley.' Tristan withdrew his hands and stood up. He picked his shirt up from the end of the bed. 'Where we shall spend our days.'

'There is to be no wedding trip, then?' Lottie hated the plaintive note to her voice. She knew their wedding was unorthodox, but she had thought they might have a trip, go somewhere before she was buried in the country. Even Henry had taken Lucy to France. A week in Calais. She was going nowhere. There were no doubt some who would say the punishment was justified, but she had always dreamt of a splendid wedding trip.

'I had not planned to marry. There are things that need my attention. The estate was left vacant for a long period. There is much to do. It will be restored to its former glory.'

'Lord Thorngrafton's coachman has gone.' Lottie

wrapped her arms about her knees. She had to be practical. She had to put aside her girlish fantasies, even if it pained her to do so. She had not married a fairy-tale prince; she had married Tristan, a man who had inherited a small, vacant estate. In time, things would improve. She had to be practical, but there remained a little piece of her that wished she didn't. The sooner they arrived at Gortner Hall, the better. A long, low wail resounded through the room and gave Lottie an idea. 'Shall we take the express? There is one that runs to Carlisle. I overheard Henry speaking about it the other night at dinner. The speeds are incredible—over forty miles per hour in some places. The first-class carriage has real armchairs.'

Tristan's hands stilled on his shirt buttons and his face once again wore his remote look. Lottie shifted slightly. Had her tongue run away with her again? What was wrong with the train? It was surely practical. She had not suggested buying a new carriage.

'That train costs large sums of money. A third of a month's wage for a labourer.'

'But you are not a labourer.' Lottie swallowed hard and struggled to breathe normally. What was Tristan saying? How poor were they? 'You are a gentleman. You were born one.'

'You have not seen what needs to be done on the estate.' He gave a slight shrug. 'My hands will soon become as rough as any farmer's.'

'You are not suggesting we walk all the way there?' Lottie strove for a laugh.

'Walking is one way of travelling. Country folk do it all the time.'

'Yes, but—'She thought about her slippers and wished she had brought her boots. She had never considered the possibility of walking. Surely he had to be joking. Her slippers would not make it and her feet would be cut to ribbons. If they were going to walk, she'd need stout boots. A train journey would cost less than stout boots. It had to. 'Gortner Hall is…in the North Tyne and we are in Scotland. It took us all night to drive here from Gilsland and we travelled with fast horses. How long would it take us to walk that distance and more? A day? Two?'

'Don't you fancy a night or two out on the open countryside—you, me and a friendly haystack?' His dark eyes danced as he expertly did up his cravat. He had once again become remote. It was as if suddenly there was a wall between them.

'Surely we are not reduced to begging.' The blanket she had been clutching to her chest fell unheeded as Lottie realised the potential. Begging. Being classed as a vagrant. Maybe if she was very unlucky, being thrown in the stocks. She would become one of the despised. There had to be a way of avoiding that fate. 'My settlement…we can borrow against that. It will be more than enough to take the first-class express.'

'I have no idea what your settlement will be.' Tristan finished dressing. The golden god of this morning had vanished and in its place was the remote man from the carriage, the one who had left her standing in the inn's yard. 'Your brother and I did not have time to discuss it. I have no doubt your brother will be fair when the time comes. Until my banker tells me it is there, Lottie, I have no wish to borrow against it. It is a good way to end up in Newgate or one of the other debtors' prisons.'

Lottie put her hand to her head. Her stomach reeled. Debtors' prison. The workhouse. She busied her hands with retrieving the thin blanket. Tried to concentrate on breathing. She could not borrow trouble. 'Have you been in one before?'

'Yes.'

The single word fell between them. Lottie put her hand to her mouth and tried to prevent the gasp. A debtors' prison. Her husband. There should be some polite remark to cover the incident, but her mind failed her. 'You have been? Were you there long? Was it as awful as they say?'

Tristan became made out of stone. Then his eyes creased and he stroked her hair, a simple touch, but comforting. Lottie resisted the urge to turn her face to his palm and rest her head.

'I was visiting a friend who had fallen on hard times. It is far from a pleasant place, Lottie.'

'You mustn't tease me like that.' Lottie released a breath and offered up a small prayer. Her husband wasn't a feckless fortune hunter. He had gone to visit a friend.

'You should believe better of me.'

'Why?' Lottie bowed her head. 'Why should I?'

'Because…I am your husband.'

'Trust is something that is earned.' She clasped her hands together. Her heart pounded in her ears. Tristan had to understand. She enjoyed expensive things, but she also understood the value of money and how quickly wealth could be lost. 'I have learnt to be cautious. Far too many men see a wealthy woman as a way to end their debts and continue with their debauched lifestyle. A debutante rapidly learns or faces the consequences.'

'You were not cautious the other night.'

'That was different.' She waved her hand. 'Other considerations were in the forefront of my mind.'

'And now you find out what I am like.' He rubbed his thumb against her mouth, a featherlight movement that sent ripples of sensation flickering throughout her body. 'I will be beholden to no man, Lottie.'

'I have some money. We can send a message to Henry…'

'I have no use for your money. Charity is nothing I have ever looked for.'

'Being proud is one thing, but this is different. I am your wife.'

'You just gave me a lecture about imprudent husbands and fortune hunters.'

'But there are certain standards one must maintain.'

'Must one?' He raised an eyebrow.

'Yes.' Lottie heard the desperation in her voice. He had to give in. He had to see. 'It must be miles to Gortner Hall. Days. Days we would waste if we walked.'

'I have enough to get us back to Gortner Hall.' His eyes were cold. 'We will take the parliamentary trains. There is a connection at Carlisle. We can get off at Hexham and catch the coach. I purchased two tickets yesterday. I thought it best to be prepared.'

A parliamentary train. One of the trains Gladstone had ordered to be run along each railway line once a day and stopping at all the stations. Lottie's heart sunk.

'But it is so slow, little faster than a stage coach, and it is all third class. All wooden benches and a tin roof.' The words escaped from Lottie's mouth. She winced as a muscle in his jaw leapt. 'Surely we can take the express. How much more expensive is it?'

'There is nothing wrong with being ordinary, Lottie. Keep your money for when it is truly needed.' He pushed the reticule away, but tugged her towards him. Her unresisting body fell into his as his arms went around her. 'It is about time you realised this. You married me. You did not marry someone like Sir Geoffrey who maintains a private railcar for his journeys. The parliamentary train with all its stops will get us there in good time.'

'I never wanted to marry him. Ever. He was old, older than Mama.' Lottie gave into temptation and placed her head against his shirt front, listened to the steady thumping of his heart. 'That was my mother's desire.'

'And what was your desire?' His fingers tilted her chin upwards and she wanted to drown in the warm pools that were his eyes. Lottie felt a tide of heat wash through her body. 'Shall we find time to explore it?'

His lips touched the corner of her mouth, one tantalizsing touch. Soft. Calling to her. She lifted her arms, placed them around his neck. Held him.

Somewhere far away heavy footsteps pounded on the stair, recalling her to where they were and what might happen if she was not careful.

'It appears that I have already explored it. I followed my desire rather than my mother's. I married you.' Lottie pushed herself away from his body. She forced her legs to carry her to where she had neatly placed her clothes last night. She rolled up her stockings, slipped on her petticoats and finally held out the corset. All she would need was to be entangled in Tristan's arms and for the door to come crashing in. For the parish constable to be standing there. She had had enough embarrassment for one week.

'Was that all you wanted—to be married to a young man?'

Lottie ignored the comment and concentrated on tying the drawstring of her petticoats. 'It would appear you will have to help me to dress if we are to leave this room and to catch the parliamentary. And I shall pack away two of my petticoats as there is bound to be little enough space on the parliamentary.'

Tristan stood very still, but his eyes burnt with a fire as if he had watched every movement and memorised it. Lottie felt the tide of a blush wash up her cheeks as she remembered some of the illustrations from *Aristotle's Complete Master Piece*. Did men like to watch women dress?

'I am only doing this because we have an innkeeper breathing down our necks.' Tristan gave the back of her neck a kiss before he rapidly laced up the corset. A warm glow infused through Lottie. It would be easy to turn and to be in his arms again. 'I would far rather spend the morning with you in this room.'

'You should pull the corset tighter.' Lottie took a deep breath in. If she concentrated, these ripples of sensation would fade.

'You will do yourself injury.'

'What is a little pain compared to fashion?' She gave a laugh. 'I thought you liked my narrow waist. I felt your hand on it when we danced. It is one of my best features.'

'What is fashion compared with pain? We are at an

impasse, Lottie, and as I have to lace you, the corset will stay loose.' His fingers spanned her waist. 'Your waist is small enough.'

'When I get my new lady's maid…'

'If you get her—who knows, you might enjoy my services.' His breath tickled her ear.

A shiver went down Lottie's back as his voice held her. The temptation to lean backwards into him nearly overpowered her. Instead she pulled her dress over her head and stood while his firm fingers fastened up the back. When he had finished, his fingers trailed along her collarbone. She held herself stiffly, refusing to give in to the sensation. 'The parliamentary.'

'I see you are determined to catch this train.'

'The innkeeper is determined to be rid of us and you delight in teasing me.'

'That much is true.'

'And if we miss this train, we will have to wait for the next one. We don't have the money for that.'

Tristan looked at her with hooded eyes. 'Do you know how much money I have, Lottie?'

Lottie drew a deep breath. She knew when she could not change things. She would have to make the best of it. Just as she had at Christmas when she was sent away or last birthday when she had been given a set of improving poems rather than the tortoiseshell combs she had longed for.

'If we must go, it is better to go now,' she said brightly. 'And who knows, I might enjoy the parliamentary. I have never been on one before. When I went to Haydon Bridge, I took the express.'

'The parliamentary is an experience.'

'My only wonder is how you managed to stay at Shaw's. My brother was at pains to point out the expense to my mother and me. Several times in the course of the afternoon and at least once more at supper.'

'Ah, Lord Thorngrafton managed that.' Tristan's eyes slid away from her. 'The suite was rented in his name.'

'But you are unkind about your cousin.' Lottie clasped her hands. Tristan had to lose his unreasonable prejudice towards his cousin. 'He obviously wanted to promote you in society. He had no cause to befriend you.'

'This much is true. My cousin did appear rather put out that I had arrived. He thought me safely on the Continent, lost for all eternity, never to set foot in England again.'

Lottie wrinkled her nose. 'You really must refrain from disparaging him. It would be dreadful if it were ever reported back. He…he even gave me money.'

'Why would he do that?' Tristan stilled. A watchfulness came about him.

'In case I changed my mind—at least, that is what his coachman said when he handed me the bank note.'

'The coachman told you this.' Tristan's voice was ice cold. 'What else did he tell you? What did Lord Thorngrafton want from you? What was the payment to be?'

'He did not inform me.' Lottie kept her head up. How could she tell Tristan that Lord Thorngrafton had thought his own cousin would abandon her? How could she divide the two further when she knew how important it was that they have good relations with him? She gave a laugh that sounded more like fingernails grating on a slate. 'Perhaps he entertained notions of me becoming his mistress in gratitude. His intentions were far from honourable last autumn. I know this. A woman can tell.'

'And you thought my intentions were honourable at Shaw's? Was that why you went out on the terrace with me?'

'I didn't think at all.' Lottie knew she had to be truthful. She could not lie to Tristan about that. 'For the first time in my life, I forgot to think about the consequences.' She paused and continued in a very small voice, 'If I had, perhaps we would not be here.'

'Perhaps.' Tristan reached down and picked up the satchel. He paused, his back towards her. 'Would you become Lord Thorngrafton's mistress? He has the reputation of being an excellent lover. The life of a mistress can be exciting to some women.'

'How can you say such things! I am your wife!'

'Lord Thorngrafton is…unique,' Tristan replied. 'Some women are entranced by a title.'

'All the more reason for not antagonising him. But rest assured that had I wanted that outcome, I would not have waited until now…until after my marriage to his cousin.'

Lottie reached for her bonnet and fastened it with expert fingers. She attempted a bright smile, but inside her blood boiled. Lord Thorngrafton held no attraction for her. The only man who had ever made her melt was standing before her, being annoying. It was as if his touch had been infected with some loving disease and all she could crave was another touch of his hand, another smile. These things had become necessary to her. And she would die before she ever admitted it. Before she would admit his failure to come to her bed last night until after she was sound asleep had hurt.

'Why did you tell me now about the money? Why didn't you tell me earlier?'

'I was ashamed.' Lottie twisted the iron ring about her finger. 'I thought you might think that I had no faith in you. That I had begged him for the money and was planning on running away at the earliest opportunity.'

'And why did you tell me just now?'

Lottie turned her head. She couldn't confess her reasons, not to him. They were too new and raw. She could not risk his mockery. 'Shall we depart? There is only one parliamentary per day.'

'You are a puzzle, Lottie Dyvelston. I would have expected you to be in tears.'

'Some things I can change, and others I can't. It is up to me to know the difference, as my old nurse used to say.' Lottie glanced back at the pillow, grateful that, after her sleep, her eyes betrayed no sign of redness. It would not do to have Tristan know that she had shed tears over him on their wedding night.

Lottie gave one last look at the mean room. There was nothing except the rumpled bedclothes to show they had ever been there. She was a married woman. She had spent a night with her husband, the first of many to come. But now she had to face the parliamentary and her fellow passengers.

Chapter Eight

Everyone crowded towards the doors when the parliamentary arrived in Carlisle, pushing past and not really caring that others might want to get off. A rather large lady elbowed Lottie in the ribs with a basket and then glared at her as she started to protest.

Lottie stepped gingerly down from the train, one of the last to disembark. Her bottom ached from the short time she had spent on the overcrowded wooden benches. She had carefully kept her skirts away from the other passengers and had declined any overtures from their fellow passengers.

'How long do we have to wait?' she asked Tristan as, with a great roar, the train chugged away, leaving them standing on the platform. She fumbled for her one remaining handkerchief. She regarded the soot-spotted cloth with distaste and put it back in her reticule.

'About two hours,' he said, checking his fob watch. 'The parliamentary to Newcastle leaves quite late in the day.'

'Isn't there a train before then?'

'Not a parliamentary.' Tristan gave her a dark look.

Lottie straightened her shoulders and took a breath. She would be dignified. 'What will happen when we get to Hexham?'

'We will find transport somehow. There has been talk of building a railway up the North Tyne, but nothing has come of it yet. There are still many more profitable places to build.'

'Then we shall have to hope there is transport.'

'I did send a letter to the hall. There should be transport waiting for us.'

'A carriage?' Lottie sent up a prayer for a well-sprung carriage, one like Lord Thorngrafton's with deep seats and a roof to keep the rain out. Not a bone-shaking pony cart that was exposed to the changeable English summer weather like the one she'd had to use at Aunt Alice's.

'Whatever Mrs Elton can arrange. It won't be the last word in luxury.'

Lottie mentally whispered goodbye to the carriage. She had to think positively—it could be worse. She had to believe in the word—transport. She lifted her chin. 'As long as I don't have to walk, I will be fine.'

'I will do my best.' Tristan put his hand under her elbow and led her to the third-class waiting room. It did not have the armchairs or the fire that the first-class waiting room did, but it was clean and neat. Respectable, but barely. 'You may wait here, if you like.'

'Where are you going?' Lottie fought to keep the note of panic from her voice.

'I am going to try to find a newspaper. W. H. Smith recently started a newspaper train to Carlisle and I would like to have a look at one of the London papers.' His eyes crinkled at the corners. 'Can I trust you to stay here in the train station? Unless you would like to tramp around the streets of Carlisle with me?'

'You pointed out before, my dress is not made for walking.' Lottie gave a shiver. She had no wish to be stared at from carriages. What if she encountered someone she knew? How they would all laugh at her. Lottie Charlton… Dyvelston, not dressed properly. She could not take the humiliation.

'If that is what you want…'

'I have learnt my lesson.' Lottie looked around the small waiting room. Several men in ill-fitting frock coats and tight collars sat reading papers, and in a corner some children played a game of marbles. Peaceful. 'It appears to be safe enough. I want to rest for a little while.'

The pads of his fingers brushed her chin, a featherlight touch, but one that stilled her, left her longing for more. 'I will keep you safe. Trust me on this.'

'You earned my trust yesterday,' Lottie whispered back. Her mouth ached for his kiss. The heat began to rise on her cheek at the boldness of her thought. Even thinking about kissing her husband in public showed how wanton and wicked she was becoming.

'Thank you for that.' He raised her gloved hand to his lips and was gone.

Lottie pressed the glove against her mouth and stared after him. Her whole body tingled, remembering what it was like to wake up in his arms. Tonight, surely, he would find time for her and she would be able to control her passion. He would not be disgusted with her behaviour again. She would not give him any excuse to leave her.

She settled down on one of the vacant benches to wait. She smoothed her dress and winced slightly at the stains and mud that were now engrained on it. No one would ever think that it was this season's silk paisley. It far more closely resembled a cast-off to a second housemaid. She gave a wry smile. At least no one would say that she shouldn't be in the third-class waiting room.

The time dragged and she began to amuse herself by making up little stories about her fellow passengers. Anything to keep her mind off Tristan and the shape of his mouth. It seemed impossible how important he had become to her already. And he was a good man. Against the odds, she had found a man who was honest and true.

'Pretty lady, can you help?' A hand tugged at her skirt. A young girl about eight stood there. Her young brother clung to her hand and regarded Lottie with big eyes in a tear-streaked face. 'Our nurse is missing.'

'I am not sure if I can do anything.'

'Please, miss, please help. You have a kind face. We are lost.'

Lottie regarded the children. Their clothes were well made but dirty and the little boy's trousers had a rip in one knee. Tracks of tears showed on the girl's face. And the boy's face was smudged with coal dust and mud as if they had scrambled about the railway yard.

'I will do what I can.' Lottie looked towards the door and wished Tristan would arrive back. 'What does she look like? And where did you lose her?'

Both children began to talk at once, chattering about this and that and how they were chased. Lottie held a finger to her lips, waiting until they fell silent. 'Please, I will help.

We shall have to find the stationmaster. He is probably in the first-class waiting room. I am sure your nurse is looking for you both right now.'

'A guard told us that we couldn't go there. He called us urchins. Chased us away. And a bad man came and tried to capture us.' A single tear ran down the girl's face.

'He was going to take us away and put us in a pie,' the little boy said. 'And I would never see Nurse or Mama or Papa again.'

'Hush, Charley.'

'But you said, Verbena. It is why we hid in the coal pile,' the boy protested.

Lottie shifted uneasily. She remembered all too clearly her experience yesterday. There were other worse things that could happen to children. She regarded the door and willed Tristan to return, but the doorway was vacant. She pressed her hands to her mouth, thinking. She had to do something. 'I will do the best that I can to reunite you with your nurse. She will be looking for you on the platform. I am sure she will.'

The children's faces cleared and the boy shyly placed a kiss on her glove. 'Thank you, pretty lady.'

'First shall we clean your faces? Make you more presentable?'

'Please, we have lost our handkerchiefs.'

Lottie took out her handkerchief and began to wipe the coal from the boy's chin. He gave a grateful smile. She handed it to his sister, who scrubbed her face before holding it out.

'Keep it. You have greater need than I do.'

She took the pair by the hands and began to look. The

nurse would be frantically searching. No doubt she would discover her or someone else on the platform.

Except for a pile of luggage and a porter, the platform was empty. Lottie stamped her foot in frustration and wished she had waited for Tristan. She had to think clearly.

It was possible she had made a mistake and that perhaps the children were meant for the first-class lounge and had become confused. The nurse might have fallen asleep and the children wandered away. It had been known to happen. She had done it once as a little girl and had been discovered crying in a livery stable.

She lifted her head and turned the knob and took the children in. A steward with a disdainful look blocked her way. He curled his lip as he looked her and the children up and down.

'Here, what are you doing with those filthy children? You are only allowed in this here room if you are a first-class passenger. I will need to see your tickets.' The steward's expression indicated that he doubted Lottie or the children would possess such a thing.

'I am looking for their nurse,' Lottie answered. 'They may have become confused and entered the third-class waiting room by mistake.'

The steward began a long lecture about the rules and regulations of the railway company and how she would have to comply. Lottie resisted the temptation to roll her eyes heavenwards. Did she look like riff-raff? At that moment, a soberly dressed elderly woman with a worried expression came up with the stationmaster. When the children saw her, they gave a glad cry and rushed into her arms.

'Bless you, my dear,' the woman said to Lottie. 'I have searched everywhere for them. They are a pair of scamps. I only took my eyes off them for an instant and they were gone. Vanished into thin air. Their mother would have been beside herself with worry. She suffers dreadfully from her nerves.'

A lump grew in Lottie's throat as the children began to talk at once. Tristan would understand why she had left the waiting room, she was sure of it. The children were so delighted to be reunited with their nurse.

'It was my pleasure,' she said when the children had finished telling their tale.

'Would you like something for your trouble?' The woman reached into her reticule.

'Nothing, thank you.' Lottie kept her back straight. No one had ever offered her money before. She had only done a good deed. 'The children's smiles are enough reward.'

'If you are sure…' The nurse held out a coin. 'You have saved my job. I shouldn't like to think what would be said.'

'Quite sure. It was my pleasure and I believe the pair have learnt their lesson.'

The two children nodded vigorously.

'If you insist, but…' The woman shook her head. 'The master won't like it. Nor will my lady. They like to help those less fortunate than themselves.'

'I do insist.' Lottie turned on her heel and started back towards the door. With any luck, Tristan would not have returned and she could explain the story with a light laugh. She intended on leaving out the bit about the offer of payment. There was no need for Tristan to know about that.

She knew she had done the correct thing. She stubbed her toe on the edge of the carpet and nearly fell.

'I am so sorry,' she said. 'I was thinking about other things.'

A fashionably dressed mother and daughter drew their skirts back as if she might contaminate them. Lottie's heart lurched. The pair could have been her own mother and her six months ago—wrapped up in their own self-importance, blind to the world around them. She wondered if those two had even seen the children and thought to stop them.

She gave her head a slight shake. The blindness and stupidity of people. A cold shiver ran down her back—how many things had she failed to see? How many things had she missed because she was too busy looking towards the best social advantage? Thankfully this time she had noticed. She shuddered and kept on walking.

'The nerve of some people, Mama.' The younger of the pair waved her fan. 'Some people think they own the railway and the station.'

'They don't know their place, dear,' the mother replied in a strident tone. 'This waiting room is supposed to be for gentle folk. Such a display of ill breeding.'

'I doubt you would know any,' Lottie muttered under her breath.

'Were you speaking to my daughter and me?' The elder of the women looked Lottie up and down. 'You should know how to speak to your betters.'

'I do and when I meet them, I shall.' Lottie lifted her chin and prepared to glide pass. There were shocked gasps from the women and a crowd began to gather around.

'Do you know who I am?' The woman had the same imperious tone that Lottie's mother used when confronted by a hostile shopkeeper.

'Does it matter? The children in question have been reunited with their nurse.' Lottie's stomach churned. Her right to be in a first-class waiting room had never been questioned before. Couldn't people tell?

'And did you know how handsome the reward would be?'

'I guessed.' Lottie gave her best social smile. 'It was very easy to work out that the children were well cared for and would be missed.'

'Shocking! She probably stole the children herself. I wouldn't put it past her,' a portly gentleman pronounced, leaning over to the two women. The elderly woman gave a smile of smug satisfaction as if she knew of her own superiority. 'The steward should be informed.'

'Yes, call the steward, Mama. I wonder I hadn't thought of that. Some people like to give themselves airs and graces. There ought to be a law.'

Lottie stared at the growing throng of unfriendly faces, all looking down their noses at her. Surely they saw her refuse the money. Surely they knew she had brought the children back out of the goodness of her heart.

'I meant their smiles and tears of joy at being reunited with their nurse. Anyone but a simpleton would know that.' Lottie tilted her head higher, ignored the steward who was steadily advancing towards her with a gleam in his piggy eyes. 'If you will excuse me, please, I believe the air is fresher in the third-class waiting room.'

She stumbled out of the first-class waiting room. Her hands were trembling as she leant against the wall and tried to collect her thoughts.

How could people be that cruel?

She put her hand over her mouth and refused to cry. Everything she did was misinterpreted. She straightened her shoulders and resolved never to behave in such a fashion herself.

When she had nearly reached the third-class waiting room, she saw Tristan striding toward her, a newspaper folded under his arm. His eyebrows were drawn together and a look like thunder was on his face. 'You have come from the first-class waiting room. Do not try to deny it. I saw the direction you scurried from.'

'Before you jump to conclusions,' Lottie said, holding up her hand, stopping his words, 'There was a very good reason for me being in there.'

'I have little doubt that you think you had a good reason for being there.' He raised an eyebrow. 'What explanation are you going to give? Were you looking for a comfortable place to sit? Somewhere where you did not have to mix with the ordinary people.'

Lottie's heart sank and she straightened the folds of her gown before answering. The irony of the situation did not escape her. She cleared her throat. 'Don't you dare try to tell me that I don't belong there. I have had quite enough of that today already. The steward protested in the strongest terms when I first went in.'

'Did you go there to prove a point?' He tapped the newspaper against his hand. 'I told you what would happen.'

'To reunite some children with their nurse,' Lottie said through gritted teeth. Then at the slight relaxation of his mouth, she quickly explained the story. Tristan listened, nodding at several points. 'And the passengers were truly horrible,' Lottie said as she finished the tale. 'I shall be pleased to return to third class.'

'What did they do to you?'

'They made it seem like I didn't know my place. The nurse even offered me some money as reward.' Lottie blinked back tears. 'Money? Me? I refused it, of course.'

Tristan put his arm around her and she drew strength from him. 'Some people only pay attention to what is on the outside.'

'But even if my gown is muddy and creased, I look presentable.' Lottie gave a huge sniff. 'It is only a few months old and the cut is highly fashionable.'

He took her chin between his fingers and raised it. 'You look presentable to me, if slightly creased. Do you want to sit in the first-class waiting room? Shall I go and make arrangements? It can be done.'

Lottie shook her head. 'Not now, not when I know what snobs populate it.'

'You have good intentions, Lottie. You did the right thing.'

'I know, but why do they always turn out to be wrong?'

'It is nearly time to board the train, Lottie. Forget about it. They are not important.'

Lottie rested her hand on his arm. 'But they were awful.'

'Now do you see what pride can do to people?' he asked and she could see a strange light burning in his eyes.

'I have never behaved like that.'

'Are you certain?'

Lottie paused. From now, she would make the effort to see the people about her and speak pleasantly without first deciding what their social status was. Her lesson had been a hard one. She would do things because they were right. But she could not explain this to Tristan. He might consider her a monster. And she wasn't that. 'No, never to my knowledge. At least, I hope I haven't.'

Chapter Nine

Tristan surveyed the Hexham railway yard with a frown. He had expected Mrs Elton to send one of the tenant farmers out with a pony cart. Not the lap of luxury, but something.

There was nothing there except a few broken-down farm carts. And Mrs Elton would not have sent one of those. They would take far too long to get to the Hall. He cursed under his breath. There was no use second-guessing the reason. He would have to adapt and cope.

'Is there something wrong, Tristan?' Lottie broke off her farewells with a farmer's widow. 'Something is amiss. I can see it in your face. The train was a half-hour late, but there's nothing we could do about that.'

'It would appear that my earlier presumption was wrong. There is no transport waiting for us. Curious, Mrs Elton is generally very efficient.'

'Perhaps the innkeeper did not send your letter. I did not trust him.'

'That is certainly one explanation.' Tristan scanned the rapidly emptying yard again, but no pony cart or conveyance magically appeared. And he had no intention of standing about, hoping that one would. 'We shall have to see if the livery stables are open. They will have a carriage for hire. I would like to get to Gortner before nightfall.'

'But won't that be expensive?'

Tristan tilted his head. Lottie had changed since this morning. She made an effort to speak to the people about her and had entertained several children with songs on their journey from Carlisle. How much was show and how much was a true change, he was not certain, but something had happened to her. He knew his plan was working. She was starting to think about others. 'Do you have a better alternative?'

'Mrs Foster's brother is a farmer. He is picking her up. He has the cart with the two white oxen.' Lottie gestured towards the widow, who gave a large beaming smile and waved back. 'Mrs Foster has offered us a place in her brother's cart. They can drop us off at the crossroads to Gortner Hall, if we like. She says it is not a far walk, a country mile or two only. And two more in the back of the cart will not make a pennyworth's of difference. I thought it best to enquire about how one proceeded up the North Tyne Valley as you appeared so vague about it.'

'I am never vague.' Tristan crossed his arms. Irritated. Lottie did not trust his ability. And Mrs Foster had her distances wrong. Gortner Hall was nearly five miles from the Wark crossroads. 'The livery stables will be able to provide something.'

'It is what ordinary people do. Do you think I am so frail that I cannot make the journey?' Lottie adjusted her bonnet. 'A mile or two is nothing to me.'

'It is more than—' Tristan stopped. Lottie wanted to do this. He would let her. It would be a good experience for her. A reinforcement of the lesson. Sometimes, one had to milk the opportunity.

'Don't be mulish, Tristan. I am saving us money.' Her lips turned up in the sweetest smile. 'Tristan, I am being ordinary.'

'Very well, Lottie, if you wish to ride in a farm cart that badly, we will. Go ahead, arrange it.'

'Way aye, it will be a right pleasure, sir,' the plump woman said, coming over. 'Your good wife and I have been exchanging recipes on making jam and chutney. She has some right interesting ideas, like. Elderflower and gooseberry. I had never thought of it, but they would go well together in jam.'

'Indeed?'

'I have always enjoyed helping out in the still room. It is one of my enthusiasms. The still room is a right and proper place for a lady.' Lottie's eyes glowed. 'I found a kindred spirit in Mrs Foster while you took refuge behind your newspaper. She likes to preserve fruit and vegetables. She even told me the best way to make sugared violets. It is a much simpler way than Lucy makes hers.'

'Your abilities never cease to surprise me.'

'I am resigned to my fate now.' Lottie smiled up at him. 'And it will be quite amusing to be the wife of a local landowner.'

Tristan tilted his head, considering the possibilities. Resigned to her fate. A form of words or the truth? Did Lottie know what she was asking? Was it a ploy because she knew he would refuse the gesture and then she would be able to insist on using her money to hire a more expensive carriage? He would play along. Nothing serious would happen and Lottie would learn to listen to him. Mrs Foster led the way to a hay cart where her brother greeted them with a genial wave and readily agreed to take them to the Gortner Hall crossroads. Tristan heard the muttered gasp beside him and the slight hesitation. Then Lottie squared her shoulders, climbed into the cart and patted the hay beside her. Her once pristine dress became covered in wisps of straw, but she appeared not to mind. 'Are you coming, Tristan? It will be fun. And you did mention hay-stacks earlier.'

'To sleep in, not to ride on.'

'As long as it gets us where we are going, I don't mind.'

He gave an inward smile of satisfaction. He doubted if Lottie had ever ridden in a cart for as long as she would have to today.

'Is the condition of the hall as bad as Mrs Foster says?' Lottie asked as the cart began to move.

'Much worse,' Tristan answered firmly.

'He would know, but I know my late husband—God rest his soul—said that all that estate needed was someone to love it,' Mrs Foster said over her shoulder. 'Mr Foster hated what had happened to it. Once, it was Lord Thorn-grafton's seat. The way the old lord treated it after…'

'I think we had best be making a move, if you want to get to Wark before nightfall,' Tristan said, not letting Mrs Foster finish. Lottie did not need to hear the exact details of the scandal from a stranger. She already knew the bare bones, but he would tell her everything in his own time.

'Allow me to help you down.'

Lottie gratefully grasped Tristan's outstretched hand as

she clambered down from the farmer's cart. The cart journey had been much rougher and had taken far longer than she had at first supposed. Every muscle in her body ached and at one point she had been sure that her teeth would be shaken loose. Mrs Foster and her brother raised their hands in farewell and started on their way again, seemingly unaffected by the bone-jarring awfulness that was the farm cart.

'I could have done it myself.' Lottie straightened the folds of her dress, picking out bits of straw and hay. Her heart sank as she regarded the windswept crossroads. 'How far is Gortner Hall from here? Mrs Foster said that it would not take very long to walk.'

'Miles. I did try to warn you, Lottie.' Tristan pointed down the desolate crossroad with not a house or horse and cart in sight. 'But you insisted that we accept this lift. It would have been churlish of me to refuse, as you quite rightly pointed out, since the lift was free.'

Lottie swallowed hard. Not even a lone farmhouse where they could beg a cup of tea stood there. It was simply the wild Northumberland moors. Even though it was late May, the wind whistled from the north. Lottie wrapped her pelisse tighter about her and wished the paisley silk had been made of heavier cloth.

Lottie watched the faint dust of the cart with a sinking heart. 'How long will the walk be?'

'Five miles, an hour or two.'

'An hour of walking?' Lottie looked down at her daintily shod foot. She had been so proud of these slippers with their bright blue ribbons when she had purchased them at Bainbridge's in Newcastle last autumn and now they would be in shreds. She should have insisted on buying boots in Gretna Green or Carlisle, on spending Lord Thorngrafton's money, but she hadn't thought beyond the train. 'Surely you must be wrong…Mrs Foster assured me…a country mile.'

'You were the one who insisted on taking up Mrs Foster's offer,' Tristan replied firmly. 'Mrs Foster is a country woman and her notion of distance is somewhat different from yours or mine. I tried to tell you differently, to hire a conveyance, but you chose to believe a stranger.'

'I am not dressed for walking. Something you pointed out to me. Only yesterday.' Lottie fought the temptation to wail. She tilted her chin and glared at his deep black eyes. 'Mama will undoubtedly send several trunks with my clothes and other items from my hope chest eventually, but I was under the impression I was eloping, not marching through the moors.'

The corner of his mouth twitched. 'Are different clothes required? I doubt we will meet anyone along this country lane and, if we do, they will forgive your strange attire.'

'I fail to see what is so funny. Nobody ever instructed me in the proper wear for an elopement. It failed to be included in my social deportment classes.' Lottie started off down the nearest track, tired of arguing with him, tired of being teased. She had been so proud of her coup, of finding a way to save money and it had all gone wrong. She had thought he might pet her and look after her, but he clearly expected her to stand on her own two feet, feet that would be blistered and torn. 'If we are going, I suppose I best begin. Each step is going to take me closer.'

'Are you often like that?'

'If I can't change things, I can make the best of them. Or at least try to. A lady should never show her distress.'

'Do you always live your life through rules?' His eyes danced.

'I like to know which rule I am breaking. It makes it much easier to live up to people's expectations.' Lottie kept her head high. He would be laughing at her now. He seemed to think this whole predicament was a big joke. He was not the person who would be suffering. 'Five miles, you say, and probably not even a cup of hot tea at the end.'

Tristan's hand closed around her upper arm, hauled her back against his hard body. His breath tickled her ear. She stilled as a wave of warmth washed over her. She swallowed hard and tried to concentrate on something other than his mouth or the way his eyebrows arched, but her mind refused to work.

'If you want to go marching off to the Hall, you might enquire the direction. Go that way, and you will only increase the distance.'

Lottie fought against the urge to relax into him and to feel the hard leanness of his body against hers once. All the way in the farm cart, he had sat next to her, his leg brushing hers. Her body tingled with awareness, with the memory of how it had felt to wake in his arms. 'Why didn't anyone come to meet us? This whole thing could have been avoided.'

Her hand lifted up and touched his cheek. He turned his face slightly, brushing her glove with his lips.

'I don't know. There was no time to get a reply to yesterday's letter. If one of the tenants was sent out and preferred to go drinking in the Railway Arms or the County, there will be hell to pay.' His hand moved up to her shoulder, stroked the sensitive skin under her chin, made her lean forwards until their breath intermingled. 'A lady— Mrs Elton does look after the Hall. She will have obeyed my request. It is not a complete ruin.'

'So we will have a roof over our heads.' Lottie glanced up at the sky. All day the grey clouds had rolled in. There was a faint chill in the late afternoon sun that foretold of rain before daybreak.

'A roof over our heads and a cup of hot tea for those who require it. Or perhaps something stronger.' His hand stroked down her shoulders until his fingers intertwined with hers. 'And a soft bed with clean sheets, lots of pillows and bed curtains to shut out the world.'

'It sounds heavenly.' Lottie concentrated on breathing. Each breath she took, she inhaled more of his spicy scent, which was intermingled with the fresh scent of the hay, an intoxicating aroma that swirled around her and held her fast. Her lips tingled as if he had kissed her. She wanted to be brazen and demand that he kiss her—out here in the open where anyone could spy them.

'Will you come with me? Some day, I promise I will get you a new dress, one far more suited to walking than that one, if you are good.'

'And you always keep your promises.'

'To the best of my ability.' He stood perfectly still, and his hands fell away from her. 'Will you come and be my bride, despite the inappropriateness of your attire?'

Lottie tried for a frown, but the corners of her mouth twitched and a great bubble of happiness burst through her. He did want her for his bride. She glanced up and saw the echoing twitch of his mouth. Their shared laughter rang out and caused several woodpigeons to take off with a noisy clap of wings.

'It would appear I am stuck with you,' she said with a catch in her throat.

'It would appear to be the case.'

He drew her unresisting body to him and lowered his head so that their foreheads brushed. The ribbons of her bonnet loosened and then fell away as he pressed butterfly kisses on her eyelids, her cheeks, the tip of her nose; finally he claimed her lips. Her arms came up and held him there. The nature of the kiss changed and he demanded more, demanded entrance. She opened and tasted the cool inner recesses of him. Molten heat ran through her, causing her body to arch and her breasts to tighten. She pressed closer, wanting, needing something, something only he could give.

'Would you settle for a haystack instead of the bed?' he said against her lips. 'You and I together with the stars for a coverlet.'

'You promised the bed.' Her voice was a raw, husky sound that she barely recognised. The hot pulsating feeling frightened her a little. 'You always keep your promises.'

His eyes searched her face with a dark intensity. She took a half-step backward. 'A bed. My wife insists on a bed.'

'A bed with clean sheets and curtains.'

'It might be possible…if you truly require it.' His thumb traced the outline of her swollen lips, sending fresh waves of molten heat through out her body. She was grateful for the steel bones of her corset as they were the only thing that kept her upright.

'You knocked my bonnet off and it is lying in a puddle,' she said to dampen down her desire.

'Awkward things, bonnets.' A smile tugged at Tristan's features.

Lottie picked up the mud-soaked straw bonnet, held it gingerly away from her body as it dripped. A sense of despair swept through her. The bonnet seemed to echo her current state—once pristine and perfect, but now grubby, soiled without hope of redemption. 'I can't wear that. Even the ribbons will be stained beyond repair. I will have to purchase a new one. This one cost me three guineas.'

'The money is needed elsewhere. You must have other bonnets.'

'It will be days before they reach here, and my nose will freckle before then. I have worked so hard to keep my complexion perfect.'

'You will look sweet with a spray of freckles.' His fingers brushed the bridge of her nose.

'Flattery will not save you. And the thought fails to make me feel better.'

'Isn't that better than trying to make you feel worse?' Tristan picked up her satchel and tied the ruined bonnet to the outside handle. 'I will examine your hat tomorrow. It may not be as bad as you think.'

'It will be worse. Mud-stained straw cannot simply be covered by retrimming. I know hats and their awkward ways.'

'We should go, Lottie. There will not be a horse and cart trundling along here, if that is why you kissed me.'

'It is not why I kissed you.' Lottie stared at him. How could he think that of her? She had been certain no one would see. She was far from being brazen or wanton. She knew that. 'I have lived in the country for the past few months. I know about country roads and how few people travel them. That could take days.'

'Why did you kiss me?'

A tide of heat washed up her face and Lottie turned on her heel. 'You are an impossible man.'

'That is no answer.'

She fluttered her eyelashes. 'So you would carry my satchel.'

Tristan set the satchel down. 'And if I refuse to carry it any further?'

'Are you asking for another kiss?' Lottie's insides trembled. Always before she had been able to play the flirtation games, but suddenly they seemed to matter. She wanted them to matter and to be about more than bandying words. 'I won't be held to bribery.'

'Then I won't be held to carrying this.' Tristan set it down.

'We send a cart for it when we get to the hall. In fact, you could go to the Hall and send back a cart for both the satchel and me.'

'A cart could take days to arrange and you will want to sample Mrs Elton's fruit cake.'

'Mrs Elton?'

'The widow who has been looking after everything for me.'

'Then she can help with my dressing.' Lottie's back became straighter. Maybe it would not be so bad. If Tristan touched her again, she knew she would melt and she was determined to show the proper amount of wifely devotion. Devotion, not passion. There was a difference.

'No, Mrs Elton will be leaving. There is little need to

employ a housekeeper at the hall when I have acquired a wife who wishes to wear expensive bonnets.'

'Mama has a housekeeper. She has had a succession of them.'

'Does your mother have a hard time keeping servants?'

'Sometimes,' Lottie said with reluctance. 'She has the tendency to hire the wrong sort.'

'Rather than hiring the wrong sort, you can learn. My mother was always her own housekeeper.'

Lottie stared at him in disbelief. Learn housekeeping? This marriage had brought many unintended changes. 'It will be a change from making patterns with pins.'

He laughed. 'Were you exceptionally fond of pinning?'

'I loathed and detested it,' Lottie said without hesitation. 'It is one of those things I did because it was expected of me.'

'Then it is best to give it up immediately. I will have no pincushion mottos at Gortner Hall.'

'Will I have no help at all? Will I have to do everything? Although I can do preserves, chutneys and jams, I am no cook. I have burnt cakes before.'

Tristan caught her hand and raised it to his lips. 'Ah, Lottie, you do say the sweetest things. If you look at me like that, I am sure I will not beat you for burning cakes.'

'Would you beat me?' Lottie hated the way her voice squeaked. She had never taken Tristan for a wife beater. Had she truly mistaken the man she had married? However, the instant she said the words, his brow darkened.

'No, and neither do I whip or indulge in any such behaviour. Although I know some consider it acceptable, I think men who resort to such measures are cowards, and I am no coward!'

'I never said you were.' A weight rolled off her back. He did not beat women. The words were said purely in jest. There was so much that they did not know about each other. So much she had to learn.

His face suddenly cleared, like the sun coming out after a thunderstorm, warming her all over. 'But what I will do is help you with your corset. I am determined to play a good lady's maid.'

A delicious shiver went through Lottie. She wanted to feel his hands on her, undressing her. A tide of fire burnt within her. She tried to hang on to her mother's words about a wife being respectable. She was his wife, not a courtesan or a mistress.

'I believe we were on our way to Gortner Hall,' she said. 'I would like to get there before it gets too dark.'

'As you wish.'

Chapter Ten

Tristan regarded the darkened house with a frown. The Gothic towers that his grandfather had installed gleamed silver against the night sky. Quite near them a barn owl swept low, pale and ghostly, winging its way into one of the broken windows and disappearing. But the house revealed few signs of human inhabitation.

He had expected Mrs Elton to have one lamp lit at least. The note he had sent before they had left Shaw's had been precise, followed by the one from Gretna Green. He had indicated the date they could be expected. The cart had been an oversight, but he had been willing to believe that one of the farmhands had become drunk and forgotten, but this was inexcusable.

'Is this the Hall?' Lottie spoke, breaking the silence she had maintained ever since they had started down the road. 'It appears straight out of a Minerva Press novel, but somehow it suits you and your reputation. I cannot see you living in a neat and tidy Georgian house or even something from Queen Anne. But it has a certain amount of charm.'

'It belonged to my uncle and I have inherited it.' Tristan advanced towards the shadowed door, fighting to keep the bitterness from his voice. 'The Duke of Northumberland's remaking of Alnwick Castle heavily influenced my grandfather. They shared a love of the Gothic. The roof badly needs repair, the guttering has seen better days and a family of owls has taken up residence in one of the upper bedrooms, but a few rooms remain habitable.'

'Beggars have little choice.'

'I had hoped you would like it.'

'No doubt in time...when I get used to it. For now it appears awfully big and...well...ruined. Still it has a roof and it can't be worse than that inn.'

'You may be right, but I am at a loss as to why Mrs Elton isn't here.'

'Perhaps your staff believed that you would need to make a run for the Continent again.' Lottie crossed her arms and gave a strangled laugh.

'Mrs Elton knows all about that. There will be some other reason.'

'You mean she doesn't consider you wicked and beyond redemption?' Tristan heard the merriment in Lottie's voice.

'She thinks of me as a little boy in long trousers who had lost his mother.'

'I am sure you were adorable as a little boy.'

'You will have to ask Mrs Elton as I can't possibly comment.' Tristan resisted the temptation to pull her into his arms. He could afford to wait for a few more minutes.

'And you are going to dismiss her because you have married me? Is that fair?'

'She will not starve.'

'You can't do that to people.' Lottie tapped her finger against her mouth and her brow furrowed. 'There must be other ways to make economies. I will go out without a new bonnet, or a new dress.'

'Why such concern for a woman you have never met?'

'Because there are standards to be upheld. The world would cease to function otherwise.' Lottie gave a little laugh, but Tristan saw through the act. Lottie was no snob. Her friendship with Mrs Foster and her concern about two lost children showed that. He knew what she meant, what she was trying to say. He reached over and squeezed her shoulder.

'Mrs Elton will thank you for your concern, once we discover where she is.'

'Please consider it, Tristan.' Lottie's arm dropped to her side and it took all of Tristan's self-control not to swing her into his arms and whisper that Mrs Elton would be well looked after and Lottie might have as many servants as she desired if only she would continue looking at him like that in the moonlight.

'I shall consider your request.' He turned away from her luminous starlit eyes and rapped sharply at the door, but there was no answering sound from within. He reached into the lantern and withdrew a key. The tiny act did much to restore his calm. He had to be resolute and to not be tempted to end the experiment before she had been truly tamed. 'Mrs Elton is usually very efficient. It is unlike her to be away.'

'I thought you recently inherited this.'

'Mrs Elton was my father's housekeeper when I was growing up. After my father's death, my uncle decided to employ her. I know the hours she keeps. We corresponded.'

'And where is the esteemed Mrs Elton? Only the thought of hot buttered toast, fruit cake and tea has kept me going this past mile or so.'

'Was it truly that difficult?' Tristan glanced at Lottie. Her face was slightly pinched with pain and she appeared to be limping. An unexpected tug of remorse hit him. Once they had begun their trek, she had not complained. He had not considered about boots or ladies' footwear until now. He pushed the thought away, surely she would have said something. Lottie had always been vocal about her discomforts before.

'I have had more pleasant days, but I coped.' Her bottom lip trembled and she blinked rapidly, but she kept her back straight. 'I had really wanted hot buttered toast and fruit cake, though.'

'I am sure I can find something. Mrs Elton will have left a cake in a tin. It is odd that she is not here.'

'Perhaps one of the tenants has taken ill,' Lottie said as he opened the heavy door, pushing his shoulder into it as it stuck slightly.

A scent of cold and damp with an undertone of beeswax polish assaulted his nose. On the small table to the right of the door stood a candelabra and a bottle of Lucifer matches. Tristan lit the lamp and scanned the note.

'Mrs Elton's niece has had twins and she has gone to look after her. She trusts I won't be inconvenienced as she expects to return by midday Thursday. Written two days ago. It explains much.'

'What happens now?' Lottie looked about the shadowy hall and shivered. Although it was neat and clean, it had not been redecorated since the war or even before. The silk

wallpaper was stained and torn in places, and the white sur-
rounds showed a yellowing that could only come with
extreme age. 'Am I supposed to find my own room? Do
we have any food?'

She hated the way her voice sounded and resisted the
temptation to cling to Tristan's arm. She also wished that
she had not read quite so many of Cousin Frances's books.
The memory of them provided little comfort. She was
tempted to jump at every sound.

'I am hardly likely to leave you on your own, Lottie. You
are my wife.' His smile increased. 'The master bedroom is
in good repair. I did spend a few days here, before I went
to visit my parents' graves.'

'The master bedroom? Husbands and wives rarely share
rooms.' Lottie focussed on the ripped silk wallpaper that
hung from the walls rather than on Tristan. They were
here. Alone. There was no excuse for him not to touch her.
She wanted him to kiss her again, like he had done on the
road. But she also knew she was untried. What if she did
disappoint? Desire and fear swamped her in equal measure.

'It is well that I do not circulate in the upper echelons
of the middle class, Lottie.' His dry voice brought her back
to the present. 'I fear the rules would bring out the rebel
in me. I will maintain my own separate dressing room, if
you require it. My parents always slept in the same bed.'

'Some of us have little choice in the matter, Mr Dyvelston. It is a matter of where we are born, and where we
aspire to be.'

'And you aspired to a life of pincushions, shell pictures,
visiting cards and At Homes.'

'It is good enough for my mother and sister-in-law.' She

held her reticule in front of her like a shield and pretended that her feet did not hurt. She did not even dare sink down on a chair and inspect her slippers. She had felt the cold seeping through during the last part of the walk and was certain a huge hole had developed in her right slipper. How could she have been so stupid to accept Mrs Foster's blithe assurance that it was an easy walk? Maybe for someone in stout boots, but in slippers, her feet ached like fire.

She had kept herself going by concentrating on the journey's end. She wanted a warming cup of hot chocolate or, failing that, tea.

Lottie regarded her hands. That was a lie. She wanted more than that. Mainly she wanted her old life back, the one she'd had before she had met Tristan. She would even like to hear one of Cousin Frances's tales. She had had enough of adventures, but she couldn't go back. She was married. And if she went back she would have to give up Tristan and his kisses.

'Mama and Lucy appear content to prick pincushions and host At Homes. I like watercolours, painting landscapes. It gives me something else to converse about.'

'That, with the greatest respect, Lottie, is not an answer. It should be what you want from life, not what other people want for you.'

Lottie regarded her gloves, picked at a smudge. 'Very few people have ever bothered to ask me what I truly want and even fewer people have listened.'

'I am listening now.' He laid a hand on her shoulder, briefly for an instant. 'Lottie, what do you want from life? What sort of life do you want to have?'

One where I am loved and can love back. The words

sprang unbidden to her mind, but she knew could not say them to Tristan. Love had nothing to do with their bargain. He had married her to save them both from the social wilderness. Love and affection played no part. She had to remember that. Maybe in time, they would reach some sort of mutual friendship. Friendship? Already she knew she wanted more than that.

'You promised me…' Lottie felt her throat begin to close. She stepped back away from him. Gave a small yelp as a splinter worked its way through a hole in her slipper. She winced, but resisted the temptation to examine the size of it.

'What have you done?' Tristan's face became hard. 'What are you not telling me, Carlotta? What are you keeping from me?'

'You said that you wouldn't call me Carlotta.' Lottie crossed her arms. This was all his fault, and he did not even care that her feet ached. He had allowed her to accept the lift, knowing full well how long of a march they would have. He had tricked her, and now he was calling her Carlotta. Tears pushed against her eyelids, threatened to spill over.

Tristan put his hand under her elbow. 'Only when you have done injury to yourself and refuse to tell me about it. Now what have you done? You can barely stand up straight.'

'Nothing, nothing at all.' Lottie jerked her elbow from his grasp. She refused to give way to tears. If she did that, she would not be able to stop, and she had no wish to make a scene.

'It looks more than nothing.'

Lottie ignored Tristan's outstretched hand and concentrated on moving slowly towards a chair. Now that they had stopped, her feet seemed to have seized up. It had been fine while they'd been walking. She had simply concentrated on putting one foot in front of the other, knew that there would be no respite and he would not give her any aid if she stumbled. But now, in this shadowy hall with its torn silk wallpaper and dusty pictures, her feet burned and ached. She knew she could not take another step, but she also did not want to give Tristan the satisfaction. He seemed to think she was spoilt and unfit for anything, but she wasn't.

'Nothing that could not have been predicted from my attire.' She gave a shrug. 'I told you that I was not dressed for marching. You knew how far it would be to Gortner Hall and you let me—'

'Sit down!'

'I am fine, I tell you.' Lottie refused to cry. She refused to allow Tristan to bully her. 'I may have lost my bonnet and my shoes may be ruined. I have not begun to examine the tears in my dress. How Mama could ever have considered lightweight silk a suitable costume for an elopement, I have no idea, but I made the mistake of listening to her. Many other people have weathered far worse storms, I am sure.'

Tristan closed his eyes, his hands balled at his sides. Lottie braced herself for an explosion but she would not apologise. She glared at him as he opened his eyes again, matching his dark, intent gaze with one of her own. Slowly, one by one, his fingers relaxed.

'Lottie, please, I beg you, sit down and allow me to look at the damage.' His voice became as smooth as silk, sliding over her skin like a caress. 'I did not think about your shoes. I wanted to teach you a lesson about assuming things and I was wrong.'

'You did what?' Lottie's breath stopped in her throat. Her brow knotted. A lesson? What right did he have to presume to teach her anything? She had thought she was helping! 'You allowed this to happen?'

'I failed to consider the condition of your shoes.'

'You knew I was not dressed for walking long distances.'

'We shall add them to the list of things that need to be replaced.'

'They were my favourite pair.' Lottie gazed down at them ruefully. 'They were beautiful.'

'I shall see what can be done.' He placed a hand on her elbow. 'But right now, my main concern is your feet. The shoes were objects. You are a person and in pain. I never meant to cause you pain. I am sorry, Lottie. Truly and abjectly sorry.'

The quick retort died on her lips. He was contrite? He had apologised? Tristan? She had been prepared to hate him and he did this. Looked at her with such intensity and regret that her heart turned over. And she knew she could forgive him almost anything.

Lottie sank gratefully down onto the small chair next to the table. He knelt beside her and eased off one of her slippers. His face darkened as the stocking revealed the extent of the damage. Lottie stared at the mess of torn stockings and her reddened feet. Tristan's mouth twisted and he shook his head.

'I made it to the hall without complaining.'

'Your feet are bleeding.' He ran a finger along the sole

of one foot. Gentle hands removed her stockings. Lottie tried not to wince as his fingers probed. Three blisters had popped. 'When were you going to tell me that your feet were this injured? Or were you enjoying playing the martyr?'

'I thought you might think me spoilt.' She glanced up at the ceiling. 'I wanted to show you that I could enter into the spirit of the thing. Maybe I should have asked.'

He knelt, holding her foot, not saying anything, simply rubbing it between his two hands. She concentrated on the blue-blackness of his hair and the way it curled slightly at the nape of his neck. She resisted the urge to bury her hands in it and to bring his face to hers.

'Tristan,' she whispered, 'are you very angry with me?'

He let go of her foot and stood up. Handed her the candle, seemingly oblivious to her torment. 'Carry this. Keep it steady. Whatever you do, don't blow it out. I have no wish to be plunged into darkness as we go up the stairs.'

'I will try not to drop it, but my feet pain me so. I am not sure how steady I will be.' Lottie regarded the long flight of stairs that seemed to stretch for ever into the blackness. She wasn't sure she could walk even five steps, let alone the whole thing.

'Concentrate and you will keep it steady. I know you can do that, Lottie.'

'You ask too much.' Lottie made a little movement with her hand. Angry tears came to her eyes. He kept asking her to do things, impossible things. Yesterday, he had left her on her own; today, he had made her take a parliamentary, spend time in a third-class waiting room, beg for a lift from a farmer's widow and then walk miles in her slippers.

Now he expected her to do more. 'I have tried, Tristan, you must believe that. But here I stay. My legs refuse your command.'

'I did not ask you to walk, only to hold a candle. You must stop assuming things, Lottie. You always make assumptions about people and things.' Without waiting for an answer, he swung her into his arms and advanced towards the stairs. His boots resounded on the marble floor. 'I never wanted to hurt you.'

'You will drop me.' Lottie hastily wrapped an arm about his neck and clung as he began to mount the stairs. He made it seem as if she were featherlight and he had not been walking as far as she had. 'I am going to fall.'

'Not with my arms about you. Keep the candle steady, Lottie, and hold it higher.' His lips were just above her hair. The sound of his heart thumped in her ears.

'Where are you taking me?'

'To the bedroom. I have something there that might ease your aches and pains.' He readjusted his hold on her, moved his arms so she was propped against his chest, but his touch was impersonal.

A liquid fire went through her limbs. She wanted to go there, but not like this. She must more closely resemble a drowned rat or a street urchin. And there would be no one to help with her clothes except for Tristan. Once again she would fail in her duty as a wife. She concentrated on the portraits, rather than on the beating of his heart. This time, she did not want to give him an excuse to leave her.

'Your family?' she asked as many of the portraits had a look of Tristan about them—a wild, untamed look as if they were ready to take on the world.

'The Dyvelstons. I am the last one.' He gave a crooked smile. 'All this history has come down to one person. One unworthy person.'

Her brain buzzed, but she was so tired that she could not think straight. All she could think was that he wasn't unworthy. He had saved her twice. Underneath everything, there was kindness. 'There is your cousin—Lord Thorngrafton.'

'I try not to think about him.'

'But surely your uncle—?' Lottie began, turning her head.

'Hold the candle steady. Do you want to plunge us into darkness? I need to see where to put my feet.'

'I am trying to.' Lottie lifted the candle higher and strange elongated shadows danced in the hallway. Then she stared at the ruined portrait of the woman dressed in clothes fashionable about a decade before. The gilt frame was lavish, but the portrait was slashed from top to bottom several times. 'Who did that?'

'Did you know that you are getting heavy?' He shifted her so that she was no longer looking at the portrait, but instead facing his lips.

'You should let me hobble. I will be too heavy for you. Cousin Frances told me that I look like a stuffed pig.'

'You have walked enough for today. Hold on tight, and you are no stuffed pig. Far too light for that.'

'I will believe you.'

He reached down and opened a door, and, banging it against the wall, he carried her into the bedroom. A large four-poster mahogany bed hung with heavy velvet curtains dominated. To one side stood a birchwood washbasin. The carpet was thick and the walls clean and cobweb free.

'This was to be my room. It is now ours. There are two dressing rooms that connect to it.'

'It is a lovely room.'

'I am glad you approve. It was my grandparents'.' He took the candle from her hand and placed it on the chair beside the bed. 'Release your arms.'

She obeyed him. His hands guided her so that she slid down the contours of his body, her curves meeting the hard planes of his muscles. A tiny spark ignited inside her, but she damped it down, telling herself that he had only wanted to set her down gently.

'And what happens next?' she asked in a voice that sounded unnaturally high to her ears as she sat, balanced precariously on the edge of the bed.

'Your feet are seen to. You should have told me about your footwear before we left Hexham.' He went over to the dressing table and pulled out a canister. 'Ointment. It was given to me by a doctor in Antioch.'

'I will put it on myself.'

'Are you sure you know how to apply it properly?'

A mental image of him stroking her feet, his long fingers curving around her calves and ankles, gliding over them, rose unbidden in her mind, infusing her with heat. She concentrated on a spot somewhere above his head. She would not make last night's mistake. She would show him that she had learnt her lesson. She knew how to behave with the decorum one would expect from a gently reared lady.

'I would prefer to do it myself. I know which blisters are the worst.'

'If that is what you want.'

'It is.' Lottie put out her hand and he placed the cold tin on her palm, then stepped back away from her.

'You only need a little bit.'

She nodded and concentrated on opening the tin, instead of on his lips. Held back the words begging him to stay. She would be dignified about it. She was not going to give in to her passion. If he touched her feet, she was sure to say something vulgar like demanding to be kissed. Her time as a proper wife started now. 'I am sure they are not as bad as they look.'

'It is no bother. I feel responsible.'

'Let me do it.' She put the ointment on her feet, rubbing it in. First one foot and then the other. Tristan had been right. The cool liquid took the fire from her feet. 'You told the truth. They are much better. In a few days, I am sure they will be vastly improved.'

'You seem to be very able and in no need of assistance from me, despite my offer.' He stood there, looking at her. 'Shall I leave the candle?'

'It would be kind of you.' Lottie hated the way her voice had become small. She stood up and held out her hand. 'Goodnight, Tristan.'

He ignored her fingers, picked up another candle and lit it. 'If that is what you want...'

Lottie bit her lip. He was about to leave. In the morning, they would be more estranged than ever. She found her earlier fears had ebbed away. She wanted to be his wife in truth. She wanted his lips to glide over hers and to have that heady fiery sensation fill her again.

She summoned all of her courage. 'Stay.'

'Why?' Tristan watched her with wary eyes. He blamed

himself for her predicament. All the words she had flung at him were correct. He had known and had not thought. He had wanted to teach her a lesson, not injure her. He found it too difficult watch her rub the ointment in, knowing she had refused his help. He had never considered her footwear, never considered it at all.

'I can't sleep in my corset.' She stood up. Fiery pain shot through her feet, crippling her, but she ignored it. She started to undo her buttons, twisting herself into a strange shape. Her cheeks were bright pink and her eyes downcast as she worked with a feverish intensity. Was that all she wanted—to be free of her confining garments? 'The button in the middle is a bit difficult.'

'You will do yourself injury…' Tristan barely recognised his own voice as he fought against his desires to tear her clothes from her body and reveal her silken skin, to explore her hidden peaks and valleys until he heard the low moaning in the back of her throat again. But he had to go slowly. A little at a time. *Her* pace.

He forced his fingers to undo the button and to draw back. She said nothing, continued to stand with her back to him as the silk dress gaped and revealed her creamy skin. He had thought when he'd carried her up the stairs that she had understood his need. He had pushed her too hard today, demanded too much of her. He would wait until tomorrow when she was less tired and her feet less painful. He had to be patient, even though his body urged him to take her into his arms…and bury himself within her.

'The first of your buttons is undone.'

'Thank you,' she breathed and her flesh quivered slightly. 'Now keep still, or otherwise you will undo the good that the ointment has done.' He counted the number of buttons and knew he could do this. He had done them up this morning. But somehow, a mean room at an inn with noises about them was very different from the hushed silence of his bedroom.

'I will try to be. I pride myself on being good. Sometimes things seem to happen.' Her voice was small and tight. She trembled, much as a thoroughbred does before a race. 'Sometimes it is very difficult to get my dresses off without assistance. The buttons go straight down my back. I have undone the first few buttons, but the ones further down are impossible.'

'Then I will do my best.'

He leant forward and let his hand slide over her collarbone. Felt her quiver beneath the pads of his fingers. The dress gave way and revealed a creamy patch of skin at the base of her throat. Soft skin that begged to be tasted. Without thinking, his head bent and he sampled the silken softness of her for an instant. Heard her sharp intake of breath, but she did not move away from him.

He risked a glance into her eyes. Waited. Her wide blue gaze stared back at him. She reached out and touched his lips with one finger.

'Lottie.' He took a step closer. Their bodies touched. She turned. Slowly and deliberately she lifted her arms, put them around his neck and pulled him forward. Their mouths touched and her lips parted. He tasted her sweetness, her innocent passion. The way her tongue bashfully entered his mouth and then retreated, only to return. This time more boldly, and to become entangled and to drink deeply. Playful, but unskilled. And all the more enticing for it.

His body responded with all the pent-up energy from their other encounters. Became hard to the point of pain. Urged him to take action, but he wanted to initiate her slowly, to show her what the true sweetness of passion could be like. He had seen what could happen if a woman was not awakened properly. It was one of the reasons why he had avoided the responsibility, but now it fell to him. She was not some courtesan or bored society beauty with an aged husband and well versed in the arts of lovemaking— she was his wife, his innocent wife, and she deserved his care.

Her passion-drugged eyes looked up at him as he withdrew his mouth. 'Is something wrong?'

'Everything is well.' He pushed the cloth from her shoulder and revealed her soft curves, curves that cried out to be savoured. 'I haven't finished your buttons yet.'

'You did promise to be my lady's maid.'

'It may take a great deal of time.'

'I never thought.' Her cheeks flamed pink and she spun around. Tristan allowed himself the exquisite torture of undoing one button at a time. Her gown fell to the floor in a whoosh and he swiftly unlaced her.

As he removed her corset, his knuckles grazed her breast. There was a sharp intake of breath, a stiffening of her spine. Tristan paused, exerted control over his body. His hands ached to caress the two mounds, to feel her nipples between his fingers, to roll them and to hear her gasp of pleasure. But he had to go at her pace.

'I can finish this,' she said with a thickening in her voice that told him she was not adverse to his touch.

'No, no, allow me. I do have some experience with

ladies' undergarments.' His hand brushed her fingers from the drawstring. He pushed the petticoat down her body, so that she stood in her chemise.

She gave a small hiccupping laugh. 'You do have the reputation of a rake.'

'Much undeserved.' He cupped her cheek with his palm. 'The ladies understood the game, but they are in the past. You are my present and my future.'

'And now?' The question escaped Lottie's throat before she could prevent it. All the time he had been undressing her, a fire had been building inside her, threatening to overwhelm her senses and good intentions. She had wanted to turn and kiss him again, but had not dared. She wanted to maintain a wifely dignity.

His hands closed on her shoulders and pulled her back against him. Her bottom met his hardness, leaving her in no doubt about his arousal. The sensation thrilled and alarmed her in equal measure. This was the deep, dark mystery.

'You are my wife. You should be in truth. There are none to interrupt us here.'

His wife. The words had a curious echo of her mother's warning. A wife was something different than a mistress. Men had different expectations. Instantly she straightened, held herself away from the tantalising pressure behind her. 'I don't need any more assistance. I can do the rest.'

His fingers turned her body so that she faced him. 'But I do.'

'I have never undressed a man before. I would not know where to begin.' She tried for humour. 'My fingers are all thumbs. I am more likely to strangle you with your stock than unwrap it.'

'As you wish…'

In one motion he had divested himself of his stock and his jacket. His shirt gaped open at the neck, revealing the strong column of his throat. His hands made short work of the buttons and the cloth slipped off his shoulders.

Her breath caught in her throat. All day she had wondered if she had imagined the breadth of his shoulders or how sculpted his muscles were, but now she saw that one brief early-morning glimpse had not been enough. She feasted her eyes on him and the way his golden skin was covered in a light dusting of dark hair, hair that pointed downwards and disappeared into his cream trousers.

A knowing smile crossed his face. She turned her head, ashamed. Perhaps such things were done at night, under the covers, but she wanted to see.

'You may look at me, if I can look at you.' He touched her chin and brought it back so her gaze went to the warm pools of his eyes.

'What do you mean?'

'Very pretty, but unnecessary.' He ran a hand along the lace, his fingers skimming the cloth and delicately stroking the swell underneath, a slow, almost lazy, touch, but one that did strange things to her insides. Instantly her breast responded to the touch, her nipples becoming tight buds, straining forwards, and a primitive longing pulsed through her.

Her hand reached out and touched his silken hair as he rained open-mouthed kisses down her throat. She held him against her skin. His lips went over the shift and circled the outline of her nipples. Circled and tugged, making the cloth wet. A gasp was torn from her throat.

'You seem to have become a bit wet. I should not want you to catch a chill.'

Her nipples were a dusky pink between the now translucent cloth. The cloth rubbed against her, making her breasts seem full and aching, and she knew that she wanted to feel his mouth on her. With trembling fingers, she raised her arms and allowed him to take the chemise off.

'I should not want you to catch cold. All alone in that big bed.' He picked her up and set her down on the bed. The faint traces of lavender and starch rose up to meet her, enveloped her in their softness. He ran a hand over her curves. 'May I join you?'

Incapable of speech, she could only nod.

The bed dipped slightly and his full length came on top of her. Warming her. Pressing her down into the lavender-scented sheets.

His mouth reclaimed hers and this time it demanded a response. A response she was willing to give. Desired.

She feasted on his lips. Their tongues tangled as her body arched and her breasts were crushed against his naked chest. Every piece of her burst into flames, molten to his touch.

Remade.

His fingers slipped down her body until they reached the apex of her thighs where her dusky triangle was, dark against the cream of her skin.

They glided into her crease, into the soft folds until they discovered the hard nub of her. Played and glided, around and round. Exquisite sensations racked her body. She lost all sense of time, all sense of everything except the touch of him against her soft hidden folds, moving along secret pathways of pleasure that she had never even guessed existed. A deep burning ache filled her. She needed something more, something to ease this burning sensation. She moaned, thrashing her head on the pillows, her hands clutching the sheet beneath her.

Her hands pulled at his shoulders, forced him upwards and reclaimed his mouth. Their tongues entangled, but it only served to increase the need inside her, instead of ending it. Her body arched in frustration, pushed up against him. Her curves met his arousal. Felt his hardness through his clothes press into her folds, press against her. Her fingers sought his waistband. She wanted to have his skin slide against hers, to experience all of it. She gave a small cry of frustration as the first button refused to give.

Hands captured hers. Held her wrists above her head. 'Patience.'

'Please.' She thrashed her head back and forth on the pillow, hardly knowing what she was asking, only knowing that she needed him.

'There is no easy way,' he said against her lips. 'I am going to have to hurt you, but it will be only for an instant. Do you trust me?'

She nodded slightly. But every portion of her body ached for him.

He undid his trousers, slid them down. Kicked them to the floor. Loomed over her, golden with a sprinkling of dark hair that, like an arrow, pointed downwards. Her mouth dried as she saw the evidence of his arousal. His masculinity. She reached out a finger and tentatively touched. Velvety hard. Burning silk over iron. She wanted to hold him and caress him. Explore his tantalising flesh.

His hand stopped her quest. 'Later.'

She withdrew her hand, chastened. She had been too bold. She swallowed hard, hating her desire and these sensations that were sweeping through her. She had done it wrong. 'I understand.'

'Sometimes, I forget how truly innocent you are.' His hand trapped hers and raised it to his lips. His mouth suckled each finger. 'I want to make this as gentle as possible.'

'You make no sense.'

'I will.'

He nudged apart her thighs, positioned himself and she felt a burning pain inside for an instant as her body opened up and allowed the length of him to enter. He lay there for a moment, inside her, joined together. His fingers slid over her skin, tracing the outline of her eyes, her nose, her mouth.

'It couldn't be helped. Your maidenhead had to be breached.' His breath tickled her ear.

'Will the pain get better?'

'Yes.' He recaptured her lips, plundering and restarted the fire that flickered inside her.

The aching deep within began again and she lifted her hips, wanting to be closer.

He appeared to understand and together they began to move, faster and faster until she felt as if she were falling. She clamped her mouth shut and stifled a scream. Tried desperately to hang on to her sanity. Failed.

'Did I hurt you much?' Tristan asked as he rolled off her, spent from his exertions. He watched her face for any sign of hidden pain. He'd held out as long as he'd dared, hoping against hope. Then his own desire had overtaken him. Now he looked at her candlelit blue eyes, searched them and saw the smouldering remains of passion.

'A bit at the start.' She squeezed his hand. 'But later it was lovely.'

He pressed his lips to her temple. An exultation filled him. He had done the right thing. He would get the sort of wife he had dreamt of. His experiment was working. Once he was sure, he would let her know the whole truth.

'It will be better next time, I promise.'

'And you always keep your promises.'

His answer was to draw her back into his arms and to stop her laughter with a kiss. Soon, soon, he would confess the truth, but he wanted to enjoy this time with her. He wanted to enjoy her innocence.

And nothing was going to stop him.

Chapter Eleven

'Why didn't you want to tell me who that portrait was? Why did you deliberately change the subject?' Lottie asked as the morning sun peeped through the curtains. She had spent the better part of an hour awake, listening to the steady sound of Tristan sleeping next to her, going over things in her mind and one piece she could not place was the portrait. Why would anyone leave a ruined portrait on the wall?

'It wasn't important,' came Tristan's sleep-laced voice. 'It still isn't. Ancient history, best forgotten. Nothing to do with you or us.'

Lottie brought her knees up to her chest and peeped at Tristan through a curtain of hair. 'I would like to know.'

His finger flicked her hair back, stroked her cheek and sent pulses of sensation coursing through her. 'It is of my uncle's former wife. You won't see it again.'

'Who destroyed it? Your uncle?' Lottie wriggled out of his embrace and sat facing him. 'It looks to be an expensive portrait.'

'You are refusing to be distracted this morning.' His

hand encircled her shoulder and pulled her firmly back against him.

'I should have asked last night, but other things occupied my mind.' She turned her face towards the pillow, rather than face Tristan. Somehow even speaking about what had passed between them seemed wicked.

'My uncle.' Tristan gave a great sigh. 'It was a portrait of his wife. He owned it. You would have to ask him exactly what went through his mind. I had left.'

'But why did he slash it? There must have been a reason.'

'You have been reading too many novels.'

'It is Cousin Frances who reads them.' Lottie propped herself on her elbow and regarded his face. A dimple showed in the corner of his mouth, which showed he was teasing her. Lottie relaxed slightly, pleased that they had reached a point where they could tease each other. 'I simply listened to her graphic tales and this…this house could easily be in one. It has that sort of atmosphere.'

'Does it indeed?'

'Oh, positively, Cousin Frances will remark on it at once when she comes…if she comes,' Lottie quickly amended. 'But how could anyone leave a house like this one to rack and ruin? It must have been well loved once.'

'Too well. My father and mother adored the house, but my father and uncle did not get on. They left when my grandfather died and went to live near Haydon Bridge.'

'You are seeking to distract me with your parents.' Lottie clasped her hands about her knees. 'Why would your uncle leave it like this?'

Tristan sat up and regarded Lottie's rosebud mouth and golden hair streaming out over the pillow. He wrapped his hands about his knees and glanced over at his wife. How much should he tell her? How much did she need to know?

'I believe my uncle never came to this house after his wife abandoned him or so Mrs Elton wrote. We were completely estranged by that point.'

'How sad. He must have been very upset when she left. He must have loved her very much.'

'The only thing my uncle loved was money—the getting and acquiring of objects. He was also devoted to preserving the dignity of the Dyvelston name, keeping it out of the scandal sheets.' Tristan's lips twitched. 'There, he failed.'

'But his wife. What did he feel for her?'

'She was simply a living and breathing object, a trophy in his old age.'

'Much as Sir Geoffrey planned for me.' Lottie brought her knees up to her chest and hid behind a curtain of hair.

'I had not given it much consideration. Sir Geoffrey did not marry you. I did.'

Tristan hoped that would be the end. He had no wish to dredge up old memories about his youthful indiscretions.

'And what she was like—your aunt?' she asked from behind her hair. 'When I meet the neighbours, they are all bound to know and there will be things alluded to. Mrs Foster said something. It will be better if you tell me first.'

'Mrs Foster was an irritant in more ways than one,' Tristan growled. 'I should never have let you accept that lift. I should have known better than to let you speak to her.'

'You are trying to change the subject. Your aunt, not

people I might meet on the parliamentary. You must have known her.'

Tristan collapsed back against the pillows and stared up at the bed hangings. How to explain about the beautiful, elusive, treacherous Suzanne? 'Beautiful, charming, much younger than my uncle. Last seen with an Italian count.'

Lottie laughed as she caught his hand and pressed it to her cheek. 'You seem to know a lot of women who were last seen with an Italian count.'

He withdrew his hand. 'Because they were one and the same.'

'You ran off with your aunt. Is it any wonder you are considered to be scandalous?' Lottie sat up, and allowed the sheet to fall to the floor unheeded.

'Hush, Lottie. It happened over ten years ago.' Tristan reached over and pulled her firmly back into his arms. 'It is nothing that concerns you. It was something between my uncle and me. Poor fool that I was—I did not understand how I was used. Both by my uncle and his wife. I was young, naive and totally convinced of my superiority and virility.'

Lottie wriggled out of his embrace and stared at him. 'Your aunt, Tristan? How could you? She must have been much older than you.'

'I never said that I was perfect, Lottie. You knew I had a scandalous past when we met.' Tristan passed his hand over his eyes. He was not ready for this conversation. There were some parts of his life that he had no desire to revisit. 'At the time, it seemed wildly romantic. She was a year old than me and much more worldly. I never considered her to be my aunt, only my uncle's wife. My uncle was aware of the fascination she held for me.' A muscle jumped in Tristan's jaw. 'He encouraged it in the beginning.'

'And he did nothing to prevent it?' Her eyes became wide with amazement.

'It is possible that my uncle felt it the best way to get a child, one with Dyvelston blood rather than one from some other family. We never discussed it. I am sorry to say that I was not terribly discreet. In my defence, I was young and blind in my arrogance.'

'How did it end?'

'Fate intervened in the shape of a disputed card game, a duel and Suzanne, his wife, elected to come with me to the Continent.' Tristan gave a bitter laugh. 'My uncle did not pursue us. I think he was pleased to be rid of her and her desire for pretty things. They had tired of each other and I was her plaything.'

'But that…that is monstrous… How could anyone be so cruel?'

'It was what my uncle was like. He wanted at all costs to have a son. It became his obsession.' Tristan's face was shadowed and Lottie was certain there was much he was keeping hidden. 'It is not a time I am proud of, Lottie, but it helped shape me.'

'But he did that to the portrait. He destroyed her portrait and he kept it hanging on the wall…for you to find.'

'For me to find, yes, but I chose to ignore it. She means nothing to me.'

A shiver ran through Lottie and she tried not to think of the woman's eyes, staring down at them, and the remains of her smile. 'How awful. He must have assumed you cared for her.'

He shrugged one shoulder. 'Suzanne ceased to matter to me years ago. I had other things on my mind when I was last here.'

'But…but…'

'It is history now, Lottie.' He trailed a hand along her flank. 'A decade ago, and I escaped the worst of it. I had come of age and there was little he could do about it. Remind me some time to tell you of my other hair-raising adventures. The scandal sheets enjoyed themselves for a few years, until I learnt my lessons and grew up.'

'And like the prodigal son, you have now returned home.'

'That is one way of putting it.'

'Is…Suzanne happy?' Lottie raised herself up on one elbow.

'She is leading a better life in the sunny clime of Italy. Italian counts with castles, money and an entrée to society were far more to her taste than young men with charming manners.' He gave a short laugh. 'A salutary lesson and one not easily forgotten.'

Lottie pressed her lips together. Was that how he had seen her at Shaw's? As someone intent on acquiring the trappings of wealth? Or as someone being sold to the highest bidder to further her mother's ambition? Another Suzanne.

'The scandal is the reason you felt unable to return home until after your uncle's death.'

'I had lots of reasons not to return here.' Tristan came over and smoothed the hair off her forehead. He placed kisses on her nose and her eyelids, soft kisses that filled her with flares of heat. 'But those have all gone. Vanished. We will make our home here—you and I. It is in my blood and I have no wish to leave it.'

'Why did he leave the house to you?'

'Because he did. But enough about history and long-ago scandals. You are here and in my bed. And that is all I need to know.' Tristan began to move his mouth along her bare shoulder, nibbling, calling up the banked fire deep within her. She turned and his tongue plundered her mouth.

It was not until much later that she realised he had never answered her question.

The sun had moved across the room when Lottie next awoke. Only the indentation in the pillow showed that Tristan had ever been there. She looked at the tell-tale streaks of dried blood on her thighs and on the sheets. Winced. Evidence if she needed it of her change from virgin to wife.

She crossed quickly to the basin and washed herself, grateful that Tristan had given her a bit of privacy. Somehow he had understood that she would need to be alone and would need time to make her *toilette*. Only she wished that he had kissed her before he had gone.

Lottie held her mud-splattered dress out with two fingers and decided that she would have to make do with the dressing gown until she could discover if there were any clothes she could make over. The dress needed a good brushing and the stitches had worked loose on the tear. It would never be the magnificent dress it had once been, but it would do after mending. There was no one here to see her except for Tristan and he had already seen her naked. Her face grew rosy at the thought.

A white cotton dressing gown was laid at the foot of the bed. Lottie slipped on a clean shift and then belted the dressing gown around that. She allowed her hair to hang down over her shoulders rather than twisting it into a simple knot.

She picked up a silver-backed mirror. Very much the well-kissed look. Almost wanton. Her mother's friends would whisper in shocked tones if they could see her and the worst of it was that she did not care. Lottie put the mirror down with a thump. She understood why brides had wedding trips. It must be the only time wives could be treated as mistresses.

Mama had been wrong to say that men did not enjoy passion from their wives. Tristan appeared to.

Lottie tapped her fingers together. Her mother had been wrong about many things. The thought failed to pain her as much today as it would have done two days ago. She had Tristan and she was determined to be the sort of wife he could be proud of. Eventually, they would make their triumphant return to society.

She would explain it all to Tristan once she found him.

A banging noise from downstairs gave her some indication where Tristan might be. It felt very strange to be in a house where she and Tristan were the only people. Generally she was surrounded by an army of servants—even at Aunt Alice's there had been three.

Lottie walked down the stairs gingerly. Her right heel still pained her, but otherwise her feet felt far better than she'd thought they would. It was the other parts of her that ached. Places where she never thought she'd had muscles.

She glanced upwards. There was a dark square of turquoise paint where Suzanne, Tristan's former aunt, had been. She thinned her lips. He had been true to his word and removed it. Lottie frowned as a stab of jealousy pierced her. Suzanne was long gone. Tristan had married *her*. They would have a good marriage based on honesty and integrity, sharing whatever the storms of fate had in store for them. She would not desert him.

She peeped into the shroud-covered rooms, looking for Tristan and mentally noting everything that had to be done. A film of dust covered most everything and garlands of cobwebs festooned the chandeliers. A family of starlings had taken up residence in the drawing room, there were definite signs of damp in the dining room and the gilt around the ceiling lay in flaked piles. But for all of the neglect, Lottie could see that it had once been a magnificent house.

It was little wonder that Tristan had been so cautious about money as it would take a fortune, if not two fortunes, to restore the house to its former glory. And it might be better simply to knock it down and start again. She would have to discuss it with Tristan. But in the meantime, there were little things, little touches she could do that would make the house appear more like a home.

The banging increased and there was a smell of bacon. Lottie's stomach rumbled, reminding her that she had not eaten.

She opened the door and stopped in surprise at the scene that confronted her. 'Are you supposed to be here?'

A wizened woman looked back at her as the tiny terrier at her feet gave a sharp bark.

'Who are you?' the woman demanded after she had quietened the dog. 'Does Lord Thorngrafton know you are here? I told him that he was not to bring any of his strumpets here, not if he wanted Mollie Elton to continue as his housekeeper.'

'The house belongs to Tristan Dyvelston.' Lottie kept her chin up and continued on a triumphant note, 'Therefore, I doubt it is any concern of Lord Thorngrafton's if I am here or not.'

Mrs Elton's eyes narrowed and she opened her mouth several times, but no sound came out. Lottie permitted a smile to cross her face. Some people had the insatiable urge to name drop, an affliction that was not simply confined to her mother or her mother's friends. Mrs Elton had to know that Lord Thorngrafton would not simply come to his cousin's house uninvited and certainly he would not bring any of his lady friends here. The notion was laughable.

'If you could manage to find me a bit of breakfast, I would appreciate it,' Lottie said to ease the awkwardness. She knelt down and waggled her fingers at the dog, who tilted its tan-and-white head and then came over to sniff her. The dog lifted its head to Lottie's fingers.

'So that's how it is, is it?' Mrs Elton cleared her throat. 'The dog's name is Joss. He's right picky about those he befriends.'

'He's sweet.' Lottie gave him another pat and tickled him under the chin as the dog lay at her feet. 'Would it be possible to have you fix me a slice of toast to share with Joss?'

Mrs Elton harrumphed, but she put two slices of toast on the range to brown. 'Does Tristan Dyvelston know you are here?'

'Of course.' Lottie waited a beat, beginning to enjoy herself. She would see the woman apologise for her rude behaviour yet. She had to remember that one caught more flies with honey than vinegar. Lottie batted her eyes and adopted her most innocent expression. 'I am his wife. We married at Gretna Green two days ago.'

'I hadn't heard. I have been away. I arrived back only an hour or so ago. I have not had time to sort through the post.' The woman made a clucking noise in the back of her throat as she turned the bread over. She looked Lottie up and down and something in her expression told Lottie that she was found wanting. 'He married you at Gretna Green? Why did he feel the need to do that? Are you in the family way?'

'You will have to ask him.' Lottie adopted her best social stare. Then she held up her hand and showed the iron ring. 'But we are married. It is a legal marriage. I am no strumpet.'

'I never doubted it. And now that I look at you I can see that I made an error. I apologise, Miss…'

'Lottie Dyvelston, Charlton as was.' Lottie held out her hand. She could be gracious, even if she was dressed informally 'We are waiting for my trunks to arrive. It was all very sudden. I didn't think you would return for a few days.'

'That I don't doubt.' Mrs Elton's face creased up and she dabbed a corner of her eye with her apron. 'It's just a surprise that is all. I had never thought Master Tristan one for marrying. Now Master Peter is a different story. He has always been determined to catch himself a wife.'

'I am acquainted with Lord Thorngrafton as well as Tristan. I have never been under the impression that he desired a wife.'

Mrs Elton gave her another queer look before she turned to bang the pots and pans about. 'That somehow was my impression.'

Lottie pinched the skin between her eyes. She knew family retainers were given a bit of latitude, but Mrs Elton was distinctly odd. She decided to try another tactic with Mrs Elton. 'As my trunks have not arrived, and my dress is entirely unsuitable for doing work around this house, perhaps I could trouble you for some clothes.'

'I never thought I would see the day that Master Tristan's wife worked in the kitchen or round the house. The late Lord Thorngrafton's wife never lifted a delicate finger. It ain't right and proper, if you will pardon my saying so.'

'I believe in being practical.' Lottie frowned. She disliked the comparison with Suzanne. She was more than a spoilt rich girl. She had always helped out at home. 'Mama believed that a woman must be useful as well as decorative. It makes it easier to direct the servants if you actually know how to do the tasks.'

'An interesting point of view.'

Mrs Elton handed her a slice of toast. Lottie broke off a small piece and gave it to Joss. The dog gave her fingers a quick wash.

'Ah, Lottie, here I find you.' Tristan came into the kitchen. Lottie felt her cheeks begin to burn. Her entire body tingled with an awareness of him and the way he had held her last night. If anything, he looked more handsome in his shirtsleeves, cream trousers and black boots. His face had a healthy glow as if he had been out walking in the morning air. It frightened her how much she had missed him in the short time they had been apart. How much she had needed to see that glow in his eyes. 'And Mrs Elton, what a surprise. I had not realised you were back.'

He caught up the housekeeper and spun her around. Her white cap with its ribbons went flying as the little dog barked.

'Master…Tristan,' Mrs Elton said in a mock-scolding voice when Tristan had set her down and she had rearranged her cap. 'That was my best cap, that was. With new ribbons and all. You are a caution. Let me have a better look at you. You have married.'

'I have indeed.' Tristan reached out and gathered Lottie to him. 'I had expected my good wife to remain in bed all day. We had a strenuous journey yesterday.'

The tide of red grew higher on Lottie's cheeks and she stepped out of Tristan's embrace. She expected to see disapproval on Mrs Elton's face, but the elderly woman positively beamed at them.

'I woke and was hungry.' She reached down and fed the last of her toast to the dog. 'I came in search of food and you. I met Mrs Elton. There was some confusion at first, but everything is sorted.'

'Confusion?' He lifted an eyebrow and his voice took on a much colder note. 'What sort of confusion?'

'Mrs Elton thought I was one of Lord Thorngrafton's fancy fillies, but I have explained everything. It was, I suppose, an easily made mistake. She was not expecting to see us.'

Tristan's eyes darkened and he shifted his stance. 'Did you now? What did you say to Mrs Elton?'

'I explained about our runaway marriage. She appeared quite overcome by it all. I have made friends with her dog.' Lottie plucked at his sleeve and dropped her voice as Mrs Elton turned back to the range and was busy banging pots and pans. 'I am not sure if she understands that you mean to get rid of her. She did not mention leaving at all. And, Tristan, she has known you since you were in short clothes. There must be a way.'

Tristan stroked his chin and his eyes became misty. 'Lottie, if you will excuse me and Mrs Elton, there is something we need to discuss.'

Lottie bit her lip. She wished she had not mentioned the housekeeping problem. It seemed wrong somehow to get rid of Mrs Elton. The woman appeared so pleased and happy to see Tristan and now her happiness was going to be dashed. But it was better that Tristan made the arrangements. Perhaps he could send her to Lord Thorngrafton—after all, the woman appeared to be fond of him. She would mention it to Tristan at the earliest opportunity.

'I can wait in the drawing room until you are finished. There are probably a thousand and one things that I need to do. Simple things to make this house more like a home.' Lottie bent down and gave Joss one more stroke of his head. 'It was very pleasant meeting you, Mrs Elton.'

'And you, my lady.' The elderly woman bobbed a curtsy. 'I will see if I can discover a serviceable gown or two for you. We are bound to have some in one of the attic rooms. It won't be up-to-the minute, like, but it will be serviceable.'

'Oh, I am not a lady. I have no title.' Lottie gave a little laugh. 'But I am handy with my needle and thread. It is amazing how quickly a dress can be transformed with a few tucks and a bit of lace.'

Tristan waited until he heard Lottie's footsteps receding down the hall. He went to close the door tighter, to be on the safe side.

'I expect you are wondering what this is about,' he said, turning to face Mrs Elton, whose face had grown dark.

'Why I should need to know anything is beyond me.' Mrs Elton gave a loud and long sniff and rattled a pan lid. 'I have only been employed in your family for three generations. Three generations, Tristan Dyvelston, and I changed your napkins when you were small. Don't you forget it!'

Tristan put his hands on the shoulders of his old nurse and looked down at her wizened face.

'I have never forgotten it, and I am grateful, but you must understand what I am trying to do here.'

'What are you attempting to do?' She cocked her head to one side. 'Don't you try to pull the wool over my old eyes. I know your ways of old, Master Tristan. There is the same sort of look about you as when you stole the cakes meant for high tea.'

'Hardly that.'

'Out with it.' Mrs Elton gestured with her spoon. 'You are not so big that I can't put you over my knee.'

'I am trying to prevent what happened to my uncle from happening to me—I don't want to be married to someone who only married me for my title and my fortune.'

'Then why did you marry her?'

'We were on the terrace,' Tristan replied carefully. 'She is a member of society. One does not ruin virgins.'

'But you think she is as spoilt as a lace table cloth.'

'I would have never married Lottie if I thought that. I have my reasons for this deception.'

'And you seriously think she knows nothing of this?'

'I am positive of it.' Tristan leant against the sideboard. 'Beyond positive. She believes that Peter is Lord Thorngrafton.'

'I gathered that might be the case.' Mrs Elton gave the fire a poke. 'I am not going to ask what sort of smoked gammon and pickles you and your cousin are up to.'

Tristan rapidly related the details to Mrs Elton, whose expression did not change throughout the recital. 'You can see why I have done it.'

'And when she finds out that you have played flummery with her?'

Tristan stared at his housekeeper. 'I haven't tricked her. I married her. And she chose to believe certain things. And once I am sure of her devotion, I will inform her of my wealth and position. She will be overcome with joy.'

'You may know railways and business, Master Tristan, but you don't know women.' Mrs Elton shook her head from side to side.

'You worry too much. Lottie likes pretty things. She wanted to marry a title. She will be delighted.'

'And I am telling you now, Tristan Dyvelston, you can never predict how a woman will react. You should never have tried this deception. She might feel hard done by and I for one wouldn't blame her.'

Tristan paused. What was between Lottie and him was far too new and fragile. He wanted to savour it a bit longer and bind her closer to him. He had to be certain. He risked losing his heart to a woman who only wanted him for his material possessions.

'I will tell her when I am ready. When I know she is devoted to me and not my title.'

'Sometimes, you have to take a risk, Master Tristan, in

love just as you do in business…if you don't mind me speaking plainly.'

'I am determined to have a marriage like my parents. My mother married my father knowing that he would more than likely not inherit the title.'

'That was a love match, that one was.'

'All I am asking you to do is to humour me. Let me be the one to explain everything and in my own time.'

'I won't lie to her. She has a good heart, that one. Real top-drawer quality.' Mrs Elton crossed her arms and glared at him. 'If that is what you are asking.'

'Mrs Elton…'

'And I won't volunteer information either, but I warn you, Master Tristan, this will end in tears and they won't be mine.'

'In my own time, Mrs Elton.'

'You are the master here.'

'That I am.' Tristan turned on his heel.

Chapter Twelve

Lottie lifted the shrouds off the furniture in the morning room. The sofa and the armchairs were highly unfashionable, probably from the reign of William IV or even earlier, but they were serviceable. And a little mahogany desk was placed in just the right position for writing letters.

Opening the lid, she discovered a supply of papers, blotter, a fountain pen and an ink well. She stretched out her hand, tempted to begin writing letters, but stopped and closed the lid down with a banging that echoed around the room.

There was much to explore in the room and how could she begin to describe the house without sounding mean or churlish towards Tristan. He could not help the state of the house.

Above all she wanted to keep busy and to keep from thinking about all the changes that would have to be made because she had married Tristan. Mrs Elton had had no notice. She knew that a good housekeeper could find work anywhere, but one as aged as Mrs Elton? It did not feel right. Lottie began to stack the cloths into a neat pile at one side of the room. With a few improvements, the room could be quite presentable.

'Mrs Elton has agreed to stay and she sends you these clothes.' Tristan strode into the room and placed a collection of clothes down on a chair. 'She thought you might like to change.'

'Agreed?' Lottie lifted an eyebrow as a weight rolled off her shoulders. She liked the little housekeeper. Tristan had seen sense. 'I thought…'

'She would not hear of it. She reminded me how long she had worked for my family.' Tristan gave a shrug and took the dust sheet from her. 'She will stay. It will give you more time to do other things. Young married women have to be cosseted, is her point of view.'

'And do you intend on cosseting me?'

'I doubt you will let me.' He gave a half-smile. 'You refused to stay in bed this morning. I had anticipated that you would remain asleep for the whole day.'

'You were gone when I woke. I went in search of you.'

'And now you have found me. Mrs Elton me told that she will put out some more clothes for you.'

'And a stout pair of boots.'

'That as well. I am determined that your feet be properly shod.' Tristan caught her hand and raised it to his lips. Lottie shivered slightly at the touch, pulled back as his eyes watched her. 'You can have a few days resting and getting to know the house, then, when your feet have fully recovered, I will show you the grounds.'

'Will I have any say in the decoration?' Lottie asked to cover her confusion. What they had done last night needed to stay in the bedroom, not be out here in the open. She was sure of that, of the impropriety of it all. 'Little things could be done to make this place more habitable. We would not need to completely refurnish.'

'Any savings would be appreciated.'

'You sound surprised.'

'If you promise not to fill it with pincushions and have numerous At Homes for farmers' wives, I would very much like you to make my house a home.'

His house, a home. Lottie hardly dared breathe. She wanted to. She wanted to show him how much she could do. 'You always bring it back to pincushions. Do you think it wrong to have an enthusiasm? What do you like to do in the evenings?'

Tristan stared at her. 'I play chess or read when I am at home.'

'I discovered a chessboard.' Lottie tapped her fingers against her mouth. 'Maybe you can teach me to play chess. I know Henry plays occasionally. The rules cannot be too difficult. Henry appears to understand them.'

'It is all right, Lottie, you don't have to learn how to play simply to please me.' Tristan's face became inscrutable. 'You may prick pincushions if that is what your heart really desires.'

'But I want to learn…' Lottie heard the desperation in her voice. She wanted to have a connection with Tristan; if that included learning to play chess, she would. Just as she would learn to make new chair covers and refrain from extravagances. She wanted to make this marriage a success. It frightened her that she was rapidly coming to want his regard. She wanted to see his eyes light up and to hear his laugh. She wanted to be with him. She had to make him understand. 'It will pass the time we have together.'

'We shall see this evening.'

Lottie hesitated and said in a great rush, 'I don't want to have a distant marriage. Mama and Papa were happy. They shared things. They played cards and went to dances at the Assembly Rooms together. Papa used to tease her about that. I think Henry and Lucy are less happy. They have little in common except for the children. If you enjoy playing chess, I would like to learn. No one bothered to teach me. How can I know if I will like something if I am kept in ignorance?'

Her voice wavered as she finished. She peeked at him over her hands.

His face had paled and his Adam's apple worked up and down several times. He started to say something, but stopped. Suddenly he appeared to regain control. He gave her an indulgent smile, like she was someone to be humored. 'I think it is about time you got dressed. Mrs Elton will be happy to assist you.'

Lottie blinked rapidly so that he would not see the hurt. Exactly what did he want from this marriage? 'I will go and change. No doubt the clothes will take some alteration. It is well that I am handy with my needle and thread, particularly as I shall not be spending my evenings playing chess.'

Tristan reached out, but she ignored his hand and he let it fall to his side. His eyes were hooded, unreadable. 'You don't have to do something just to please me.'

'I know, but I did want to learn. It will give me something to do in the evenings. I doubt we will be going to any balls. Or if we do, I shall take a stout pair of boots with me. I will become a regular country lass yet.' She gave a weak laugh at the feebleness of her joke. Tristan's brow became darker and she wondered what she had done wrong and longed to do away with convention and ask him to take her in his arms. Instead, she swallowed hard and wrapped the shreds of her dignity about her. 'I had best make myself presentable.'

She walked quickly from the room before her tongue humiliated her further, before she asked him to kiss her. When she was in his arms, everything appeared fine. It was when they met outside the bedroom that things became more strained. She would show him that she could keep economies and could be an asset as he tried to revive this estate. Then this fragile bond between them could grow. All she wanted to do was have him like her and think well of her. To want to spend time with her, just as she wanted to spend time with him.

Tristan only partly listened to Lottie's earnest money-making schemes as they walked through the grounds two days later with increasing uneasiness at their situation. It was getting harder and harder to tell her half-truths.

He had no need of the schemes. His business was healthy. The estate could be and would be easily restored, but he was impressed that she cared enough to make suggestions. Several of her suggestions, like cutting down stands of mature trees to open the view and selling off the timber, warranted a second look.

Was Mrs Elton right? Would Lottie react badly when she

learnt the true state of his wealth? Tristan rejected the idea as preposterous. She would be relieved. Yet he hesitated, unwilling to take the risk.

He became aware that she had stopped speaking quite as excitedly and was staring at him with a quizzical glance.

'You are not attending me, Tristan. And I did beat you at chess last night. Remember?'

'How could I forget?'

'Then attend, please.'

'And after we sell the timber, what do we do?' he asked, enjoying the way the afternoon sunlight caught her curls and turned them to burnished gold. His fingers remembered their silken texture and he itched to smooth them from her face, itched to feel her curves against him and go down the secret pathways of desire with her.

'I have gone beyond the possibility of timber.' Lottie waved her hand. 'You are humouring me, just as Henry does when I try to speak of funds. He seems to think that railway stocks will keep going up and up, but they can't as who is going to be able to afford them?'

'I happen to believe the same as you about the railways. And I am not humouring you.' Tristan touched her hand with his. 'Maybe just a little bit. You are so full of ideas that you are like a bee flitting from flower to flower, rarely stopping to enjoy.'

'I would have preferred a butterfly.' Lottie made a little moue with her mouth and Tristan remembered the slide of her lips against his. He managed to hang on to his sanity and not draw her into his arms. 'Besides, I was not speaking of timber at all. I was speaking about a way in which we could return triumphant to Newcastle and then I spied that hut.'

He moved closer and prepared to lead her away from the shadowy summer house where Suzanne used to entertain her lovers and complain of the boring countryside. He should have thought of it before they turned this way. He was unwilling to seduce her there.

'Shall we go and investigate it? I feel the intrepid explorer.'

'Why should you want to do that? It might be better off sold.'

Lottie pressed her gloved hand against his. 'It will be amusing to tell my friends about it when we return to Newcastle.'

'We shall be living here.'

She tilted her head. 'Surely you will allow me to visit my mother and sister-in-law? And if we sell that stand of timber, it will provide—'

'Do you always try this hard? Does it really matter if you know everything about this estate today?'

Lottie blinked and a puzzled frown appeared between her eyebrows. 'I wanted to seem interested. I wanted to get to know you and the estate you inherited.'

'Seeming and being are two different things.'

'But I *am* interested.' Lottie rubbed a hand across her eyes. She forced her lips to curve upwards. 'And the hut is intriguing. What do you think it was used for? Smuggling?'

'Lottie.' He moved closer and savoured her fresh scent, her innocence. He knew what that hut had been made for. He closed his eyes and saw every portion of it. The leering cupids, the artfully placed mirror. The peepholes for his uncle's spying. It was not what he wanted for Lottie. 'We have time. You don't have to learn everything in the first week. Your feet must pain you.'

'My feet will be fine. I am excited about what could be done to this estate and how it could be brought back to life. That is all.' Lottie clasped her hands together and her face took on an earnest expression. 'I want to make this marriage a real partnership with no secrets between us. Is that too much to ask?'

Tristan shifted uncomfortably. Secrets. There were beginning to be far too many secrets. He kept finding reasons to put off telling her and explaining. They were growing closer and he had no wish to jeopardise that. He wanted to be certain that her desire for him was more than the duty she felt a wife owed her husband.

'A marriage is a marriage.' His hands closed over her shoulders. 'You don't have to try with me. Be yourself. You don't need to spend time coming up with schemes, plots and plans if you don't want to. The estate will take care of itself.'

'But what should I do if I want to please you?'

'Kiss me.'

She raised herself up on her tiptoes and kissed his cheek. A quick hard peck. A dutiful kiss, not a spontaneous one. 'There, I have done that, now will you take me to see this mysterious temple? There must be a story behind it. It looks so lost and forlorn. I want to be able to tell everyone, Martha Irons especially, as she thinks the countryside is boredom personified.'

'You can give me a better kiss than that. It was like one you would give an uncle you are not overly fond of.' Tristan touched cheek.

'Someone might see.' She lightly danced out of his reach. 'Mrs Elton might be looking from the upper windows.'

'She knows we made a runaway match. We are new-lyweds.'

'And of course there is the little girl who does the scullery, and the laundress and…' Lottie began ticking names off on her fingers. Excuses rather than true concerns. Tristan knew it with a sinking heart. She had no desire to kiss him. She was attempting to change the subject. The Lottie of the daytime was not the passionate woman he held in his arms at night, and yet he knew she lurked there, waiting to be unleashed.

'How did you learn about these people?'

'I have eyes, Tristan. I saw them over the past few days, when you were busy riding out on the estate. Mrs Elton does not do her own laundry. Everybody sends it out. And her hands are too smooth to do the pots and pans. It stands to reason.'

'But they are of no significance.'

Tristan waved a hand. Had she guessed how many people were actually imployed by the estate? Or had she even considered it? Had she begun to wonder? And why hadn't she asked him about it? How long did they have left together in this innocence?

Tristan knew he was not ready to welcome the world back in, not without knowing how she truly felt about him. He wanted her to desire him all the time, to be passionate, without thinking whether it was the right or dutiful thing to do. Without planning how she would conquer society.

'Tristan, they are servants and servants are people.' Lottie pressed her fingers to the bridge of her nose. It was no wonder that things were in a muddle if he did not know how many people Mrs Elton employed. He shouldn't be arrogant. 'A woman always needs to know the number and names of people in her employ. It is basic common sense. Otherwise she might make a hash of the accounts.'

'I can help you with the accounts, but you are changing the subject. Tell me the true reason. Why do you feel the need to boast and brag about the estate to your friends?'

'Boasting?' Lottie hesitated. 'I want people to hear of your accomplishments. I have no wish for people to pity me.'

'You know little of my accomplishments.'

'Then tell me. I am your wife. There should be no secrets between us.'

'When the time is right.' Tristan's eyes became harder than black obsidian. 'Not when you want to feed your vanity.'

'My vanity?' Lottie stared at him. 'I am your wife.'

'Then you should kiss me properly, instead of wondering about how to make your life in the country sound more exciting to your friends.'

'Not where the servants might see.' Lottie hoped he'd understand what she was trying to say. 'It is terribly bad form. I don't think I have ever seen Henry being affectionate towards Lucy. Oh, he cares about her, and they have children but I have never seen them kissing…not the way you kissed me.'

'Then Henry is an ass.'

'He is my brother.' Lottie gritted her teeth. 'You should not speak that way about my brother. Only I am allowed to speak about him that way.'

'But the kiss you gave me was more like one you would give your brother.'

She cursed the heat rising on her cheeks, and then she

tilted her chin in the air. 'What sort of kiss did you have in mind? Then I will know for the next time and keep it in the repertoire.'

His mouth swooped down and captured hers, plundering it, feasting and calling up all the primitive sensations that Lottie had fought so hard to keep inside her today. His hands cupped her buttocks, pulled her close and left her in no doubt about the state of his arousal.

'Tristan, shouldn't we go somewhere? Somewhere more private?' she murmured against his lips as her eyes flickered towards the house.

His answer was to increase the kiss, to plunder more deeply until her hands curled around his neck and held him there as her back arched towards him. Her breasts swelled and pushed against the cotton. She gave a small mewl in the back of her throat.

He lifted his head, stepped away from her at the exact instant that her bones began to melt and she ceased to care where they were. The cool air rushed between them. His lips took on a cynical twist and his eyes travelled slowly down her form, taking in the state of her clothing.

'Now do you understand the sort of a kiss a wife should give her husband of only a few days? Without being asked?'

Lottie's hands struggled to rearrange her clothes. She wanted her pulse to stop racing.

'I did not want to presume,' she said in a low voice.

'Not presume? You are my wife, my bride!'

Lottie recoiled from the suddenness of his outburst and from the way his eyebrows drew together. Her heartbeat slowed and her breath caught in her throat. 'I am your wife and not your lover.'

'And there is a difference?' He lifted his eyebrow. 'Pray tell me, wife, what have we been doing in our bedroom every evening? Or does that come under wifely duties?'

She bit her lip, not wanting to show how much he had hurt her. Wifely duty—was that all it was to him? 'There are certain expectations…'

'Who has these expectations? Society? Me?'

'I do.' Lottie drew a deep breath, struggled to contain her temper. 'I mean to be a success. And I have noticed that men treat their wives differently from their paramours.'

'You have a lot to learn, Lottie. When two people desire each other, it is natural they should want to touch each other. There is nothing wrong with kissing in the open air.'

Desire, but not love. Lottie put her arms about her waist. Desire faded, love lasted. And in love was the one thing Tristan was not with her. He might desire her. He might even indulge her, but he was not in love with her.

All the breath left her body as she silently acknowledged that she was falling in love with him. That she loved him. Over a week ago she had not even known he existed and now her whole world was starting to revolve around him and his quest to restore this estate. She wanted to be a good wife, but she also wanted him to look at her with passion. She wanted to be important to him, and not just an object. She wanted this marriage to be a partnership, a meeting of two people who respected each other.

'I understand.' She kept her chin up and did not allow her voice to wobble.

For an instant Tristan's urbane mask slipped and she saw fury. 'You understand nothing.'

'I understand more than you give me credit for.' Lottie

kept her back straight and her voice even, despite the knots in her stomach. 'Back at the hotel, you saw me as another Suzanne—a woman whose family wanted to marry her to the first lord who offered. You sought to save me from that fate by kissing me and unfortunately we got caught. We were forced to marry. You played my knight because of your uncle's wife's experience. It had nothing to do with me.'

'No one forced me to marry you.'

'You need not have worried. I would have found a way to avoid Sir Geoffrey Lea.' Lottie paused and summoned all her courage. She had to lance this boil. 'You must stop seeing her in me. Your uncle's wife sounds like a perfect beast.'

'She was spoilt and demanding.' He lifted an eyebrow. 'Has anyone called you that? Have I?'

'I am not spoilt,' Lottie said between gritted teeth. 'I may like pretty things and enjoy parties, but I am hardly spoilt. I give generously to the poor. I devote myself tirelessly to good works. I even helped out at last year's bazaar and I did not demand the ribbons and bows stall but helped Mrs Hedigan out with her Scents of Araby stall.'

'Are you worried that people think you spoilt? Is that why you are so quick to defend yourself. It is the first time I have ever heard a scents stall used to bolster an argument.' The coldness of his smile increased. 'What else shall you use? Do you give your cast-off gowns to your maids?'

'I shared a maid with Mama. It was what was expected. The maid was grateful for them, I am sure.' Lottie bit out each word.

'You shared a maid. Was that a measure of your economising?'

Lottie longed to throw something. He was laughing at her. Belittling her.

'If you feel that way, I wonder that you married me, spoilt child that you thought I was.' She clenched her fists. Counted to ten and forced her fingers to open one by one. 'Why did you marry me? Was I to be the jewel in the estate? You were going to save me, because you could not save the other woman? I did not need your sacrifice, Tristan.'

Tristan was silent. He stood there, glowering at her while a muscle worked in his jaw. A lump began to grow in Lottie's throat. She wanted him to take her into his arms, but he wouldn't. She turned on her heel and began walking away from him before she made an even bigger fool of herself.

'Where are you going?' he said in an icy voice. 'Our discussion is far from over.'

'There is little point in discussing it further,' she said, after she had regained control of her emotions. She kept her chin high and looked down her nose. 'I am going to write letters, lots and lots of letters.'

'Telling your friends how hard done by you are. What a mistake you made. How you are buried alive in the countryside.' His lip curled back and his eyes had turned glacial.

'No, telling them how wonderful this estate is and how pleasant my wedding trip was.' She paused and drew a deep breath. 'And maybe, just maybe, if I write it out enough times, I will begin to believe it. Good day to you, sir.'

'Wait.' His hand captured her wrist, held her there. She looked at his hand and one by one, his fingers released her.

She stood there, rubbing it. 'The hut was used ten years ago by my uncle's wife. It was where she entertained her lovers. It is no place where I would like my wife to be. I never want you to feel sordid and illicit.'

'It would have been helpful if you had told me that in the first place.' Lottie attempted to maintain an icy dignity as a flash of jealousy went through her. Her accusation had been close to the mark. She was a symbol to him, nothing more. 'Far be it from me to disturb the memories of your youth.'

'This has nothing to do with my youth! This has everything to do with you and your need to conform. Your need to find excuses for people's behaviour.'

'How dare you say such a thing! You forget who you are, Tristan Dyvelston!'

'I am your husband and we will live where I say!'

'I was attempting to help! Why do you seek to hide things from me? Maybe if you had told me the truth…'

'Good day to you, ma'am. When you decide to apologise, we can speak.'

Tristan stalked off, leaving her standing staring after him. Open-mouthed. Furious. How dare he suggest that she apologise. She had behaved properly!

Lottie's temper had improved considerably several hours later when she had finished writing her letters to various friends and relatives, telling them about the marriage. With each line she wrote, it became harder and harder to be positive and enthusiastic about her situation. There were only so many ways she could describe the utter horror of the house without it sounding awful.

She chewed the end of the fountain pen and tried again in her letter to Lucy. She described the wonderful battlements on which her nephews would enjoy playing soldiers and how Lucy herself would enjoy strolling in the gardens with its many delights and follies.

She paused and then, gripping the pen more tightly, she wrote: *And, dearest Lucy, Mama is so scatterbrained these days that I fear she will have forgotten to send my trunks. I know how good you were at sending my things on to Haydon Bridge—could you please make the necessary arrangements now?* A problem solved, simply and neatly without having to confess after all.

Lottie tucked a strand of hair behind her ear and began her next letter, the one she had been putting off. She drew out the bank note from her reticule. Placed it on the desk and picked up her fountain pen again.

Dear Lord Thorngrafton, Many thanks.

Her pen paused over the paper, creating an ink blot. She would do this. She would send the money back to Lord Thorngrafton with a pleasant note, inviting him to Gortner Hall whenever he desired to visit. A little pleasantry, but one that could go a long way towards easing tensions between Tristan and his titled cousin. For too long the feud had gone on. She had to show that there was no simmering resentment, and this provided her with the perfect opportunity.

She put the blotter over the paper, folded it with the note inside and sealed it. But where to send it? She frowned. She could hardly ask Tristan. This would be a wonderful surprise for him when she unveiled it. She tapped the pen against the edge of the desk.

Then it came to her—the perfect solution.

Swiftly she addressed the outside to Lord Thorngrafton, care of Shaw's Hotel, Gilsland. If Lord Thorngrafton had left the hotel, he was sure to have provided a forwarding address. Lottie smiled and allowed her shoulders to relax.

The scheme was flawless. She would demonstrate to Tristan that she could be useful. She took her duties as a wife seriously. The social contact was far more than a duty. It was a pleasure.

Lottie remained floating on the air of sainthood when she discovered Mrs Elton in the kitchen. 'I presume there is someone who picks up the post.'

'Way aye, there is, the lad should be coming for it in under an hour, but the master—'

'I have no wish to trouble Tris…Mr Dyvelston.' Lottie gave her best smile. She didn't want to explain about their earlier quarrel. She would be polite, but distant. Mrs Elton had no cause to hear of her troubles. It was far better that the staff were kept in ignorance of such things. She gave a little wave of her hand. 'He undoubtedly has a thousand-and-one better things to be doing than seeing to my correspondence.'

She waited, trying not to hop from foot to foot like a child. Mrs Elton had to take the letters. The thought of going bonnet in hand to Tristan would ruin the whole surprise.

'Aye, I can see your reasoning,' Mrs Elton said, tightening her shawl about her shoulders. 'He does have a lot on his mind at the moment.'

'There is a letter to his cousin that I am especially anxious to have sent out. There has been much bad feeling between Lord Thorngrafton and Mr Dyvelston; I suspect, left to their devices, neither will make the first gesture of reconciliation.'

'You are a good soul, ma'am. That you are. I knew it the moment you came into the kitchen. Joss is a sound judge of character.'

'Joss is a wonderful dog.'

The small dog gave a little yap at the sound of his name as Mrs Elton's face took on a queer expression, as if she might be about to burst into tears.

'I will see that the letter is sent. You may count on me, ma'am. I have no doubt that it will go a long way towards reconciling them.'

'Do you?' Lottie rocked back on her heels and resisted the urge to pat her hair. 'I do hope so. It is awful to be at loggerheads with one's relations. I want peace and harmony between Tristan and Lord Thorngrafton. It will make it easier in the long run.'

'I do so agree, ma'am.'

Lottie played with the little dog for a few more moments before she returned to the morning room to await Tristan's apology. She would be forgiving with regal dignity. Gracious without being condescending. She would let him kiss her properly as they were indoors and she would make him forget his past.

Lottie picked the perfect spot to wait—the sofa facing the door. The chessboard was ready and waiting. She would offer him a wager, once the unpleasant business of his apology was over.

Twice heavy male footsteps stopped at the door and her breath caught as she lifted her mouth ready for her kiss. But after a moment, they carried on.

* * *

When the clock struck nine, she realised that he was not going to come. Lottie rose, enlisted Mrs Elton's aid in loosening her corset and went upstairs. She chose her prettiest shift and left her hair unbound. A golden carpet, he had whispered only last night, running his hands through it. And then she began her vigil again, watching the candle wax slowly drip.

This time, he would appear.

She heard the distinct click of his dressing-room door and the sound of his boots and then his clothes hitting the floor. Every particle of her froze. He would come to her.

She willed him to open the door and stride toward her. Hastily she blew out the candle, readied herself.

Then she heard the creak of the divan in his dressing room. Silence. She waited and waited. Listened to the distant ticking of a clock.

A single tear ran down her cheek as her eyelids fluttered closed. He never came. She had never had a chance to accept his apology.

Never had the chance to whisper her own to him.

Chapter Thirteen

The door to the library was firmly shut. Unwelcoming. Lottie paused and listened for any faint sounds coming from within. Tristan had been excessively polite when she encountered him finishing his breakfast. They had even managed to speak about inconsequential things. Lottie had given him several opportunities and openings to apologise, but he had declined to take them, choosing instead to excuse himself at the earliest opportunity.

Out here in the hallway, faced with a closed door and a day that stretched before her, she knew what she had to do—the unthinkable. She had to swallow her pride and apologise for her behaviour first.

Her peck on the cheek when he had asked for more had been wrong. She should have kissed him. Properly. Without prompting. She should have listened to her body. She should have considered his pride when she mentioned her friends. She had to share some of the blame for their quarrel.

Living like this—alone in this great ruin of a house with

the barest of conversations—was not really living, not when she desired more.

She wanted his company. She missed his smile, the way his eyes danced. And how, despite the adversities that life had sent him and his straitened circumstances, he worried about others, sought to take care. He was a man she could respect. A man she desired. A man she loved, even if he did not feel the same.

It was more than she could hope for in a marriage.

It had been stupid and pointless of her to be jealous of some long-ago woman. Changing the past was not a possibility, but she could work with Tristan and, in time, they could grow together and reach an understanding.

She pressed her hands together to keep them from trembling. This was worse than her first ball. She wanted to go back to what they had had before. She wanted to experience that passion again.

Was that so wrong of her?

She went over her speech one more time. She had practised it in front of the dressing-room mirror five times before she knew it was perfect. It had to be perfect. It would be. She took a deep breath and rapped sharply on the door.

'Enter.'

Lottie slowly opened the door. She started her speech and made the mistake of looking at him full in the face. A single lock of black hair dangling over his forehead captured her attention and drove every other thought from her brain. Her fingers itched to smooth it away. It was all she could do to stand and stare at him.

'Was there something you required?'

You. The word leapt to her mind. Hung there. She trembled, worried that she might have said it aloud. Tried to remember her speech, but the words kept sliding away from her and all she could do was stare and mumble slightly. She swallowed hard. 'Tristan, I have come into the room—'

She stopped, her mind once again becoming a blank as he continued to regard her with a stony expression. The temptation to turn around and flee back to her room became overpowering, but she made her mouth turn up at the corners. Hopefully he would understand her unspoken message.

'Do you always state the obvious?' He raised a single eyebrow and her smile faded under the sternness of his gaze. 'Or am I suppose to guess your true purpose?'

'No…that is…I wanted to speak to you about something of great urgency.'

He pointedly rearranged the papers on the table where he was working. A distinct rustle of paper to show her that he was busy, had little time for her. A pang went through Lottie's heart. This was getting increasingly more difficult.

'Do you have another money-making scheme that you wish to discuss? Another way in which you can show off to your friends? Am I going to have to play a game of questions?'

Lottie shut the door with a bang. 'I have closed the door.'

'I can see that.' His hands stilled on the stack of papers. 'A start. You wish to speak to me in private.'

'This is not how this interview was supposed to go.' Lottie gave a small stamp of her foot. 'It is not how I practised it.'

'And what is wrong with it? What small detail? What *duty* have you forgotten?'

'You are not making it easy for me. You were supposed to make it easy for me.'

Tristan stood up. His height towered over her. His dark hair contrasted with the white of his shirt front. One stray strand looped over his forehead, giving him a boyish appearance. But there was nothing boyish about his guarded expression. 'Should I make it easy for you?'

She moved closer to the table, closer to him. She lifted her face towards him, a clear invitation. 'I have come to apologise.'

His face changed for an instant before the mask went down again. 'What do you need to apologise for? What misdemeanour have you done, Carlotta?'

Lottie winced at the Carlotta. He wanted to provoke her, but she had to take this chance or always wonder what might have happened.

'I should have kissed you properly. I was too far gone in sensibilities. I was wrong.' Lottie stopped. Her brow wrinkled. She had said it and he made no move towards her. Had she left it too late?

'Will you kiss me now?' The words were so softly said that she did not know if she had imagined them.

'Yes.' She took a few steps forward, curled an arm about his neck and brought his head down to hers. His cool lips touched hers. Soft at first, but becoming hard as she teased them with her tongue. His arms came around her and held her. The kiss seemed to stretch for ages. Slow. Satisfying.

'Was this the sort of kiss you had in mind?' she whispered.

'It will do for the starters.' His hands cupped her face. 'I accept your apology.'

'I did say that I would try.' She stepped back, uncertain

suddenly. 'Having kissed you, I should leave you to your work. You are very busy with papers.'

'Appearances can be deceptive.'

'Can they?' She struggled to breathe as a delicious pulse of warmth spread through her.

'They can.' He threaded his fingers through hers and pulled her unresisting body back against his. His hands worked on her buttons and she felt her dress begin to loosen. 'Very deceptive.'

He caught her face in his hands. Ran his fingers through her hair. Pressed a kiss against her temple. 'You should not be frightened with me, Lottie. I want to protect you.'

Lottie stiffened. Was Tristan going to carry her up to the bedroom again? What if Mrs Elton or the scullery maid saw? How could she face them? And yet, she knew that she wanted this. She wanted to feel Tristan's body against hers. She wanted to prove to him that she did desire him. 'There is no bed here.'

'We don't need a bed.' He gave a husky laugh. 'Sometimes, I forget how innocent you truly are, sweet Lottie. How much I can look forward to teaching you. Lovemaking can happen anywhere.'

'On the floor?' She didn't want to think how hard the floor was. She didn't want to think at all. She wanted Tristan to kiss her, to hold her. 'Please, Tristan, not the floor.'

'Here.' He lowered his mouth and she felt herself falling back against the table. With one sweeping motion he sent the papers crashing to the carpet.

'Your work!' Lottie turned her head. Paper was now littered all over the floor. 'What can you be thinking of, Tristan?'

'Leave it. Stay there. On the table.' His eyes were smouldering as he pushed her dress down, revealing the cream of her shoulder.

Lottie froze, but she was unable to prevent the warm tingles that were flooding through her. What did he mean to do? She made a little gesture. 'But they are jumbled and you were busy. You will be neglecting—'

'The best place for them. I have more important uses for this table now. You are at the correct height.' His voice was molten honey, flowing over her, lapping at her senses. Lulling her.

Lottie struggled to concentrate. 'Just the height for what?'

'Trust me.' Tristan looked down at her pale oval face, her blonde hair golden against the deep red-brown of the desk. All his muscles tensed. Patience. He wanted to get this right.

She had come to him, had kissed far more passionately than he had expected, but he wanted her to understand that passion was not something that had to be hidden in the dark. He wanted her to surrender to him. Fully. Here. Now.

His hands grasped her shoes, eased them off. One, then the other. He forced himself to go slow. Rolled her stockings down, tracing the outline of her calf with steady fingers, and listened to her intake of breath. He balanced her pink feet on his hands. Small. Vulnerable. A finger slowly touched the now healing blisters. Her foot arched towards him and he placed a quick kiss on its instep. Tasted the smoothness of her perfect skin. His actions had damaged it, but it was healing.

He glanced up. Beyond her feet was the lace edging of her drawers and then the white froth of her petticoat. His body ached with need. He had to go slow. He had to savour this.

'What are you doing?' She raised herself up on her elbows and her hands began to smooth her skirts down.

'Lie back on the table. I want to see how your feet are healing.'

'I could have told you that.' She gave a half smile as her hand tucked a stray ringlet behind her ear. 'Your ointment worked wonders. I have obeyed your instructions.'

'I wanted to make sure. Let me examine your feet.' His fingers encircled her ankle. Held her still. 'Indulge me.'

'Are you sure it is safe?'

'You were the one to close the door.'

Her shoulders relaxed slightly. 'Yes, I suppose you are right.'

He put out a finger and traced the outline of her bottom lip, felt it tremble beneath his touch.

Tristan lifted her right foot and massaged it with strong steady fingers. His fingers circled and stroked and gradually her foot began to relax and her eyes became hooded.

'Tristan, I hardly think a table is the right place for this.' Her voice had deepened to husky rasp. 'There is a sofa over there.'

'It is exactly the right place for what I have in mind. Trust me.'

'I do trust you. You are my husband.'

Tristan raised the foot to his mouth, closed his lips around her big toe and suckled. He heard a gasp of pleasure and reached out to catch her questing hand. Her fingers curled around his as he trailed his tongue down the instep of her foot. He squeezed them as he heard a moan of pleasure come from her throat.

Slowly he put one of her feet on his shoulder. Lifted the

other. Trailed open-mouthed kisses from her heel to her toe. Heard her gasp of anticipation as his mouth hovered over her, teasing her toe with his tongue while his hands drew circles on her calves. He stopped. Looked towards her. Her skirts flowed around them and her drawers gaped opened, revealing her dark tangle of curls and her innermost folds—pink, glistening. Tempting him. His groin ached to breaking point.

He caught his breath and feasted on the sight as the urge to take her threatened to swamp him.

His body throbbed with need, but he drew on his reserves of self-control. He had to remember that she was not experienced. He would introduce her slowly to pleasure. Show her what it could be like between a man and a woman. Show her that a wife could experience passion with her husband. That it should be more than simply a duty—it could be the most pleasurable thing in the world.

'Are you finished?' Her voice brought him back from the brink.

'Finished?' He ran his fingers up her calf, under the fine linen, caressing her curves. 'I have barely begun. Now you shall discover what you can do with a table. Why it is more necessary than a sofa or a bed. What its true purpose is.'

'True purpose?' Her tongue ran over her lips, making them glisten.

'Relax and enjoy.' He reached out and touched her hand. 'But if, at any point, you wish to say stop, do so and I will. I want to give you pleasure.'

'Pleasure.' Her husky voice sent a quiver of desire

through him. And he barely retained his self-control. 'I will hold you to your promise.'

His fingers travelled up her legs over the drawers, this time, skimming until they reached her warm, moist cleft. He took his finger and very deliberately stroked along its length. Listened to her gasp. Forced himself to wait. To see if she could take more. To see if she wanted more. Her eyes were closed, her mouth full, but she uttered no protest.

He stroked more firmly, deeper. Saw her hips rise and her head began to writhe on the wood as her hands searched for purchase.

He slid one finger in and her body arched to meet him. Tightening around him. Soft. Warm.

He withdrew, bent his head and slid her forward and up until his breath touched her hidden folds. He felt the shiver go through her. His body tensed, waited, as her face was hidden from him in a froth of white. But her only reaction was to tighten her legs about his neck, urge him closer.

His tongue darted forward and lapped at her crease.

She gasped and wriggled as another wave of pleasure hit her senses. He put a hand on her stomach, held her there to allow her time to absorb the sensation. 'Tristan.'

'Do you like this?' he asked as his deep gaze penetrated hers. She could only nod. Every particle of her seemed focused on this one spot. She knew many would be horrified, but his tongue against her innermost folds created a need within her. She wanted more. Her innermost being cried out for more as her body writhed against the silken smooth wood.

'Please.' It was no more than a breath.

He lowered his head and resumed his lazy exploration

of her folds and hidden places. Taking her to the brink and retreating. She gave an inarticulate cry and her body bucked upwards as he found her innermost core and suckled. A great molten wave washed through her and her hands clung to the table top as her body arched upwards to meet him, to seek more of the sensation.

Her world exploded.

Her hands gripped the edge of the table, held on as his mouth continued to play between her thighs.

Then, when she felt herself begin to break, he raised his head. Stopped, looked at her. Leant forward. Placed a gentle kiss against her mouth.

'I need…'

'Soon. Soon.' He slowly and deliberately unbuttoned his trousers. Lowered her legs to his waist, put his hands on her hips and brought her forwards. Entered her. Impaling himself. Her body opened for him, lifted up, urged him to drive deeper.

All around her stars burst as he called the rhythm. Faster and faster she felt the table slide under her bottom. She held on to him with her legs. Drove him deeper. Needing him. Needing to feel the length of him. Then, with a great cry, the world exploded for a second time. She heard his cry echo hers as together they reached that exquisite plateau.

He lowered her back down to the table. And she lay there, panting, looking up at the white confection of the ceiling. A deep languor went through her body. She reached out a hand, brought his fingers to her face. Pressed them against her cheek as no words could describe what she felt. She wanted this floating to continue for ever.

He traced the outline of her swollen mouth with his thumb, gathered her in his arms and carried her to the sofa. Tristan sat down with her nestled in his lap. Her head rested on his shirt and her hand played with the buttons.

'Now do you see what a table can be used for?' his lazy voice whispered against her ears.

'I am beginning to understand.' She gave a slight laugh. 'But perhaps I can have a reminder every now and then. From my husband. Tristan.'

Tristan felt the husky laugh go through him. He wanted to shout and dance. He had done it. He had tamed her. She wanted him for herself, not for his title or for his money. His plan had succeeded.

'Do you like it here?'

A crease came between her eyebrows. 'It has potential. Does the sofa have other uses as well?'

Tristan paused. He wanted her again, but he also wanted her to understand about her misconceptions. How she had to stop leaping to judgements. He wanted her to trust him. Completely. There should be no secrets between them. But how? Would she understand why he had done it this way? Gently he eased her off his lap. 'I meant the house.'

'The house is fine, but I want to be with you, Tristan.'

'We need to speak, Lottie.' He lifted a damp curl from her face. 'About the future. About what happens next. After the honeymoon. After the wedding trip.'

She sat up straight, her hands primly in her lap. Her eyes became troubled. 'To speak? Is there something wrong, Tristan? What have I done? This is our home, isn't it?'

'No, nothing is wrong. Everything is very right.' He gathered her hands in his. 'There are a few things—'

His voice was drowned out by the steady knocking on the door. 'Master, master,' Mrs Elton called. 'A man has come to see you and he swears it is urgent.'

'I will see him later.'

There was some mumbling. 'He says that he is from Misters McGowan and Saidy, sir. Urgent, like. Important.'

Tristan ran his fingers through his hair, glanced back at where Lottie perched. If McGowan and Saidy had summoned him, it was because Peter had not held true to his promise. Tristan would have to make Peter understand there were consequences to his actions.

Lottie would have to wait. He wondered idly what she would look like dressed in nothing but a strand of pearls. They would be his gift to her. A way to explain. An omen for the future.

'I have to go, Lottie.' He kissed her cheek. 'Trust me on this.'

'Go where?'

'Away on business. I should be back within a day.'

Her bottom lip trembled. 'I will miss you.'

'And I you,' Tristan said, looking down at her. She started to rearrange her clothes, but he caught her hands. 'Stay like that until after I have gone. Let me make a memory of you like that. My passionate wife.'

Her cheeks flushed scarlet.

Tristan forced his body to turn and leave her. In a few short hours everything would be clear between them.

'He's in there, or at least I think he is. McGowan and I slung in him there,' Saidy said, jerking his head towards the stable when Tristan arrived at Mumps Ha', the notorious hedge alehouse about a mile from Gilsland. It had lost none of the gloom and secrecy that Sir Walter Scott had noted in his novel about the area. 'Bawling his eyes out like a girl. I would have expected better of a relation of yours, Thorngrafton.'

'Have you harmed him?' Tristan asked, handing the reins of his horse to the waiting groom. The ride from Gortner Hall had taken several hours and the weather had turned nasty. A sharp wind howled down from the north and the alehouse appeared permanently wrapped in mist. 'I told you that I did not want him attacked, and you were only to approach him if he approached first.'

'He came in, all swaggering and puffed up. Throwing his weight around in a manner he had no right to.' Saidy twisted his hat in his hands. 'Even told us that he were you, like.'

'That he should not have done.' Tristan examined his gloves.

'I thought so. I says to McGowan, I says, this here man is our pigeon. That one that Thorngrafton told us to look out. He ain't no right to that name.' Saidy's smile increased, revealing his broken teeth. 'He had the stake, no need for a vowel there. Then the games really began. Fancied himself an expert. And it became right interesting for a while...'

'But have you injured him? I wanted no physical violence.'

'It weren't necessary. Hurt his pride, mayhap, but other than that we obeyed orders. He became overconfident. Thought we were a couple of amateurs. It was like taking bonbons from a girl.' Saidy puffed out his chest. 'He lost and lost badly.'

'Who has his vowels?'

'The vowels are here. Ready for purchase.' The man's face took on a crafty aspect.

'I will pay you for them.' Tristan held a pile of notes out. 'Unless you'd care to play cards for it.'

Saidy's hand went out. He looked at the stables, then back at Tristan. 'Cards? With you? Not on your life. Not after the other night. You know when to stop. A trick I intend to employ more often.'

'I thank you for the compliment,' Tristan said as Saidy handed him Peter's debts. 'It is the amount we agreed... the other night. I trust there are no added extras or incidentals.'

Saidy's face took on an expression of outraged innocence. 'I don't need to count it, you know. We were working for you and you do have a certain reputation.'

'A well-deserved reputation,' McGowan said as he came out from the stables. 'That there punch that you laid on Den Casey is the talk of Gretna Green. He were a champion, he were. And don't deny it were you.'

Tristan nodded. 'I will see him now.'

The stables were little more than a hovel. A figure crouched on the ground, pleading as Tristan walked in.

'You have everything. I don't have anything more.'

'I warned you what would happen if you attempted to use my name.'

'I had a letter from Lottie Dyvelston. Addressed to Lord Thorngrafton. I took it as providence.'

'You had a letter from Lottie?' Tristan started in surprise. What was Lottie up to? 'I don't believe you.'

'She sent the touching epistle to Shaw's and enclosed a considerable sum of money.' Peter gave a watery smile. 'She was under the impression I had asked your coachman to give it to her in case she needed to escape. Yours, I take it.'

'Robinson was in an over-generous mood. And a little over-zealous in carrying out my orders.'

'You should maintain better control of your manservant.'

'Normally I do.'

Peter tapped the side of his nose. 'Ah, but Lottie has very fine blue eyes.'

'I have no wish to discuss the state of my wife's eyes with you. Or with any other man!' Tristan barely retained control of his temper.

'Is your little deception running into difficulties, then, Tristan? Lottie is not feeble-minded. She saw through my stratagem with ease last November.'

'I have no idea what you are talking about.' Tristan crossed his arms. 'I came here to offer you the chance at redemption. A chance to get out of this stinking hellhole and start a new life, away from here.'

'Your wife appears not to know your proper title and begs me to join you at table when next I am in the area,' Peter continued as if he had not heard Tristan speak. 'It would appear that I am not in need of redemption, but you are. You have misled your wife, Tristan.'

'That is the drink talking, Peter.' Tristan tapped the vowels against his thigh. 'I hold your debts.'

Peter's laughter echoed around the stables as he shook his head.

'I fail to see the merriment in this situation.'

'Your wife.'

'My wife?' Tristan stared at his cousin in astonishment. 'What does Lottie have to do with it?'

Peter pressed his fingertips together. 'I am a gentleman, Tristan. And as such never borrow money from ladies. I sent the money back to Lady Thorngrafton with my compliments. Now who is ruined?'

'You sent Lottie the money?' Tristan bit out each word, not able to believe his ears.

'It seemed the right and proper thing to do. A magnanimous gesture to appease the goddess of fortune.' Peter put his hands behind his head. 'I am not without family feeling.'

'You did it to spite me.'

Peter's smile increased. 'That, too.'

Tristan weighed his options. The die was cast. He wanted to be the one to tell Lottie. He might get there before the letter arrived, if he hurried. 'You are incorrigible.'

'I am the only kin you have.' Peter wiped a handkerchief across his face. 'Now, are you going to give me my vowels back? You need me. I will happily explain that I forced you into the situation. Otherwise, what explanation will you be able to offer her?'

Tristan crossed his arms, stared at his cousin. He could not lie to Lottie. 'The truth. She deserves nothing less.'

'But…but…'

'I am going to give you a chance to start afresh, Peter.' Tristan tapped the pieces of paper against his leg. 'Next time, the man you lose to might not be so generous.'

'You are giving them back to me.' Peter's face shone in the pale light. He ran a hand through his hair. 'I never expected it from you.'

'No, I am keeping them as insurance. You owe me first before anyone else.' Tristan felt a pool of cold anger surge through him. Peter had so much, every advantage, and he chose to squander it on this. 'You will not gamble again. You will go elsewhere and start a new life.'

'But…but…'

'Do you have the money to pay me?'

Peter hung his head. 'No. My estates are all mortgaged. I even pawned the family jewels. But you will forgive me. You are my cousin.'

'I did warn you not to use my title. What is mine stays mine.'

'You remind me more and more of our uncle, Tristan.'

'I am not him. His fate is not mine!' Tristan bit out each word. He pressed his hands into his eyes, regained control. 'Peter, I do want what is best for you, so you can prosper.'

Peter hung his head, defeated. 'Where? Where should I go?'

'I will provide you passage to one of the colonies. Prove yourself and you will go far away from here. I am not without mercy, Peter.' Tristan permitted a smile to cross his face.

'And what did you get, Tristan? Was it worth the price?'

'That is for me to decide.' Tristan turned on his heel and left his cousin bleating in the grimy stables.

Chapter Fourteen

Lottie sat on the library sofa with her feet curled under her for a long time. Her body ached from the passion she had shared with Tristan, and she worried slightly about what he wanted to tell her. She had nearly whispered her love for him and for one awful moment had thought she had.

He must care something for her. What they had shared had gone beyond all understanding.

If those men had not come for him on urgent business, perhaps he would have said more. All she could do now was wonder what he had meant about after the honeymoon. This was not a wedding trip. This was where they were going to live—both of them together. He wasn't going to abandon her here, was he?

A small sigh escaped her. Perhaps she had ruined everything and he did not care for her. Perhaps he wanted to escape her. He had been warm and caring before the men had arrived, but then he had changed. It was as if the shutters had come down again, and he wanted to keep parts of his life from her. Was it too greedy of her to want to be involved in everything? She wanted to be his chief confidante, the one he would turn to first. That was the sort of marriage she had dreamt about, one that seemed like a castle in the clouds.

Unable to sit and let her doubts overwhelm her, she began to straighten the library and to plan ways of improving it. The sofa needed pillows and the table legs should be covered.

Her hand hovered over the mess of papers. Tristan had told her to leave them, but that was when... Her cheeks grew hot. Surely he could not have meant these to be left on the floor indefinitely. She picked them up and placed them on the table, making a neat pile. Idly she picked up one and began to read, starting in surprise. She flicked through the next few. They were all addressed to Lord Thorngrafton. Papers that Lord Thorngrafton should have, not Tristan. Or maybe his man of business. It was not unknown for a lord to employ one of his relations to take charge of the day-to-day running of his business so that he could concentrate on those that mattered to him. Lottie pressed her hand against her mouth, comprehension dawning.

Why had Tristan pretended that he and Lord Thorngrafton were not close, when in fact he was his man of business? He had to be. It was the only explanation. It was why Lord Thorngrafton had Tristan at his side at Shaw's Hotel and why Lord Thorngrafton provided the carriage. A tiny pain developed behind her eyes. It had to be the explanation. There could not be any other.

She didn't want to think about Tristan acquiring papers that were not rightfully his, deceiving someone as to his true identity. Tristan had far too much integrity for such a thing. Lottie put her hand to her throat. But that did not explain the queer look he had given her when they'd first met and she said that she knew Lord Thorngrafton. Unless… She dismissed the idea as irrational and the product of a fevered imagination. Tristan would have told her. He would have had to have given his full name to the blacksmith when they married.

She ran out to the hallway and gazed at the portraits. A long line of Dyvelstons. This was no minor estate. And why had the former Lord Thorngrafton left it to Tristan when he hated him so? Had he had a choice? She reached out and grasped the banister, struggled to hang on to the fact that she had met the new Lord Thorngrafton.

Her footsteps echoed down the corridor as she hurried to the kitchens and barged into Mrs Elton.

'You startled me, pet,' the older woman said, smoothing her apron and cap. 'You appear distressed. Master Tristan will be back as soon as he can be.'

Lottie pressed her hands against her stomach and took a deep breath as she fought to keep the nervous tone from her voice. 'I wanted to learn more about Tristan's family.'

'His family, ma'am?' Mrs Elton developed an interest in her apron. 'Shouldn't you ask Master Tristan about them? Begging your pardon, ma'am, but he might be the right and proper person.'

'Tristan has gone off on business and failed to tell me when he might return. I require some information, now.' Lottie paused and counted to ten. 'His father. I wanted to learn more about his father.'

'Lucas Dyvelston?' Mrs Elton's face cleared. 'Mr Dy-

velston was a kind master, unlike his brother. He had time
for people. It was such a shame that he died so young and
his dear wife as well. A tragedy. And such a love story.
Tristan was their only child.'

'Exactly what was his relation to Lord Thorngrafton? I
know Tristan told me, but I have forgotten.' Lottie batted
her eyelashes and gave her winsome smile. 'My mind can
be like a sieve.'

'Lucas was the younger brother. He married against his
father's wishes and was cut off, but managed to amass a
small fortune.'

'Were there only the two brothers in the family?' Lottie
made her voice sound light. 'You said—younger brother.'

'Did I? There were three children in the family. Lord
Thorngrafton was the eldest.'

Lottie felt certain that Mrs Elton could hear her heart
thumping. 'Ah, that explains it. I was wondering where Peter
Dyvelston, the present Lord Thorngrafton, fit into the
picture. I understand that Tristan's uncle did not have any
children.'

'Master Peter?' The woman's eyes flicked about the
room and her hands plucked at her apron. 'Now, that
reminds me—something did come for you and what with
Master Tristan departing and everything, I forgot to give
it to you.'

She hurried over to the butcher's block and held up a
letter.

'Who could be sending me things?' Lottie turned it
over. 'I don't recognise the handwriting.'

'Master Peter sent it. I'd recognise his writing anywhere.'

'Why has he sent me a letter?' Lottie pressed her lips

together. First the money and now this. Every single time she encountered Lord Thorngrafton, something went wrong.

'An answer to your letter, maybe?'

Lottie smacked her hand against her forehead. 'Dear, sweet Mrs Elton. Of course. I had not even considered the possibility. That must be what it is. Lord Thorngrafton is being gentlemanly.' Lottie turned the parcel over in her hand. 'And Tristan was wrong. Lord Thorngrafton does want to be friends.'

'Master Tristan and Master Peter were boys together.'

Lottie sat down on the kitchen bench and began to attack the parcel, tearing the letter to reveal the bank note. Was this a hint? Another move in his attempt to make her his mistress? The thought made her flesh crawl. The only man she wanted to touch her was Tristan.

'I shall have to send it back. Immediately.'

'Shouldn't you wait to hear what Master Tristan says?'

'I have no desire to have Tristan find out about this.' Lottie shoved them away from her. 'There are enough problems with Lord Thorngrafton as it is. One simply does not send money like that to a married acquaintance.'

'Maybe Master Peter sent a note. He must have a reason for sending it.' Mrs Elton pressed her hands together. 'You may say many things about Master Peter, but he was never deliberately rude. His heart is in the right place. He used to idolise Master Tristan, follow him around.'

Lottie rubbed her eyes. She wanted to cry. Families and their politics. Tristan's sounded worse than her own. The only thing she was pleased about was that Tristan was not here. He need never know.

Lottie searched through the packaging and found a

calling card inscribed: *To Lady Thorngrafton, who has done me much honour by loaning me money, but I am not so lost in feeling to borrow from a lady.*

'Is he mad?' Lottie held the card away from her. 'I am not Lady Thorngrafton. I have never been and will never be. I am married to Tristan!'

'And…' Mrs Elton made a motion with her hand.

Lottie stopped. Stared at Mrs Elton. 'Who is Peter Dyvelston? What relation is he to Lord Thorngrafton?'

'They are cousins. Peter's mother was Lucas Dyvelston's sister. He was born Peter Burford, but changed his name to inherit Lord Thorngrafton's wealth, that portion that wasn't covered by the entail.'

The words hung in the air and Lottie's brain buzzed. Cousins. 'First cousins? And Tristan was the son of the next male heir?'

'Yes.'

'But that would make Tristan Lord Thorngrafton, and he isn't.' Lottie backed away from the table, the full horror starting to dawn on her. Had she made a dreadful error all those months ago? Had she assumed wrongly? 'Is he?'

Mrs Elton nodded. 'I promised Lord Thorngrafton that I would not lie, nor would I volunteer the information, but my lady, it would appear that you have guessed correctly.'

'But why? Why did Tristan…Lord Thorngrafton do this?' Lottie looked at the money. 'What purpose did this whole charade serve?'

'That, my lady, is something that you will have to ask his lordship.' Mrs Elton shook her head. 'I did warn him, you know.'

My lady. Lady. Lady Thorngrafton. She had a title, or

so Mrs Elton assumed. The words tasted like bile in Lottie's mouth. She might have a title, but Tristan had lied to her. Deliberately lied to her. How did he plan to keep her in ignorance? Had he truly intended to abandon her here?

'I have been so blind.' Lottie put her hands on either side of her head to block out the echo of Lady Thorngrafton in her head.

What else had he hidden from her?

She paused and wondered how delicately she could ask the question about Tristan's finances. She wanted to rush back to the library and examine his business papers, but that would be prying. Henry had not allowed her to be entirely ignorant of business matters. She could read a balance sheet, but not much else. She had to maintain some sense of dignity.

'Not blind, my lady, simply misled.'

'I don't understand.'

'Lord Thorngrafton had the reputation of being a fearsome card player in his youth, my lady.' Concern creased Mrs Elton's face. 'He keeps hidden what he wants hidden. I did warn him that you might guess.'

'Am I to understand that Lord Thorngrafton can restore this estate without recourse to my fortune?'

'It would not be for me to say, my lady, but I believe his lordship has been very successful in his endeavours. He knew the late lordship's position and knew that he would be inheriting a plundered estate.'

'Do you know what he has business in?'

'Railways. He was much enamoured of the waggon-ways when he was a boy, but I could be wrong. And I ain't said nothing.'

Railways. He was a railway king. Lottie closed her eyes. She should have known something was up when he mentioned Jack Stanton. They were friends, close business associates. She had never even considered the possibility. She had been so quick to label him an adventurer.

'Thank you, Mrs Elton.'

Lottie stumbled out of the kitchen and into the morning room. She sat down on the little armchair and put her face in her hands. Tristan was titled and had money. Everything she thought she had ever wanted, except he had chosen to hide it from her.

He had led her to believe they were penniless. Why had he done that? Why had he deceived her? All the things that he had allowed to happen to her! All the things she had accepted with a cheerful smile, never suspecting that he might be laughing at her.

He had betrayed her trust. And she had believed in him. Her heart still wanted to believe in him.

A cold fury descended on her. She would show him that she was not to be treated in such a cavalier fashion.

The early morning sun's golden rays had reached the top of Gortner Hall's tower when Tristan arrived back. The single shaft of sunlight gave the stone a slight pinkish tinge. A white mist shrouded the walls. A slumbering fairy castle. But was it worth restoring? Would Lottie prefer a new house made to her specifications with all the latest modern conveniences? She could be happy here. He knew she could be.

He'd ask her after he had explained about the slight deception. She would be delighted, he was positive, to know that she had received a somewhat mistaken impression of their finances. He would do it his way and she would understand the reasoning. First he wanted to waken her as she lay slumbering.

His boots resounded in the entrance. Tristan stopped and stared. Lottie was seated at the end of the entrance-way, dressed in her much-mended afternoon dress, with her satchel at her feet and a determined glint in her eye.

'Tristan, you have returned.'

'Don't tell me that you waited up all night.' Tristan attempted a smile, tried to banish the faint feeling of unease.

'I felt it was important.'

'It was kind of you, but unnecessary.'

'I am a considerate person. I am a generous person. Everyone says so.'

'I know, but someone has to look after you.' He reached out and gathered her hands in his, pulled her to her feet. He wanted to smooth away the wrinkle between her brows. 'Aren't you going to greet me properly?'

He captured her cool lips with his. She made no resistance, but her kiss did not hold its usual passion. He let her go and she stepped away from him as if he had burnt her. She put her hands on her cheeks and turned her face away. Tristan frowned as he noticed she wore gloves as if she was about to depart on a round of visiting. A shiver ran down his back. 'Is there something wrong, Lottie? Has something happened?'

'Should there be anything wrong, Tristan?' Her voice sounded tight and high and her eyes were far too bright.

'I am in no mood to play a game of riddles.'

'Funnily enough, neither am I.' Lottie crossed her arms. 'I am not enamoured with riddles and masquerades.'

A wave of tiredness washed over Tristan. He had no wish to start a fight. All he wanted to do was to go to bed with Lottie, sink into her softness. Then when he awoke with her in his arms, he'd explain everything. When she was in his arms, he knew that she'd forgive him.

'Nothing should be wrong.' Tristan rubbed the back of his neck. He wanted the feeling to go. 'I have been up all night, but my business has been resolved satisfactorily.'

'That is good. I am glad.'

She continued to stand there. Did not take the hint that he might like to retire to bed...with her.

'What has happened, Lottie?'

'A letter arrived while you were out. A letter addressed to Lady Thorngrafton.'

'Peter told me that he had sent it.' Tristan silently cursed his cousin. He would consign Peter to whichever hell was appropriate. He was not ready for the conversation. When they had the conversation, he had planned how it would go and it would not involve his misbegotten cousin. 'He enjoys playing practical jokes. I think he saw the humour in it. I had hoped that it had been delayed.'

'Humour? Sending a large sum of money to a married woman is humorous? Some people would take offence at being given such a gift.'

'Peter knows who Lady Thorngrafton is.'

'And she is? I will send the money directly to her.' Lottie ignored the trembling of her stomach. She had given Tristan an opportunity. She had not accused him, but had given him a chance. Even now, she wanted to believe that there had been some horrible misunderstanding, that he had not attempted to deceive her.

'The wife of Lord Thorngrafton.' Tristan regarded her with dark eyes and an enigmatic expression but the tone of his voice told her that the matter had ended.

It had not. It would only end when she had her answers.

Lottie drew herself up to her full height, squared her shoulders. She would do this. She had a right to know the truth. 'Are you Lord Thorngrafton?'

'You would not be asking the question if you had not already made up your mind. What do you believe, Lottie?'

He reached towards her, but she stepped backwards, away from him. Lottie knew if she went into his arms, she would forgive him, even before he asked her to. She was not yet ready to forgive. He had to suffer. She wanted him to suffer. He needed to learn that she was not to be trifled with in this manner. She had stopped playing his game, had stopped dancing to his tune. He had hurt her. 'Belief has nothing to do with it. It is a simple fact of life. Who is the current Lord Thorngrafton?'

'Do you want me to be?' he asked softly. 'Is that what you desire? A title? Or do you desire your husband?'

'Do not answer my question with another question!' She slammed her fist against her open palm. Her voice broke as anger rushed through her. 'I want the truth! I deserve the truth!'

'I am Lord Thorngrafton.'

Lottie's stomach reeled for instant before righting itself. A wall of ice came down, surrounded her. Not red-hot, but ice-cold fury. He was Lord Thorngrafton. He had deliberately tried to make her believe otherwise. He had tried to make her think that he was a pauper without any prospects. He had made a fool of her. He had lied to her. She had trusted him, and he had lied. 'Then why did you deny it?'

'I have never denied my title. How could I? It is something I inherited. It is something I obtained because of my birth.' He gave a small shrug. 'Can I help what others think? I never said to you one way or the other. You simply assumed.'

'You actively encouraged me to think differently. That was wrong.' Lottie clenched her fist. 'Very wrong.'

'I was not aware that you needed any encouragement.' His eyes were cold hard lumps of black granite. 'You seemed intent on believing that my cousin was Lord Thorngrafton.'

'He told me that he was.' Lottie kept her head straight and her voice even, but inside she wanted to weep. He blamed her for the mix-up. Her! She refused to start screeching. She would behave rationally. 'He told everyone. He presented credentials in Newcastle. I had no reason to doubt it.'

'He lied.'

'But at Shaw's? You were there. You should have taken steps.' She pressed her fingers against her temple. This time she would not forget what she was going to say. She would discover the truth. She had to. 'This whole misunderstanding is your fault. Do not attempt to twist the truth.'

'I did what I thought I had to do.' Something flared in Tristan's eyes. 'I wanted to protect myself. I feared if your mother knew about our earlier encounter as well as my title…'

'So instead, you seduced me.'

His mouth fell open.

'You have no ready answer for that.' Lottie tapped her foot. 'I am no cad.'

'Did your uncle leave you money?' She forced her voice to be hard. 'Did you mislead me about that as well? Did you?'

'My uncle sought to leave me an empty title and a broken-down estate.'

'That is no answer!' She lifted her foot and then stopped, slowly lowered it. She was not going to start stamping like an overgrown child despite her fury at her husband.

'It is the best you will get for now!'

'I want an answer, Tristan. I demand an answer! Did your uncle succeed?'

'Look around you.' Tristan gestured to the house. 'It is a shadow of what it once was. Gortner Hall was the grandest house in the district once. It is a ruin.'

'There is more to it.' Lottie crossed her arms as anger surged through her once again. 'Even now, you seek to twist my words. It was your coachman who gave me money at Gretna Green, wasn't it? He was acting under your orders, I presume, when he handed me the money. You wanted me to go. You had no intention of marrying me.'

'I found you! I rescued you!' He stretched his hands out to her, a gesture designed to placate her.

'Only because you abandoned me in the first place!' She crossed her arms tighter, held them in place. Refused to be manipulated. 'Why did you look for me, Tristan?'

'You are only asking because you want to pretend to be angry with me.'

'There is no pretence about my anger, Lord Thorngrafton.'

A huge great crater opened up in her middle. She met

his gaze measure for measure. Did not look away. His shoulders sagged. He ran a hand over his face. 'Do we have to stand here, arguing like fishwives? I have been up all night, Carlotta. Allow me some sleep and we will speak. We have much to discuss. But later, sensibly. I can explain everything, if you will let me. I had to be certain.'

'No!' Lottie kept her head high. Inside, her heart had shattered into a thousand shards. She doubted that she would ever feel whole and secure again. She had loved him. Trusted him. It would be very tempting with him here to allow everything to be postponed. She could feel the tug of attraction, but she knew what was right. And what he had done to her. How he had treated her. 'We have nothing to discuss later, Tristan. We discuss this now.'

'No?' He took a step towards her. His hands were outstretched, but she moved away from him and his hands fell to his sides. 'We are married.'

'Are we even married? You never said your title.' Hot tears sprung to her eyes. She blinked rapidly. 'Or were you going to discard me when you'd had your fun?'

'Yes, we are married. You were there. We married over the blacksmith's anvil. I gave my full name. It is a legal marriage, Lottie. You are my wife.'

'You decided to test me.' Lottie stared at him. The full horror of what he had done sinking in. 'You did those things to me deliberately. At the inn. Those men who attacked me.'

'You did those things yourself. You paid no heed to my advice. You would have come to no harm.'

'You left me there!'

'I was going to tell you the truth, Lottie.'

'When? You had ample opportunity. It is not as if we have never spoken.'

Tristan's lips became a thin white line. 'Once I was sure. This was our wedding trip. Our chance to get to know each other before the world crowded in.'

'You never even attempted to get to know me.' Lottie picked up her satchel. 'I am leaving you, Tristan. I am going back to my world. This was a false world. What we shared was false. You tricked me.'

'There is an explanation.'

'You only think there is an explanation.' Lottie's stomach ached and she knew the lump in her throat was growing beyond all proportion. And if it became too large, she would burst into noisy floods of tears. She refused to cry in front of Tristan and to show how deeply he had wounded her. She wanted to be strong. 'I have gone over and over in my head the possibilities and have come to the conclusion that you thought me proud. That I needed to be punished. You had no right to do that, Tristan.'

'I had every right!'

'The man I thought I married would never have done that,' Lottie replied quietly, in control of her emotions once more. 'He had integrity.'

'What are you going to do about it? I can't change the past.'

'I am leaving you, Tristan. You can stay in this ruined hall with your memories, but I am going back to my world, the world where I belong, the world where people love me. If this is marriage, it comes at far too high a cost.'

'I thought I pleased you.' He pulled her into his arms, lowered his face, but she turned her head and pushed at his chest. His hands let her go. He stood stock still, chin lifted high, a remote expression on his face.

Lottie swallowed hard. He was seeking to manipulate her. Again. This time it was not going to happen. This time she would win.

'Physical attraction vanishes, Tristan, when you betray someone. And you betrayed me in the worst way.' She picked up her satchel and held it in front of her like a shield. If he made another move towards her, she would be tempted to melt and she was determined not to do that. She wanted him to understand what she had gone through. 'You decided that I was a blank slate to write on, to mould and shape however you wanted. You never asked me if I wanted that.'

'I may have been highhanded, but it was for the best. I needed to know.'

'May have been? Definitely you were.' Lottie composed her features. She had made her plans in that long dark night. She was not some desperate woman, intent on having her man at any cost. Tristan had to want her and her alone. 'Goodbye, Lord Thorngrafton.'

'Goodbye? We have not yet begun!' The roar of his words resounded in her ears. 'You are not going anywhere, Carlotta. I forbid it.'

'I have always hated that name, Lord Thorngrafton.' Lottie held out her hand briefly. She saw that he ignored it, preferring to stand there glowering at her. She composed her features and refused to show any sign of weakness.

'I thought our time together would show me who you really were. And it has!' Tristan turned on his heels and closed the door behind him with a thundering crash.

Lottie waited for a moment, head tilted. She heard the sound of heavy footsteps mounting the stairs. A great feeling of loss welled up inside her. Angrily, she brushed away her tears. He thought he could end the argument by simply leaving the room and that she would obey him. He had another thing coming.

She twisted off her iron wedding ring and placed it on the marble-topped table by the entrance. Tristan would be sure to find it, if he looked.

'It was so very pleasant to have had this time with you, Lord Thorngrafton. Truly enlightening. I do so hate pro-longed goodbyes. I wish you great joy in the future,' she said to the empty hall.

Chapter Fifteen

Tristan sat in the empty morning room, turning the tiny iron ring over and over in his hand. The room seemed lifeless without Lottie's presence. It was surprising how in a few short days, he had come to rely on her being there, hearing her excited chatter and listening to her latest scheme. It was as if a large part of him had gone with her.

Lottie would return. This was a grandiose gesture on her part. She would not even get as far as Hexham station. All he had to do was wait.

'Mrs Elton,' he called. 'What train was Lottie leaving on?'

'The express. For Newcastle.'

Tristan glanced up at the clock. A great emptiness opened inside him. If she was going to return, she would have been back by now.

She had gone. Left. Without a backward glance, without waiting to hear his explanation.

This was not how it was supposed to have happened. He had calculated that she might be slightly angry with him, but that she would have been pleased to have all her dreams come true.

He took one last look at the ring and placed it in his pocket. He would lock it away somewhere, keep it in a box and never take it out again. And he would go far from here. Never to return.

He pressed his hands against the mantelpiece. Was this what his uncle had felt when Suzanne had left him? Was he only seeking to possess Lottie? Should he just go about his business as if Lottie had never entered his life?

Tristan gave a wry smile. It was almost as if his uncle had set a trap for him, one that he had blindly walked into. Had he become his uncle?

Instantly Tristan rejected the notion. He did not want to possess Lottie. He wanted her in his life. His life would be an empty place without her. And he had never even asked her to stay.

His fingers went to his other coat pocket where her Claude glass resided, had resided ever since he'd found it.

He would get her back. He would fight for her. He was finished with games and riddles. Lottie was too valuable for such things. He only wished that he had realised that before.

He would get her back…even if it took a lifetime.

She did not stand a chance.

He had to be patient and draw on all the lessons he had learnt. Only now it seemed that he was playing for the highest stakes—Lottie's love.

'And is that the end of your tale?' Lucy Charlton leant forward and touched Lottie's hand. Her sister-in-law's face was wreathed in worry lines as Lottie finished recounting her tale later that afternoon in Newcastle.

'I came here.'

Lottie put her head back against the armchair in the familiar comfort of Lucy and Henry's dining room. It was a place where nothing bad was ever allowed to happen. The walls were painted the most fashionable shade of Dragon's Blood red. White lace hung over the backs of chairs and pincushions with their mottos carefully pricked by Lucy's friends were arranged so that they could be admired. Familiar. Safe, but somehow stifling. All the way back to Newcastle Lottie had thought that if she made it here, everything would be fine. But she had been wrong. Everything was far from fine.

Every bone in her body ached and a great weariness swept over her. She would cry except she believed she no longer had any tears left inside her. She had shed those last night while she'd waited for Tristan's return. Now she felt like a dried-out husk. She doubted whether she would ever feel anything again.

'But surely Lord Thorngrafton tried to stop you.'

'No, Lucy, he made no effort. The journey was quite straightforward. Mrs Elton had arranged for a pony cart. The express arrived swiftly and I caught a cab to your house.'

'Mother Charlton remains at Shaw's. She is hopeful of Sir Geoffrey Lea for herself. She is very proud of your marriage, you know.'

'She knew about Tristan's title?'

'Not at first. I believe Sir Geoffrey used the knowledge to comfort her later.'

'Sir Geoffrey knew? Why didn't he warn me?'

'Who would you rather be married to?' Lucy's eyes danced.

To Tristan, came the immediate answer. *To the man I said yes to. The man I am afraid doesn't exist.* Lottie managed to hold back the words. 'That question is not relevant, Lucy. I would have found a way. Mama was being stubborn.'

'You have your title, Lottie. Isn't that what you said you would always have?'

'Times change.' Lottie rubbed a hand across her face. 'I had very little sleep last night and almost none on the train. I am so sorry for my poor company, Lucy. You must think me dreadfully dull, going on in this manner.'

Lucy reached over and squeezed Lottie's hand. 'But the problem remains unresolved—what are you going to do with your future now that you have left Lord Thorngrafton?'

Somehow the fact that Lucy used Tristan's title made things easier. Lottie knew she had never been in love with Lord Thorngrafton. It had been Tristan she'd loved. And every time she closed her eyes, she saw his face. That one last terrible look he had given her. Cold and unforgiving. Had he even seen her, or had he merely seen the reflection of Suzanne? Deep within her, Lottie knew that she was far from being that sort of person and that was what hurt most. He had judged her and found her wanting.

'I had rather thought to go on as before.'

'You are married, Lottie. There may be consequences…'

Lottie put her hand to her mouth. 'I had never thought about such things as babies.'

'You should do. From what Henry wrote me, you and Lord Thorngrafton have been engaged in an activity that is likely to result in children.'

'Lucy! I never!'

'Well, it is why you married, isn't it?' Lucy folded her hands on her laps. 'One might as well be practical about such things. We are both old married women now. You know what goes on behind closed bedroom doors.'

A small warm bubble built inside her. She would like to be a mother and to hold Tristan's child in her arms. But then it popped. She had stopped believing in dreams. Right now that would be the worst thing for her. Tristan would have complete rights over the child. She would have nothing. Life was cruel to do that to women. It was wrong. She pushed away her fears, composed her thoughts. 'I will cross that bridge when I come to it.'

'If that is the way you feel.' Lucy bent her head and kissed Lottie's cheek.

'And the question remains what am I to do now?'

'You are quite resolved not to return to Lord Thorngrafton?'

'There is no point. There is nothing in that relationship, Lucy. He does not respect me.' Lottie fought hard to keep her voice calm. 'I discovered that I wanted more from my marriage than he was prepared to give. I deserved more.'

'You, of course, may stay here for the time being. A woman alone in Mother Charlton's house would not be suitable. If you are determined to take this course.'

'I am quite determined, I have done nothing to feel ashamed of.'

'Good, then you will come with me to the At Homes. You always enjoyed such things.' Lucy proceeded to list the ones that were happening the next day.

Lottie shook her head. 'I couldn't bear it. No, not yet, Lucy. Give me a few days. I need to rest after my journey.'

'You did say you were tired.' Lucy's eyes were speculative. 'I will give you some time before you go back into society, but your true friends will stand by you, as I will.'

Lottie turned her head and tried not to think about what might have been, that green and pleasant land shimmering just beyond her reach.

Lottie sought to hide a yawn. Her fourth conversation about the weather in as many stops. She should never have agreed to join Lucy for today's At Home round. They still had two more stops, including Emma Stanton's first At Home since she'd returned with her new husband from Italy.

'I hear you have married, Lottie.' Mrs Fletcher, one of the leading matrons of Newcastle, advanced towards her, leaning heavily on a cane. A woman who had often shown little regard for her mother.

'Very suddenly.'

Mrs Fletcher peered around her. 'And your new husband, he is not with you? I understand you are making your first calls after your marriage.'

'Yes, I am. It is amazing how many people have remarked on that.' Lottie leant forward, swallowing the annoyance that rose in her throat. 'But enough about me— tell me, how is your bad leg? Has it started to heal? I was speaking with Mrs Elton, my husband's housekeeper, about such matters and she swears by a special ointment.'

Mrs Fletcher started on a long rambling explanation and Lottie breathed a little easier. She would write to Mrs Elton and get the recipe for Mrs Fletcher. It would give her something to do. She would have preferred not to do the calls on her own, but she could. And it was only those people who were not truly her friends who mentioned the lack of a husband by her side. Her friends were either happy for her or concerned that she appeared pale.

'You know my dear…' Mrs Fletcher had finished her story '…I never realised before what a good listener you are.'

'I like hearing about other people. I am interested in them and tend to want to find a solution to their problems. It is one of my most glaring defects.'

'Hardly a defect and time will curb your impulses. I must have you and your new husband to dinner. You remind me of myself when I was a young bride.'

'That would be lovely.' Lottie pasted on a smile. 'I shall have to consult Tristan.'

'And what does Mr Dyvelston do?'

'She means Lord Thorngrafton, Mother.' Mrs Fletcher's younger daughter came up hurrying up. 'Lucy has just told me that you married a lord!'

'You are a dark horse, Lady Thorngrafton.' Mrs Fletcher inclined her head. 'I do hope we will get to know each other better. I fear I may have misjudged you. You must be ecstatic.'

'Supremely happy in every way.' Lottie forced the words from her throat. 'All of my girlish dreams have come true. And what more could I ask for?'

'And will we see your husband at the summer ball, Lady Thorngrafton?' The younger Miss Fletcher gave a sharp-toothed smile. 'I do so long to meet him and see the man who swept the incomparable Lottie Charlton off her feet.'

Lottie found it difficult to breathe. She had hoped to avoid the subject of Tristan. Each time he was mentioned, it was like a dagger to her heart, opening the wound once more. Someday, it might close, but for now it was physically painful.

'Lottie has no idea when Lord Thorngrafton's business will be finished.' Lucy's arm went around her waist and Lottie regretted every solitary cruel thought that she had ever had about Lucy. Lucy was kind and Henry was lucky to have her as his wife. She could hear the real affection that Lucy had for Henry.

Was affection enough? Was she wrong to hope for more? Was she wrong to want more?

'Lottie, don't you agree?' Lucy was looking at her with a quizzical expression. 'About the ball?'

'Yes, yes, I am positive it will be wonderful.' Lottie firmly but politely changed the subject back to the weather.

'Do you think I can skip the next few calls, Lucy?' Lottie asked as they left the Dresser household. 'My head is beginning to pain me.'

'I never thought to hear you say that.' Her sister-in-law paused as she was getting into the carriage. 'You do not appear to be enjoying today's round of calling. I thought you lived for it and home was dull, dull, dull. Isn't that what you wrote me when you first arrived in Haydon Bridge?'

'It must be some other Lottie that you are speaking of.' Lottie pressed her hand against Lucy's. 'Have I told you lately how dear you are to me? And how much I appreciate the things you have done for me lately.'

Lucy's cheeks turned a rosy pink and she became

almost beautiful. Lottie could suddenly see why her brother had married her and why *he* was the lucky one and not the other way around.

'I do declare, Lady Thorngrafton, marriage has been good for you.'

'Sometimes, one learns lessons the hard way, lessons you did not even know you needed to learn.'

Lucy settled herself in the carriage. 'As long as you are rested for the ball tonight. Henry has promised that he will be back in time from Durham.'

'I shall sit on the sidelines and keep you company. Lottie, the very respectable matron.'

'Here, I was looking forward to seeing you dance.'

'I am not sure…' Lottie allowed her voice to trail away. How could she go to a dance without thinking about Tristan and the last time they had waltzed together? She would find an excuse later in the day. She had no desire to go the Assembly Rooms today or any time soon. It was not the pity that she would see in people's faces when she took her place among the matrons. Or the inevitable sitting out of every dance because her husband wasn't there. Her reasons were far more personal. She was not ready to face the emptiness in her heart. 'I wanted to thank you for your intervention back there.'

'Don't let the harridans bother you, Lottie.'

'Mrs Fletcher and her kind don't, Lucy. She is actually very nice once you begin speaking with her. Honestly, I would be a pretty poor person if I based my self-worth on the judgement of a few. It is just…' Lottie gave a small hand wave as her throat closed.

'We can go straight to the Stantons if you wish. I know

both Emma and Mr Stanton will be looking forward to seeing you.'

'I hardly think that.' Lottie smiled, regaining her composure now that the danger had passed. She was certain that she could act normally until the next time something reminded her. 'I only hope that Emma has forgiven me for my inopportune comments.'

'Emma and Mr Stanton are very much in love. I for one have revised my opinion of those comments. They were precisely what was needed.'

'Very well, we shall press on.'

The crush at the Stantons was worse than Lottie had anticipated. Everyone who was anyone in Newcastle appeared to have descended on Emma and Jack Stanton's At Home. Everyone would know that she was making calls without her husband.

Lottie had to admit that she had been wrong about Emma being ancient. She looked so lovely and happy, standing next to her doting husband that Lottie felt a distinct twinge of jealousy. She did not mind the gossip about Tristan not being there. She wanted him to be there for her own well-being. She wanted Tristan to look at her like that. She wanted to feel his hand about her waist and see his eyes fill with warmth and good humour. Not that it was possible. She had been at Lucy's for more than a week now. And with each passing moment, she missed him more. But he had not sent word. It would not be difficult to find her, if he desired it.

A well-upholstered lady moved and she spied a pair of broad shoulders encased in a form-fitting frock coat. Lottie rubbed her eyes. And she was seeing things now. Tristan here? Impossible. Her nerves were becoming addled.

'I wanted to say how sorry I was about my outburst after the skating party,' Lottie said in an undertone to Emma. 'It was wrong of me. I understand now how these things can happen.'

'On the contrary, I am now grateful for it. Jack and I married and resolved our differences. It changed my life.' Emma smiled at her. 'Think on it no more. I understand you have become a lady now.'

'That is correct.' Lottie braced herself for the inevitable question—where was her husband? She had already seen several people pointedly nudging each other. 'I married Tristan Dyvelston, Lord Thorngrafton, a few weeks ago… Undoubtedly Lucy told you the circumstances.'

'Jack says that Thorngrafton is a good and able man. High praise indeed from Jack. I wish you all the happiness.' Emma pressed Lottie's hand. 'I can see a change in you. There is a certain glow that wasn't there before.'

'Thank you,' Lottie said around the sudden lump in her throat.

'And where has—?'

'There you are, Lottie. At last I discover you.' Tristan's voice slid over and around her.

Lottie hardly dared breathe, let alone turn and see him. But he was here. In this room. She had to be hearing things. Tristan would never go to an At Home and certainly not one with her. It was beyond imagining. His fingers grasped her elbow. And she knew this was no dream. 'Tristan.'

'Lottie left before I could accompany her on her rounds,' Tristan explained to Emma. 'I am so pleased that my hunch was correct and that you were so gracious to allow me to wait here for her.'

'Grace and politeness had nothing to do with it. It gave Jack and my father someone to converse with. Jack hates these sorts of gatherings, but even he recognised the importance of the first At Home to a bride.' Emma gave another smile and swept off to greet some more callers, leaving Lottie to stand awkwardly, facing Tristan.

Eagerly her eyes searched his face. His mouth appeared slightly pinched and his eyes hollowed, but that could have been the result of anything.

'You left without saying goodbye.'

'I said goodbye to the empty hallway.'

'That does not count, Lottie. You should have said goodbye to my face.'

'I have no wish for a scene, Lord Thorngrafton.' Lottie made her voice cold.

Tristan's response was to press his lips together. The silence between them grew.

'Tristan,' Lottie said into the silence, striving for normalcy, 'I have told everyone you were away on business.'

'What sort of husband leaves his bride alone so quickly after the wedding?' Tristan smiled down at her. His eyes were warm and pleasant. A show for others. It had to be. 'You forgot your ring.'

He held it out. Lottie's heart lurched. She longed to grab it. Her hand felt too light and empty without it, but it was impossible. There was too much between them. She forced her hand to remain still.

'Keep it. It represents a lie.'

'As you wish…for now.' His eyes were inscrutable as he smoothly returned the ring to his pocket.

'But why come here? Why not to the house?' Lottie could hear her voice begin to rise as she ruthlessly crushed any hope. Tristan had shown up at this At Home. He was in Newcastle and he had not bothered to visit her first.

Several of the more elderly ladies turned towards them. Lottie saw at least one disapproving glance as they lifted their hands to gossip.

'Do you want to make a scene?' Tristan asked out of the side of his mouth. 'I am here. I arrived in Newcastle after you went out this morning, after you began your round of calling. I did promise that you would not be humiliated.'

'And you always keep your promises,' Lottie said carefully.

'Always.' His eyes crinkled at the corners. 'You did say that the first At Homes a woman attends after her marriage are among her most important.'

Lottie resisted the urge to smile back. She wanted there to be another reason why he was here. A reason beyond simply keeping his promise and she wanted the reason to be her.

Then it hit her like a physical blow to her stomach. Tristan had not attempted to find her earlier. He had appeared at Jack Stanton's At Home, and had been here far longer than propriety suggested necessary. Jack Stanton was the key to everything. He was a business associate of Tristan's. He was here because of Jack Stanton and not because of her. And he had known of her association with Jack when they met at Shaw's. It did not take a genius to see who he was wary of offending. Whose society he wanted to be accepted in. The irony of the situation failed to make her laugh.

'Did you have trouble finding me?'

'Finding you?' He raised one eyebrow and his body stilled. 'Not particularly, I suspected you would be here.'

'Ah, Thorngrafton, I see your wife has appeared.' Jack Stanton came up and clapped Tristan on the back. 'Good, good, Emma will be relieved. She was a bit worried when you appeared earlier without her.'

'Yes, Stanton, Lottie has finally arrived. You know how the ladies are. Stubborn and insistent.'

'I do, indeed. But Emma would have it that I am the stubborn one.' Jack Stanton inclined his head. 'We must compare notes some time.'

'I look forward to it.'

Jack Stanton moved on, greeting other people. Lottie waited until he was out of earshot and lowered her voice. 'Is he a close business associate of yours?'

'A business associate and a friend for more years than I would like to remember. We share an interest in railways and progress.' Tristan's hand caught her elbow, moved her closer to him and out of the way of a maundering matron who was intent on greeting her friends. The brief collision of their bodies caused Lottie's heart to leap. 'He was vastly amused when he learned we had married and the manner of our marriage.'

'Amused.' Lottie shifted uneasily. She could well imagine Jack Stanton's amusement.

'I believe he said something about pots calling kettles black.'

'I explained about that.' Lottie plucked at her glove. 'It

was an error of judgement on my part. I have apologised to Emma, but she simply laughed.'

'His wife suits him. I don't think I have seen him look this happy and contented before.'

The pain between Lottie's eyes threatened to overwhelm her. She bit her lip, wondering what she could say. 'My time is nearly up.'

'Time? We have scarcely begun.'

'Fifteen minutes is the proper length for a call. Enough for a cup of tea and a conversation about the weather.' Lottie tilted her head. 'I have no wish to trespass on the Stantons' hospitality.'

'I will take you home.'

Home. The word echoed through her body, conjuring so many memories. But she knew that she could not simply go with Tristan. Nothing was settled between then, and she refused to go back to what they had. It was an infatuation, that was all, and it would pass in time.

'I came with Lucy.'

His eyes clouded and then cleared. 'I understand.'

He did not move away from her.

'Oh, Lottie, Lady Thorngrafton, Lord Thorngrafton. Your prediction from last summer came true after all.' Martha Irons came up, giggling, and Lottie wondered if murder was ever justifiable. 'Do you realise that you will have to lead the quadrille at tonight's dance at the Assembly Rooms? How does it feel to have your dreams come true? All your predictions?'

'I am very happy and looking forward to the ball,' Lottie replied woodenly as she resolved herself to a crashing headache.

'Are we going to the ball tonight?' He raised an eye-brow, looked down at her.

To go to the ball with Tristan. On his arm. Did he want to go? Lottie hesitated. The lure of waltzing again with Tristan was powerful, if only for a few moments. She would have to guard her heart, but she knew she would be unable to resist. 'I suppose we are. Everyone will be there.'

'It does seem to be the talk of the At Home.'

Lottie's smile froze. She had forgotten about Jack Stanton and the need to be correct. The formality of being titled and keeping up appearances. She wanted to throw down her gloves and stomp off. She wanted Tristan to waltz with her because he wanted to, not because it was expected of him.

'Balls and the like always excite the gossips.'

'And do they excite you, Lottie?'

'Sometimes.' Lottie examined the handle of her reticule. Then she glanced up into Tristan's face. There was a wariness about his expression. 'I believe I shall enjoy this ball after all.'

'I will take you in my carriage. We do not wish to cause talk.'

'If you wish…'

'I positively insist.' Tristan raised her hand to his lips and turned it over. His tongue briefly found the gap in her glove and touched her bare skin. Heat seared up her arm and she gave a brief gasp. His eyes took on a cynical look. 'Not in-different to me, then, Lottie.'

'Lucy is signalling, Tristan. I must go.' Silently Lottie cursed her wayward body. She would forget her passion for him in time.

'I will bid you *adieu*, then.'

Lottie forced her legs to carry her to Lucy's waiting carriage and did not look back.

Chapter Sixteen

'**W**hy has he done that?' Lottie frowned as the carriage returned to the Charltons' home. 'Why has he sent the carriage so early?'

Outside the Charltons' drive, with his arms clearly emblazoned on it, stood Tristan's carriage. On the ride back from the Stantons', Lottie had sat stone-faced, concentrating on tonight. What she would wear and how she would show Tristan that she was indifferent to him.

'Done what?' Lucy leant forwards and gave a pleased smile and a little clap of her hands. 'I thought he might do that! Emma said that he had arrived early to the At Home. I am certain that he wants to mend this quarrel between you two. Quarrels often happen in the early part of a marriage, Lottie.'

'This was why you insisted we make the small stop at the milliner's.' Lottie's heart sank. Lucy had decided to meddle and fix the quarrel. She had tried to keep most of the trouble to herself, not wanting to overburden Lucy, but now it appeared that Lucy considered the chasm between them to be a mere tiff and had encouraged Tristan to call at the house. It wasn't. It was something far more fundamental. She was not some sort of blank slate to be written on, to be shaped and moulded as Tristan saw fit.

'I wanted to see the new bonnets, but I also wanted to give your husband time. I hoped he would be here when we returned after I hinted at it. I am so pleased he understood.' Lucy reached over and patted Lottie's hand. 'You have spent long enough hiding in your room. Even Henry remarked on it two nights ago.'

'Remarked? He positively bellowed.' Lottie attempted to peer around Lucy and discover exactly where Tristan was and in what sort of mood. 'A rogue elephant would have had more subtlety and tact.'

'You do your brother a disservice. He simply feels that you should have given your marriage a chance. He does care about you. He is willing to provide a home for you, if that is what you require.'

'Thank you. I know this is your doing.' Lottie placed a kiss on Lucy's cheek. 'You can move mountains in your quiet way. I never quite appreciated how well you manage him.'

'Sometimes, one accomplishes more.' Lucy reached over and straightened Lottie's bonnet. 'Now, enough of this. You have a husband, standing there waiting for you.'

'Will you stay with me?' Lottie asked, suddenly nervous. What more could Tristan have to say to her?

'It is far better to speak to your husband in private before the ball.' Lucy's eyes turned grave. 'It saves scenes. It is better for all concerned this way.'

'There is really very little to speak about.' Lottie

climbed down from the carriage. Her insides trembled. 'Our marriage is over.'

'Is that you want? Or are you going to fight?'

'There is nothing to fight for.'

'Ah, Lottie, you return at last.' Tristan came up and put his hand on her shoulder.

'Have you been waiting long?' Lottie forced her voice to be normal.

'I decided to bow to your expertise on At Homes and left.'

'Are you staying somewhere in Newcastle?'

'I arrived this morning, but have arranged for lodgings at the Royal Hotel. I felt you might prefer it that way.'

Lottie's heart twisted. Rooms without her. There was no indication that he intended that she should live with him. They would maintain separate lives and establishments, how many in the aristocracy behaved. 'Are you planning on staying long in Newcastle?'

'It depends on how long my *business* in Newcastle takes.' His jaw tightened and his eyes became hooded. 'We will have to appear as husband and wife, Lottie. Society will demand it.'

'I hardly intend on cutting you, Lord Thorngrafton. We are married. There would be talk and I have no intention of causing unnecessary scandal. It would reflect badly on my family.'

'You relieve me no end.' He inclined his head. 'Now, do we continue this discussion on the pavement or do you wish to take a ride in my carriage?'

A ride in his carriage. Lottie's head pounded. She was not ready to be alone with him. It brought back far too many memories of the other carriage ride out to Gretna Green. 'I am tired, Tristan. Anything you need to say can be said in Lucy and Henry's drawing room.'

'If that is what you wish…' He inclined his head.

'I do,' Lottie said firmly. 'Our marriage is of great concern to me. We need to determine how best we go on from here.'

'Yes, you wouldn't want anyone to think anything was amiss.' Tristan stared at his wife, drinking in her form. Not a hair was out of place. It was as if she was encased in armour. There had to be a way of reaching Lottie, of making her understand that he had never intended to hurt her.

'Appearances can be deceptive, Lord Thorngrafton.'

A muscle jumped in Tristan's cheek as her barb struck home. He had hoped that she might show some signs of missing of him. Had he inadvertently destroyed everything between them? 'Indeed they can.'

Lottie led the way into a drawing room that groaned with knick-knacks and pincushions. Every chair leg was carefully hidden. Up-to-the-minute good taste and sensibility, but somehow, despite its fussiness, it also seemed comforting.

'Your sister-in-law provides a comforting home,' Tristan said to fill the silence as Lottie removed her bonnet and gloves, handing them to the butler.

'Henry and Lucy are proud of it, but it is too cluttered for my taste.' Lottie began straightening the cushions and moving the figurines.

'You would decorate differently?'

'I shall have to see when the time comes.' Her eyes

twinkled. 'There again, perhaps I will develop a sudden affinity for neatly picked-out mottos and shell pictures.'

'Mottos and shell pictures.' Tristan was unable to stop the brief shudder of horror as Lottie's eyes twinkled.

'As I am unlikely to have my own establishment, it is not a problem.'

'There is Gortner Hall,' Tristan said quietly and waited.

'That belongs to you. You may reside there if you wish.'

'But you are my wife. You should be making my house into a home; while I may not care for the decoration of this house precisely, it does exude a homely atmosphere.'

He went to close the door, but she held up her hand, stopping him. 'Leave the door open, please.'

His hand lingered on the doorknob. Not as indifferent as she might pretend. He had something to work with, something to build on. 'Who is it that you don't trust, Lottie, you or me?'

'That sort of teasing is obvious, Tristan.' Lottie wrapped her arms about her waist. 'And unworthy of you.'

'I merely asked the question.' Tristan took a step closer, invaded her space. She had called him Tristan. It was the tiniest sliver of hope and he found his mind clinging to it with all its energy. 'You refused a ride in my carriage and now insist on the door remaining open.'

'I should not like anyone to think that you are taking advantage.'

'I promise you that I have not come here to ravish you.' Tristan adopted his most innocent face. Not here. Not until he had her on his own, without fear of being disturbed. He wanted to show her that he intended to devote his life to her.

'Why have you come?' She toyed with a Dresden shepherd.

'Because our conversation at the Stantons' was unsatisfactory,' Tristan said, looking at her and trying to think beyond kissing her mouth. He had missed her more than he thought it was possible to miss anyone and she appeared not to have missed him one bit. 'I wanted to speak to you about more than the weather.'

'This morning has been very enlightening to me.'

She placed the china dog closer to the shepherd, arranged them in a pleasing tableau, taking her time, concentrating on the figurines instead of him. Tristan watched her long tapering fingers. The memory of how they felt against his skin swept thorough him, nearly destroying his sanity. 'Has it? I am afraid I found the whole proceeding deadly dull.'

'Yes, it has now become clear to me why we married. I was blind before.' She widened her eyes and gave him a brilliant smile.

'Pray enlighten me, Lottie.' Tristan leant against the door frame with crossed arms. Exactly how much had she guessed? And, more importantly, how could he show her the true reason? 'Why did I marry you?'

'You are a business associate of Jack Stanton's.' Lottie began ticking the reasons off on her fingers. 'You had no wish to be outside his society. It could be bad for business. You were very unsubtle today, Tristan.'

'You are very blind.' Tristan clung on to his temper. How dare she think that!

'Not blind now,' she retorted, her voice becoming chips of ice. 'Once, definitely. I have stopped believing in fairy tales.'

Tristan stared at her in amazement. He had thought to show her that he was willing to meet her halfway and she had twisted it! He gritted his teeth. His plan was not going the way he had intended. 'This is what you have decided. Irrevocably.'

'Yes, and, as such, I can see why you feel that we need to show our marriage is a success.' Lottie pressed her hands together. 'Why we need to show a united front. Why you are here in Newcastle, rather than staying on the estate or wherever you wanted to be.'

'And you are willing to accept this sort of marriage?' Tristan asked as every fibre of his being strained to hear her response.

'Yes,' she whispered and then her voice grew firmer. 'It is the only solution to the problem. An annulment is not possible.'

'Why not?' Tristan felt the tension drain from his shoulders. She wanted to stay married. It was a small straw. He had to have patience, despite the desire of his body. He could not force her. She had to come to him, to forgive him.

'Because I am unwilling to lie. I am no longer a virgin.'

'And this is what you want. A formal marriage.'

'For now.' Lottie kept her head high. 'I will make a good hostess, but I have no wish to be buried alive in the country.'

'I can see that.'

'We will lead separate discreet lives.'

'If that is what you wish…' Tristan clenched his hands. Refrained from shaking her. There had to be a way of getting her to see that it was not what he wanted. This interview was going much worse than he had planned. This was her territory, her bolt hole. He had to hope the surprise he had planned worked. That she would realise what he wanted.

'It is the only solution.'

'I can see that there is nothing to speak about. You have decided everything.'

'It is the way it has to be.'

'For now.' Tristan put his hand in his pocket and withdrew a slim box. 'I would ask you to wear the Dyvelston pearls, even if you don't want to wear my ring. Every Dyvelston bride has worn them. I retrieved them from Peter's pawnbrokers.'

'They do not appear to have brought the Dyvelstons much luck.' Lottie held the box with two fingers.

'Nevertheless, wear them. It is expected.' Tristan replaced his hat on his head. 'I will take you to the ball, Lottie, and then we will discuss our exact marriage arrangements.'

Lottie touched the pearls that hung about her neck as she waited for the first quadrille of the Assembly's Summer Ball to begin. She did not like the pearls any better now than when she had first seen them, but she had worn them, determined to show Tristan that she could play her part. She wanted to be his wife. Her rose silk with its décolleté neckline did set them off, but she made sure the lace was properly tucked and that she looked more like a matron than a debutante.

Her stomach clenched slightly as she struggled to remember the intricate steps. She had always thought that leading the dancing must be the pinnacle of success. Now she knew it for a hollow sham. It had nothing to do with what sort of person she was.

'What are you doing in Newcastle, Tristan?'

'Waiting for the quadrille to begin, standing next to my wife.'

'You did not even know this gathering existed before Martha said something.' Lottie gave a little laugh. She tried to ignore how handsome Tristan looked in his evening clothes. How, without him even touching her, every bit of her was aware of him. 'I don't need the pretence, Tristan. I have had enough of that.'

'You are wrong there. I knew about this ball before this morning,' he said firmly. 'Do be quiet and let the man start the ball, Lottie. The sooner the speeches are over, the sooner the dancing can begin.'

And the sooner they would be finished. Lottie heard the unspoken words. With every breath she took, this charade of being happy became more and more difficult. The candles blazed down on them, throwing heat into an already crowded room. It appeared everybody who was anybody in Newcastle was there, and all eyes were turned towards her and Tristan. She wanted to run screaming from the ball. This was all fake, all shadows and mirrors without any real substance. This was not life.

The master of ceremonies began speaking. Lottie listened with half an ear and then froze as the man proceeded to thank Lord and Lady Thorngrafton for their generous support.

She glanced up and saw the amused twinkle in Tristan's eye. 'But why did you do that?'

'I was determined to force you into the first quadrille. It is what you want—to be a social success.'

'I wanted it once.' Lottie began to dance and was

grateful that the steps led her away from Tristan, away from danger. She had considered her heart immune this afternoon, but here she knew it was not. She had pieced it back together, determined to keep it whole, but within a few hours of seeing him again, she was making castles in clouds.

'Did you miss me?' he asked when they next joined hands.

'How can I miss someone I don't know?' Lottie tilted her head and peered up at him. 'Lord Thorngrafton is a stranger to me. We have never been formally introduced.'

He missed a step, Lottie noted with satisfaction, but his bland mask remained firmly in place.

'I asked you to call me Tristan,' he said finally. 'It is the name I want to hear from your lips.'

'But which one are you?' Lottie's steps faltered and his hand went to hold her up. 'Lord Thorngrafton or Tristan?'

'I am your husband.'

The dance swept them apart again and Lottie made pointless conversation with the other man in the set. Then the music stopped and the quadrille ended.

Lottie stood there, ready to begin the long march over to the side to join the other matrons, but Tristan's hand closed about her wrist, held her there. Imprisoned.

'The dance is finished.' Lottie gave a slight tug on her hand, but his fingers slipped down her palm, held it gently.

'The newlyweds' waltz is about to begin.' Tristan gave a brief smile. 'I have made my enquiries. Everything has been carefully explained to me. Jack and Emma Stanton are on the floor. You would not want to give people cause to comment.'

Lottie pressed her lips together. She remembered how once she had dreamed of dancing with her titled husband, being the envy of all the unwed women. How she had boasted that she would do that at this very ball. It seemed so childish now. Titles and money were not as important as the person. She knew that if Tristan had neither, she would still be proud of him, still want to be here in his arms.

She wet her lips and held her head high. She could do this. She could waltz with Tristan, without remembering exactly what it meant to be in his arms. And why it could never happen again.

'If we must keep up appearances, then I will.'

She put her hand into Tristan's, felt his other hand touch her waist. Immediately her head reeled. It was one thing to dance a very formal quadrille with him and quite another to dance an intimate dance like a waltz. The music rose up and surrounded them. All the air whooshed from her lungs and she struggled against her corset to take a deep enough breath to replace it. A coincidence, it had to be that.

The orchestra were playing the same Strauss waltz that they had first waltzed to.

'Do you like it?' Tristan asked, and his body seemed tense.

'It has a beautiful melody,' Lottie replied carefully as the memories swamped her.

'It has become one of my favourites.' His hand tightened on her waist. 'Since that evening at Shaw's.'

'Did you know they were going to play it?'

'I was consulted.' A faint smile touched his lips as he inclined his head.

Her heart began to pound in her ears. He had been consulted and had chosen this waltz, a waltz that had recently become his favourite.

What exactly was he doing? Was this another game? Another lesson she had to learn? She had finished her lessons.

She wanted to hope that he cared something for her but she was too scared. How he had cynically treated her was too raw.

Distantly she heard the sound of clapping hands as they circled around the dance floor. She forced her feet to keep moving, but it became harder and harder. Her head became light. When she thought she must fall down, the music stopped. And with it, she knew that she could not be in a loveless marriage. She could not participate in a sham. She had no use for games.

She slipped out of his arms and fled, not caring about the shocked gasps that echoed after her.

Out in the corridor, she pushed past people until she reached an empty room, one that would be used later for cards. She sank down on a chair and put her face in her hands. Everything was over. All her dreams were gone. She was never going to find love because the man she loved did not care about her. She allowed the tears to fall on to her gown, creating large red blotches.

'Lottie?' Tristan's shadowed figure loomed in the doorway. 'Are you ill?'

'I can't go on.' She raised a tear-stained face to his. 'I have tried, Tristan, but I can't. It is all pretend and make-believe out there. It has no meaning beyond the music and the twinkling lights of the chandelier.'

'Many people enjoy such things.'

'But I don't…not anymore. It feels false. Everyone

clapping and me pretending to be happy, when I am miserable, utterly miserable.'

'You look pale, Lottie. Have something to drink.' Tristan thrust a flask into her hand. 'It will do you good. Restore your confidence. It was bridal nerves. When you are ready, we can go back.'

'My head is spinning enough as it is.' Lottie shook her head and waved the flask away. 'You are being very kind.'

'It is my job to take care of you. Let me.'

He put an arm about her shoulder and Lottie indulged herself by leaning there, drawing strength from him. If she closed her eyes, she could pretend…then she discovered that she did not want to pretend anymore. She had to explain to Tristan her feelings for him.

'Did the crowds give you a funny turn?' He came forward and caught her hands in his. Warming them. 'You could be breeding.'

'It is far too soon to know such a thing.' Lottie withdrew her hands. Ice encased her. He was looking after her because she might be bearing his child. An heir, and he was the last one. She should have thought. 'I will let you know if I am. I understand how much you must want an heir.'

'I am not my uncle, Lottie. The getting of an heir became an obsession with him. In the end, it destroyed him. I have no wish to follow in his footsteps. I intend on living my life, my way.'

Lottie closed her eyes. She had to know. 'What happens if I am pregnant?'

'For my part, I hope you are not…not yet,' he amended with a smile.

He wanted to end everything. A quick break was

probably best. 'Have you found a way to end our marriage without a scandal?'

He knelt beside her. 'Lottie, very selfishly I want to have more time with you, to get to know you far better before we have children.'

'But you wanted a sham of a marriage.'

'It is you who wants that. I agreed because if that is the only way to have you, I will, but I want more than that. I will always be praying for more than that.' Tristan paused and brushed her hair from her forehead, allowing his words to sink in. A small fluttering of hope built within her breast. Did he want more from the marriage? Did he actually care for her? 'And I hoped tonight that I showed that I wanted anything but. Lottie, I need you in my life.'

'You care for me?'

'You are determined to have your pound of flesh.' Tristan gathered her into his arms. He was vulnerable in a way she had never seen before. Naked with longing. 'I love you, Lottie Dyvelston. I want you in my life as my wife in truth. I want you and not some reflection of you. I want you to be you and not try to twist yourself into someone you are not. You are my world and I need you to be with me to make me complete.'

'What are you saying?' Lottie breathed, afraid that this might be some sort of cruel dream.

'I was wrong, Lottie,' Tristan said humbly. 'Utterly and inexcusably wrong. I have come here to beg your forgiveness and to ask if we can begin again. If there is any hope for me. Can you care for me?'

'Tristan…' Lottie tried to let his words sink in but her heart was pounding far too loudly and her limbs were trembling. He was asking her to forgive him. Her! 'But why? Why did you do this?'

Tristan reached into his coat pocket and drew out a small oval object. He placed it in her hand. 'This might help you to understand.'

'My Claude glass? How did you…? When did you…?' Lottie stared at it in astonishment. 'Why are you giving it to me now?'

'Because it is the only way I can explain.'

'Explain about what?'

'I found it that first day after you had gone from the graveyard.' He curled her finger around it. 'Lottie, I accused you of looking at life through a mirror and not really living it.' He paused. 'It was not you who was doing that, but me.'

'You?'

'I had made sure that I was self-sufficient, that nothing and no one could hurt me again.' Tristan stood and moved away from her. His eyes became shadowed, and Lottie could see the pain etched on his face. 'I was wrong. It wasn't really living. But I arrogantly thought it was. That I knew better than anyone else how my life should be lived. I was determined not to repeat my uncle's mistakes. But without realising it, I was slowly becoming him— bitter and twisted, thinking of no one but myself.'

'I think you are being too harsh on yourself. I know the sort of man I met that day in Haydon Bridge.' Lottie moved over towards him, knowing that she had to go to him. She had to show him that she cared.

'You think far too highly of me.' His fingers touched her cheek. 'I began living again when you became upset about the state of my parents' graves.'

'It was a little thing. It was wrong of me.' She squeezed his hand.

'It was utterly right of you. And then when we met again at Shaw's, I knew that I could not let you marry anyone else. I knew you were the right woman for me.'

'You did that to save me from Sir Geoffrey Lea, because you did not want me to be tied to an old man… like Suzanne was.'

'You think so little of my abilities that I could not find another way of saving my reputation, besides marrying you.' He gave a slight laugh, but his hand went about her waist and pulled her close. Lottie laid her head against his chest and listened to the steady thumping of his heart. 'I wanted to secure you for myself and not have to worry about anyone else taking you away from me.'

'Is that why you married me?' she whispered, unable to trust her ears. Tristan had married her because he desired her.

'Yes, and selfishly I wanted you to want me too. I wanted you to care for me, not just my title or my wealth.' Tristan tilted her chin so she gazed up into his deep black eyes, burning with an intensity and desire that she had not seen before. 'Can you? Can you forgive me for what I did?'

'There is nothing to forgive,' Lottie said and knew it was the truth. She could understand now why he had done it. She could forgive him now she knew that he loved her.

'I want to spend the rest of my life making it up to you.' There was a humble note in Tristan's voice that she had not heard before. 'Please tell me that there is a little bit of your life that you are willing to share with me. That it is not all duty for you. Please take my ring back.'

'With pleasure. My hand has missed it so very much.'

He took off her glove and slipped it on her finger. She gave a contented sigh as the weight settled once again on her hand. 'I love you, Lord Thorngrafton.'

His response was to lower his head and claim her lips. She brought her arms up and arched her body towards his, savouring him. Wanting him. Demanding him. Here. Now.

The door clicked and Lottie jumped away from Tristan, hurriedly tried to straighten her gown, but knew she looked thoroughly kissed. Tristan moved to shield her.

'Excuse us.' Emma Stanton's musical voice floated from the door. 'We thought to find a quiet room, but I see this one is otherwise occupied.'

'I thank you for that,' Tristan said, and started to draw Lottie into his arms again.

'And you need not worry, Lady Thorngrafton, our lips are sealed.' Jack Stanton gave a laugh as the door closed once more.

'Tristan,' Lottie whispered.

'I am afraid your reputation is ruined, Lottie. It is just as well we are married.'

'That is true.' Lottie laughed as she reached up and pulled his face next to hers. 'They already know what a hopeless pair we are.'

'And do we go back to the ball?' he asked against her temple. 'This room is not exactly secure. I have no desire to be interrupted again.'

'I was hoping for a little more.' She peeped at him from under her lashes.

'Shall I take you home?'

'But you are in lodgings.' Lottie attempted to keep the disappointment from her voice. She could not imagine taking him back to Henry and Lucy's. It would be unbearable.

'I have a small confession.' Tristan laced his fingers with hers, and pulled her close. 'I think that the principal suite in the Royal Hotel would be suitable for you…for now.'

'And for later?'

'We can live in Newcastle if you wish. I also have homes in London, Paris and Rome.'

Paris. Rome. London. Places that had she once dreamt of and had boasted she would see, but they held little appeal now. The only place she wanted to be was in Tristan's arms.

'But the estate?' Lottie paused, thinking of that once-loved place and how much it mattered to Tristan. 'What about Mrs Elton? And the rest of the servants? You wanted to restore it, or was that another ruse?'

'I will restore it in time, but we will live where you want to live.'

'Let's go home to Gortner Hall, Tristan—tomorrow. I find I am weary of society and long for my bed. And my husband in it.'

'Done!'

Their mutual laughter rang off the walls of the little room. Lottie smiled up at her husband and knew that somehow, despite all the misconceptions and mistakes they had both made, all her dreams had come true.

* * * * *

Immerse yourself in the glitter of Regency times and follow the lives and romantic escapades of Stephanie Laurens' Lester family

15th February 2008

21st March 2008

16th May 2008

20th June 2008

www.mirabooks.co.uk

The much-anticipated finale to the Moreland quartet!

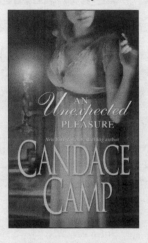

London, 1879

Had Theo Moreland, the Marquess of Raine, killed her brother? American journalist Megan Mulcahey had to know. But to find out, she needed to infiltrate the marquess's household.

The new American governess intrigued Theo. Miss Mulcahey had come to Broughton House to teach his young siblings. Now the strange pull of their immediate desire both troubled and excited him. But why was this delicious vision snooping around his mansion like a common thief?

Available 19th September 2008

Celebrate 100 years of pure reading pleasure with Mills & Boon®

To mark our centenary, each month we're publishing a special 100th Birthday Edition. These celebratory editions are packed with extra features and include a FREE bonus story.

Plus, you have the chance to enter a fabulous monthly prize draw. See 100th Birthday Edition books for details.

Now that's worth celebrating!

September 2008
Crazy about her Spanish Boss by Rebecca Winters
Includes FREE bonus story
Rafael's Convenient Proposal

November 2008
**The Rancher's Christmas Baby
by Cathy Gillen Thacker**
Includes FREE bonus story *Baby's First Christmas*

December 2008
One Magical Christmas by Carol Marinelli
Includes FREE bonus story *Emergency at Bayside*

Look for Mills & Boon® 100th Birthday Editions at your favourite bookseller or visit
www.millsandboon.co.uk

0908/CENTENARY_2-IN-1

FREE!

2 Books
and a surprise gift!

We would like to take this opportunity to thank you for reading this Mills & Boon® book by offering you the chance to take TWO more specially selected titles from the Historical series absolutely FREE! We're also making this offer to introduce you to the benefits of the Mills & Boon® Book Club—

- ★ FREE home delivery
- ★ FREE gifts and competitions
- ★ FREE monthly Newsletter
- ★ Exclusive Mills & Boon Book Club offers
- ★ Books available before they're in the shops

Accepting these FREE books and gift places you under no obligation to buy, you may cancel at any time, even after receiving your free shipment. Simply complete your details below and return the entire page to the address below. You don't even need a stamp!

YES! Please send me 2 free Historical books and a surprise gift. I understand that unless you hear from me, I will receive 4 superb new titles every month for just £3.69 each, postage and packing free. I am under no obligation to purchase any books and may cancel my subscription at any time. The free books and gift will be mine to keep in any case.

H8ZEF

Ms/Mrs/Miss/Mr ....Initials ....

Surname ....

Address .... **BLOCK CAPITALS PLEASE**

....

....Postcode ....

Send this whole page to:
UK: FREEPOST CN81, Croydon, CR9 3WZ